One girl could lay the world at his feet . . . Elizabeth could only offer her heart.

The fabulously wealthy Grant Jarvis decided to employ a girl to accompany him to Australia to pose as his fiancée—so that designing women, the bane of his life, would not pursue him. But it turned out to be an unfortunate, if not disastrous whim . . .

Unfortunate, because the girl he chose fell deeply in love with him; disastrous, because the rich girl who intended to marry him was impatiently awaiting his return . . .

ROMANTIC NOVELS by

Lucy Walker

THE CALL OF THE PINES
COME HOME, DEAR
DISTANT HILLS
FOLLOW YOUR STAR
HEAVEN IS HERE
HOME AT SUNDOWN
LOVE IN A CLOUD
A MAN CALLED MASTERS
THE ONE WHO KISSES
THE OTHER GIRL
REACHING FOR THE STARS
THE RIVER IS DOWN
THE STRANGER FROM THE NORTH
SWEET AND FARAWAY
THE MAN FROM OUTBACK
DOWN IN THE FOREST
THE MOONSHINER
THE RANGER IN THE HILLS
WIFE TO ORDER
THE GONE-AWAY MAN
SHINING RIVER
SIX FOR HEAVEN
THE LOVING HEART
KINGDOM OF THE HEART

Available from Beagle Books

THE
LOVING HEART

Lucy Walker

BEAGLE BOOKS • NEW YORK
An Intext Publisher

CHAPTER ONE

ELIZABETH HEATON worked as a typist in a woolbuyers' firm in the City of London. She had been in this office four years now . . . ever since she was eighteen, in fact. It was on her twenty-second birthday that something strange, wonderful, and earth-shaking happened to her.

She was sitting before her typewriter, just before ten o'clock in the morning, when the most junior typist, who often acted as office girl, came into the main office.

"Elizabeth," she said. "Mr. Ashby wants to see you. *At once*, he said."

Elizabeth knew that when Mr. Ashby said *at once* he meant instantly, regardless of what you were doing at the moment. Mr. Ashby was the staff manager for Small and Smallwoods, woolbuyers for the British Isles and Continent. His word was law and his position in relation to the girls in the office was that of omnipotence.

Elizabeth Heaton was a shy girl with light brown curly hair and pretty forget-me-not eyes, a sensitive mouth and a generous smile. In the four years she had been with "Small's" she had held an unpretentious place in an office full of girls who, she thought, had much more glamour than herself. The other girls seemed to get engaged and then married off, mostly to the woolbuyers engaged by the firm who travelled to remote places like Australia, Spain and South Africa in pursuit of their firm's business. The girls had then been able to go off globe-trotting with their husbands.

Elizabeth was not envious of these successes in the marriage market because tucked quietly away in her background home in Mereton, north of London, was Ralph Dalton.

Ralph was a Mereton boy with whom Elizabeth had grown up. They had been inseparable friends ever since Sunday School days and village tennis played once a week in the summer at the vicarage. Ralph was a young man of strong purpose who sometimes assumed a flippant attitude to other people's important problems.

When Elizabeth had been seventeen and Ralph twenty

5

they had talked about marriage. For two years after that they had talked *around* marriage. For two years now there had been silence on the subject and Elizabeth knew it was because Ralph was trying to establish himself firmly as a law clerk before he undertook responsibilities that would be a financial strain. Elizabeth lived in a lovely rose-bowered cottage with her widowed mother; her salary at Small's helped in keeping that tiny menage in a degree of comfort. Patiently she waited for Ralph to "establish" himself.

Now on Elizabeth's twenty-second birthday, a cold March morning, the staff manager sent for her. *At once.*

In the office of Small and Smallwoods it was known, in a strange grapevine way, that the wife of a senior partner in the firm had come home to England from one of the firm's big sheep stations in Australia. Mrs. Seaton Morgan was a woman of great charm, distinction and wealth. They also knew she had been travelling backwards and forwards between England and Australia all her life. The most junior employee of the firm knew that the finest merino wool was grown in Australia and a big share in Australia's merino wool clip was grown on one or two stations owned or financed by the company that also owned Small's.

Mrs. Morgan's presence in England was one of those titillating pieces of gossip that kept the ebb and flow of office life alive. She was a director of Small's in her own right.

Mrs. Morgan, Mr. Ashby told her, had fallen and fractured her hip and broken her right wrist on the steps of a West End store. She was in a Kengsington nursing home and wanted a stenographer to do her correspondence for her.

Mr. Ashby did not ask Elizabeth would she go. He merely said:

"Here is the address, Miss Heaton. See if you can be back and get the correspondence typed off by lunchtime and back to Mrs. Morgan for her signature early this afternoon. Take a taxi both ways. And Miss Heaton . . ."

"Yes, Mr. Ashby?"

"You are the quietest of the typists so I thought you would be the best person to send forward to a patient in a nursing home. Especially," he added meaningly, "to Mrs. Seaton Morgan who is, I believe, suffering a great deal of pain."

"I understand, Mr. Ashby," Elizabeth said gravely.

"Good girl," he said, for once unbending.

As Elizabeth put on her coat and small head-hugging hat and drew on her gloves she had thought that this was the first time being "quiet" had proved to be an asset.

She was not only going to see the fabulous Mrs. Morgan, but Mr. Ashby had trusted her to carry out what was probably a diplomatic mission.

On the way to the nursing home Elizabeth conjured up visions of a haughty aristocratic lady made slightly difficult by injury and pain.

When Mrs. Morgan's special nurse showed Elizabeth into the flower-bedecked rooms she received one of the pleasantest surprises of her life. Mrs. Morgan, a handsome, middle-aged woman with dark questing eyes and a humorous mouth, was sitting up against her pillows, her head only just appearing over the great cradle that protected her splinted leg from the bedclothes and her bandaged wrist and hand resting on a pillow beside her.

"Come in, my dear," she said gaily. "So you're the stenographer. I hope you can bear with the sight of this frightful hump in the middle of the bed. If you can't, my dear, just keep your eyes on the flowers. Aren't they gorgeous? And in England, at this time of the year!"

One quick glance at the roses, sweet peas and carnations told Elizabeth they either came out of a hothouse or didn't come out of England at all. Delivered by air from one of the Continental agencies of Small's probably.

"How do you do, Mrs. Morgan?" Elizabeth said gravely. "I'm Elizabeth Heaton and Mr. Ashby sent me from the head office. May I be of assistance to you?"

Mrs. Morgan put her head on one side and regarded Elizabeth with a smile.

"As long as you're not too serious about it, my dear. What I really want is someone young to cheer me up. Did you know that every Small, Smallwood and Morgan in the firm is over sixty? Not that they haven't been blessedly kind to me. They have. But I miss my young people out there in Australia."

Elizabeth smiled. Mrs. Morgan reflected the smile and suddenly Elizabeth's smile had reached her eyes, her lovely white teeth gleamed in a face made young and pretty.

"I'm so sorry about your accident," Elizabeth said. "I can quite understand how you miss your family . . ."

"They're not exactly my family. They're all my friends' families. Have you ever been on a sheep station? But, of course not. Well, my dear, a big station is just a mass of families. There's the manager, the overseer, the stockmen . . . all with wives and families. I regard them all as my own."

Mrs. Morgan indicated a chair and Elizabeth sat down.

"Take off your coat, Elizabeth. May I call you Elizabeth? You'll get too hot in this centrally heated room and then be cold when you go outside."

While Elizabeth was taking off her gloves and coat and taking out her note-book and pencil Mrs. Morgan went on to explain how she wrote every week to "all her families" and told them about her adventures in England.

"Of course I'm an Englishwoman," she said, "but every time I come back I find fresh wonders in a country where I was born and educated and married. Does that seem strange to you, Elizabeth?"

Elizabeth shook her head.

"I don't think anyone would live long enough to know England so well there was nothing fresh left to discover and love," she said.

"Ah, but you should go away, my dear. It is the coming back that is so truly wonderful."

Elizabeth remembered her mother's wish that she, Elizabeth, should take a holiday on the Continent. She said nothing, however, but smiled and prepared to take down the invalid's letters.

Elizabeth was both charmed and fascinated by Mrs. Morgan and when presently she began to take the dictation she found herself quietly enjoying her employer's descriptive and amusing accounts of all she had been seeing and doing in the week before her accident. Elizabeth found a new and entrancing view of London that warmed her own heart. Mrs. Morgan's account of her accident made it sound light and trivial, even amusing.

The longer Elizabeth stayed in this woman's presence the more she both liked and admired her.

When it was time to pack up and go Elizabeth thanked the other for her kind welcome and said she had really enjoyed the visit.

"Of course you did," said Mrs. Morgan unexpectedly.

"I could see you laughing behind that correct stenographer's manner of yours. I enjoyed watching you thaw out too, my dear. Now tell Mr. Ashby you're to come back next week and we'll have some more smiles together. Now, off you go. I'm not going to let them send you back in this raw weather to-day. I'll telephone Mr. Ashby from my bedside to send a messenger boy back with the letters."

Mrs. Morgan had been so gay Elizabeth did not know whether she should shake hands on departure or not. The older woman had been more like a friend than an employer and for this very reason Elizabeth was anxious not to overstep the bounds set down by Mrs. Morgan herself.

The patient resolved the matter by just waving her own hand, so Elizabeth smiled, drew on her gloves and walked quietly to the door.

"I shall tell Mr. Ashby to send you next week," Mrs. Morgan said again.

Elizabeth went through the door and down the lift out into the street. There she took in a deep breath of cold March air. It was all the more bracing because she felt she had just left the delight of a warm cosy fireside.

On two other occasions Elizabeth went to the nursing home to take Mrs. Morgan's letters. Then the outings ceased as the patient was transferred to her own home at Leath Manor with a trained nurse.

The three weeks had been like a holiday to Elizabeth because she had had the pleasure of this unusual work and then later the joy of recounting her experience first to Ralph, waiting for her at the appointed spot outside the Underground, and then her mother over the supper table.

The only chill in the whole encounter was the casual reception Ralph gave to the accounts of it. Elizabeth had a vague feeling that Ralph either disapproved or was not impressed by Elizabeth keeping company with people who were rich and powerful in the wool industry. Perhaps he thought it would all go to her head. Well, she would soon show him she was capable of accepting the experience joyfully and then putting it away without regrets when it was over.

Six weeks later the junior typist came in and said once again:

"Elizabeth, Mr. Ashby wants you. *At once*."

The *at once* made Elizabeth think it was not advisable to delay even to draw out the typing she was now engaged on. She felt a lilt of excitement and anticipation. Last time that order had come she had had the delightful experience of working for Mrs. Morgan. What now? But such good luck couldn't happen twice!

She pushed back her chair and went quickly to the door.

"Don't run, Elizabeth," laughed Bessie Wainwright—another girl who had just become engaged to a woolbuyer from one of the Continental firms. She wore an enormous single diamond engagement ring that had made even Elizabeth feel faintly envious. It wasn't the size of the ring so much as the brave advertisement that soon the hat would go round in the office for another typist about to turn into a young matron. And there would be gift parties and presently little cartons of wedding cake for every member of the staff.

One day perhaps . . . she and Ralph . . .

"Don't run," Bessie Wainwright laughed. "It won't be a second director's wife with a broken hip."

When Elizabeth entered the staff manager's office he stood up and offered her a seat. He smiled on her.

"Well, I've news for you, Miss Heaton," he said. "First, you live alone with your mother, don't you? Could she spare you for six or eight weeks? Is there any reason why you should not go abroad on the firm's business for a period as long as that?"

Elizabeth looked her astonishment. The only people in "Small's" who were important enough to go abroad on the firm's business were the woolbuyers and the directors.

"Aboard, Mr. Ashby?" she stammered.

The staff manager watched the girl closely as he added his next words.

"Mrs. Seaton Morgan, to whom you have already rendered some service, is returning to Australia. The firm has agreed to send someone with her as she is still not able to use her right hand or walk without the help of sticks. She has specifically asked for you."

Elizabeth felt as if she had been hit on the head with a million-pound note.

She did her best to maintain her correct stenographer's demeanour but her words came stammering out.

"You mean . . . go away with Mrs. Morgan, Mr. Ashby?"

To the place from whence the best merino wool came . . . and from which Small and Smallwoods made its fortune? The place that was so far down under the curve of the world that it was in another world altogether?

And as these bewildered questions flashed through her head there came fleeting images of Ralph waiting outside the Underground for her; and her mother sitting alone at the supper table in the rose-bowered cottage.

Her mother would be glad, she knew that instantly. But Ralph? She remembered his flippant disapproval of her happy visits to Mrs. Morgan in the nursing home. She saw mental images of Ralph walking home alone . . . and later, perhaps, growing used to it. Used to freedom. Perhaps not wanting to return to the tie of a companionship that had lost the gay rainbow colours that had once adorned it.

In the midst of her surprise and bewildering pleasure at the request, she knew fear.

Six or eight weeks was a long time. Perhaps Ralph might . . .

The colour mounted in Elizabeth's cheeks. Mr. Ashby was talking about the arrangements for passages, a travelling allowance and a dress allowance in order that Elizabeth should be suitably clothed for the voyage. Elizabeth heard it all yet her mind was fleeing away down long dark tunnels of thought. How long had this fear of Ralph's lack of adventurousness in the matter of an engagement and later marriage really troubled her?

How long had she known, deep in her heart, that Ralph had got too used to her? As her mother once had said . . . like an old cloak?

The only other friends she had were more pleasant acquaintances with whom she and Ralph played tennis at the vicarage. Without him her whole world would wobble off its axis.

"I see this has come as a shock to you, Miss Heaton," Mr. Ashby said. "I want you to leave what work you are doing now. I'll get Miss Wainwright to take it over. You had better take the rest of the day off in order to consult your mother. I'd like you to telephone me as to her reaction by two o'clock and then take a quick train out to Leath Manor and get there for tea with Mrs. Morgan by four-thirty. Can you arrange to do that?"

"Yes, certainly, Mr. Ashby," Elizabeth said quietly. How disappointed, even annoyed, he would be if he knew that though her heart had bounded when he first made his statement it was now somewhere down in the nether regions of her diaphragm.

"Good." He stood up to signal the interview was at an end. He performed the unprecedented act of walking with her to the door.

"Miss Heaton," he said, looking at her closely as he stood by the door. "You understand, of course, that this excursion is something more than a voyage abroad? You have the considerable responsibility of looking after Mrs. Morgan's welfare and of maintaining Small and Smallwoods' standard of efficient work."

"Of course, Mr. Ashby. I won't forget that for a moment."

When she returned to the main office she was still too dazed to explain to the other girls what had happened. She knew they were looking at her curiously as she took her hat and coat from the stand at the end of the room.

"Not another director's wife on the sick list?" Bessie Wainwright asked jokingly. "You seem to have missed your vocation, Elizabeth. You should have been a nurse."

Elizabeth shook her head.

"It *is* Mrs. Seaton Morgan . . . but she is better. She is going back to Australia. Mr. Ashby wants you to carry on with my work, Bessie. I have to . . . I have to go and see Mrs. Morgan. . . ."

And with that she fled.

As she hurried towards the Underground she knew she had let her office colleagues down by not giving them a full explanation. But how could she explain to them why she was not quite jumping over the moon with excitement?

As a matter of fact she very nearly was. One moment her spirits rose like something effervescent in a corked bottle. The next they sank.

If only Ralph . . .

She took her seat in the Underground and permitted herself one happy daydream.

Perhaps Ralph, too, might mind the parting. He might suggest they become engaged now . . . before her departure. Ah, if only he would do that. There would be all the heavenly thrill of writing to one another; planning her return;

planning a wedding. Perhaps she could bring back from all those eastern ports of call some pretty things for their home.

Brasses, hand-beaten silver, silks, camphorwood boxes. A silk sari threaded with gold or silver!

How often in her years at Small's had she seen these lovely things brought into the office by returning woolbuyers and their wives?

And now it might be her turn.

The happiness of these thoughts released her from her fear and she was able to turn her mind to Mrs. Seaton Morgan, that gay invalid who had liked her well enough to ask for her companionship on that voyage.

They were to leave Southampton in the liner *Albany*. Mrs. Morgan would leave the ship at Fremantle, the Australian port on the Indian Ocean, as that was the nearest port to the sheep station to which she was returning. Elizabeth was to remain on the ship while it made its call at other Australian ports and return on it to England. In other words, Mrs. Morgan thought it was better for her to return on the ship that carried them outward bound because Elizabeth would, by that time, be at home on it and the return voyage would not be lonely. Mrs. Morgan thought of everything.

The travelling allowance was in the form of her salary in advance in a lump sum; and a set wardrobe was to be arranged for at the stores to which Mrs. Morgan would direct her. In addition she was to receive double salary in the next two weeks of preparation because of the anticipated costs of running backwards and forwards to the West End shopping.

It was quite fabulous. In fact it could be an Arabian Night's dream, if it weren't for the shadowy figure of Ralph in the background.

Elizabeth arrived home to find her mother, and her aunt who lived in a nearby cottage, waiting for her with hot tea and freshly-made biscuits.

Mrs. Morgan had indeed thought of everything. She had sent Mrs. Heaton a telegram asking for the loan of her daughter for the duration of a voyage to Australia.

In the face of their pleasure and excitement Elizabeth could only match it with her own.

"Darling," her mother said, "I'm so proud of you. It is a wonderful compliment. Small and Smallwoods must think very highly of you."

She looked at her daughter fondly and thought that at last Elizabeth had got her chance of something rare and fine happening to her. Elizabeth was good and kind, but sometimes a little too quiet. Ralph Dalton was a fine young man and Mrs. Heaton would be quite happy to see her daughter married to him, if only he realised what a pearl he had got. And she had no patience with his dilly-dallying. To let such a pearl slip between his fingers! And he might. He very easily might. Elizabeth might meet someone else once she got away from the one-path routine of her life!

For the first time in years, Elizabeth was not at the Underground to meet Ralph. Mrs. Morgan had not released Elizabeth from their conversation piece over the teacups early enough for her to keep her usual appointment.

Ralph Dalton, a tall young man with brown hair and handsome, lively eyes in an equally handsome face, waited for half an hour. He had never had to wait more than the usual five minutes for Elizabeth before and he suffered irritation. Then perturbation set in and he walked along the main street making up his mind whether he would go out of his way to call in at Rose Cottage or whether he would go on home, have his supper and make inquiries later.

Common sense told him that if anything had happened to Elizabeth he would have been telephoned by Mrs. Heaton at his law office during the day.

What, he wondered, could the girl be up to?

He had often contemplated breaking this habitual meeting. Sometimes he found himself hankering for the pleasures of independence, but somehow the thought of Elizabeth's puzzled face had deterred him. She was a nice kid. He'd quite forgotten how many years had passed since he first got amusement watching the expressions on Elizabeth's mobile face.

He supposed they really ought to think about getting married. As it was, things were very comfortable and it gave him opportunity to save money. Money, he had realised in the course of his work in a legal office, could make more money than hard work could make. That is, if you had enough of it.

Not that he wasn't fond of hard work. He was. In fact work was more his god and his life than anything else. He had ambitions. Ambitions were wise things to encourage in a troubled and divided world. Given time he would be very secure financially by the time he was forty. Play safe first, then play merrily last—that was Ralph's current motto.

In actual fact he would be better off without any obligations to anybody. As a lone wolf he could go further. Make more money that would make money for him.

Yet every time he thought this way Elizabeth's sweet and faintly troubled face would come before his inward eye and he knew that he couldn't give her up. Often, as he watched the passengers streaming out of the Underground he would see Elizabeth before she saw him. He would see the eager searching look on her face and the faintly anxious eyes. Then she would see him and her whole face would light up and there would be a gladness there that would soften something in his own heart.

And really, it was quite enough. Let the future look to itself. They could go on like this for quite a long time yet. Meantime . . .

Meantime, where was Elizabeth to-night? Off to that Mrs. Seaton Morgan who had been filling her with foolish ideas of stockmen and rodeos and gymkhanas; of millions of acres and thousands of sheep flocks. Of gold and asbestos and uranium and manganese found lying open on the ground in lonely mountain ranges and untraversed desert places.

This wouldn't do at all. Elizabeth should take a realistic view of life . . . which was very much centred on Mereton.

Ralph thought it had been unwise of Small's to send anyone as inexperienced in life as Elizabeth to listen to a worldly woman like Mrs. Seaton Morgan.

No. Very definitely he would not walk round to Rose Cottage. If Elizabeth had defected from her usual habits it must be she who made the explanations, and voluntarily.

When eight o'clock struck and there was neither a message nor a visit from Rose Cottage Ralph decided at length to walk around there. This silence was unprecedented and perhaps something had befallen them there.

As he neared the cottage and saw it ablaze with light he did not understand the disturbance in himself. Supposing something had happened? Elizabeth was a sweet kid!

A Rolls-Royce was drawn up by the small gateway. Ralph had not seen it in the darkness until, as he drew near, a uniformed chauffeur emerged from the shadows of the gate, got into the car and switched on the engine and the drive lights. Before Ralph could reach the other side of the road the car had swung round and purred noiselessly away.

It must have something to do with that director's wife, after all. Ralph felt instead of perturbation a mounting irritation. If she was not ill, or hurt . . . then surely Elizabeth could have let him know. How many years was it he had been waiting outside that Underground? And never once defected or kept Elizabeth waiting? How many other fellows would stick around like that?

As he stepped on to the porch, it was Elizabeth, hearing his step, who flung open the door.

"Oh, Ralph!" she cried, and with an involuntary movement ran into his arms.

Only then, when he felt her head cradled against his shoulder, did Ralph realise that in spite of that Rolls-Royce he had been really worried. A sense of relief pervaded his whole being as he felt the warmth of the girl's soft body against his own. It was easier to keep on this way, he reflected, than let her go.

Even as he let his lips rest on her head she looked up quickly.

"Ralph, darling, I'm so glad you came. I rang the office from Leath Manor but you had just that minute left. I'm so terribly sorry. Did you wait long? And it's such a cold night. It's just that Mrs. Morgan doesn't keep a clock in her drawing-room and my watch is at the jewellers'. And even if I'd known I don't think I would have dared to ask . . . although she is such a lovely person I'm sure she wouldn't have minded. But it's hard to know quite how to behave. You see, I'm *employed*, after all . . ."

The words tumbled out pell-mell. There were laughter, tears, happiness and regret in Elizabeth's voice. Above everything else there was excitement that had got just a little bit out of hand. If Ralph was looking straight into her heart he would have read there that far more important to her than this trip abroad was the signature of his approval and of a promise that love and the fulfilment of love was awaiting her return.

Ralph looked up to see Mrs. Heaton's smiling face in the doorway.

"She is going abroad, Ralph," Mrs. Heaton said. "With

Mrs. Seaton Morgan. What do you think of that? Isn't it wonderful! She'll be quite eight weeks away. Three weeks there and three weeks back. Fourteen days round the southern coast of Australia at least. . . ."

He might have known it would be something like this. The nonsense these rich women thought up!

CHAPTER TWO

WHEN THE *Albany* steamed grandly out of Southampton Water into the Channel, and Elizabeth had stowed away her things in the bright little single-berth cabin opposite Mrs. Morgan's suite, she had time to think of that night when Ralph had come to Rose Cottage a few minutes after Mrs. Morgan's chauffeur had driven her home.

How incredibly wonderful would be this cabin with its modern fittings, the built-in wardrobe, the wash basin alcove, its bedside telephone, the lamp over her bed and the clock, synchronised to the official ship's time, set high up in the panelled walls where she could see it the minute she opened her eyes in the morning—if it hadn't been for that tinge of sadness and the little probing finger of fear that came to her when she thought of Ralph. And she thought of Ralph often.

What a crazy thing was love, she thought as she sat on the soft springy bed with its gay pink cover, and brushed her hair.

Mrs. Morgan was being attended to by her maid. She had told Elizabeth to "run along and discover the ship, my dear. It's a world on its own."

First Elizabeth had unpacked and put her clothes in the wardrobe and chest of drawers. She had glimpsed the promenade decks and the fabulous sun deck and vast lounge of the ship when they had come on board. There had been a lot of hand baggage to supervise on its way to Mrs. Morgan's suite and then, because of the step over the companionways, the entrance to the lift and the step into the suite, there had been need for both Elizabeth and the maid, Hetty, to help Mrs. Morgan. The invalid could walk without any trouble on an even surface but because her right hand was still out of action she did not trust herself to take steps over things without help. She couldn't lean on her right hand·for assistance.

Then Mrs. Morgan had dismissed Elizabeth with a gay wave of her hand and a command to "discover the ship."

Now Elizabeth had changed out of her coat into one of the new long line sweaters she had bought on her shopping spree, and a simple but well-cut straight skirt, the nicest part of which, Elizabeth thought, was the cheeky kick pleat in the centre back. She had washed her face and hands and reapplied some powder and a touch of lipstick. Then because pulling on the sweater had disarranged her hair she put a plastic cape round her shoulders and sat on her bed to brush her hair.

Always her mother had taught her to brush her hair well.

"Bring out the lights . . ." her mother had always said.

Elizabeth's hair was always shining.

So she sat there, the brush swishing, half of her longing to be done with it and to run out on a tour of inspection, the other half of her wishing she could give all this away and remain at Ralph's side.

Ever since the night she had come home from Leath Manor and Ralph had come into the cottage and shown only an unusual amusement in his face she had wished she could back out of the whole venture. It would be a wonderful experience, of course. But not worth the losing of Ralph. She knew now that that was what she feared. If Ralph had wanted her the way she wanted him he would have said something about it before her departure.

Then why, she asked herself, did she want to go on clinging to him?

Because she had no other life. For five years every waking moment had one way or another been spent in some kind of communication, real or spiritual, with him. For five years his companionship had cost her the close companionship of others and she had never learned to find a society other than his. Without him there would be no ground under her feet. She would not know how to make other friends. She saw her life one long endless chain of meetings outside the Underground at nights. She saw herself and Ralph growing older . . . first the wrinkles coming and then the grey hair . . . plodding nightly, side by side, their way home from work. Their separate homes.

It wasn't good enough, she knew. But there wasn't anyone else, or any other way of life. She didn't know how to make a life without the old routine.

And she loved him. You can't spend five of your best years that way without the habit and the need becoming ingrained in the very fabric of your life.

She loved him, and the only thing wrong was that Ralph did not say . . . "It's about time we thought of getting married and settling down."

Now she was leaving him in a vacuum for eight weeks. What would he do? Her heart ached for his possible loneliness—if he really loved her. She would wish he could find other companionship to fill the gap. Some other girl?

Elizabeth brushed her hair and swallowed hard.

I must go and see the ship, she thought. Mrs. Morgan will ask me about it. She will want to write all about it to all those friends and their children on the sheep station.

The *Albany* was a good deal like every other luxury liner that steamed a route through the Mediterranean, the Red Sea and the Arabian Sea and so down the green and blue and gold of the Indian Ocean, but as Elizabeth had never been on any kind of liner before, it was all new and wonderful and quite fabulous to her. She temporarily forgot Ralph and her private sorrows as an amazing vista of lounge, sun deck, observation lounge, cocktail bar, sports deck, opened out one from another before her questing eyes.

She realised at once it would probably take her a week to find her way about the upper decks alone. Was there never any end to his great ship? Just how *long* was it?

While she was pondering this question, walking the outside, glassed-in deck, stealing curious but polite glances at her fellow travellers, she heard the lunch bugle.

What exactly did she do now? she wondered. Mrs. Morgan had told her to take her lunch in the dining-saloon. Where was it? She had seen it somewhere half a mile back on her travels . . . a wonderful panelled room, big as a ballroom, with flower-decked tables shining with silver and glassware and cradles of exotic fruit on several sideboards.

A deck steward was coming towards her and must have

read on her face the uncertainty he expected in inexperienced travellers.

"Are you taking lunch, madam? May I show you the way?"

And he did, with such a flourish of kindly deference that Elizabeth immediately was at ease. Inside the dining-saloon the steward inquired her name and then referred her to the chief dining-steward.

"Certainly, Miss Heaton," he said. "Will you follow me? A place had been reserved for you at Dr. Grant Jarvis's table."

At that moment the ship's doctor, resplendent in naval blue with the gold and red rings of his profession round his sleeve cuff, came in from another companionway. He took his place, at the head of a table set for six. Elizabeth found herself on his left hand.

"Good morning, Miss Heaton," he said with a whimsical smile. "I see the Channel is not going to frighten you off your first meal on board."

He was a middle-aged man of medium height, slightly reddish hair, blue sailor's eyes in a suntanned face and a smile with a touch of mischief in it.

"Am I supposed to feel seasick already?" Elizabeth asked in surprise. "I did notice the waves seem quite high outside but I don't feel any motion at all."

"There isn't any," the doctor assured her. "We're stabilised against motion. Those who feel seasick only think they do . . . if you know what I mean."

They exchanged smiles and Elizabeth suddenly felt she was going to enjoy her mealtimes. The twinkle in the doctor's eye made a fellow conspirator of her.

"How did you know I was Elizabeth Heaton?" she asked him.

"It was all arranged," he replied. "I tell the chief steward I want someone young and charming. Of course he immediately carries out my wishes. But there's a catch in his readiness. He then puts some solid opposition farther down the table . . . just to keep your eyes averted from me."

Elizabeth glanced round but so far the only other occupant of the table was a young woman of her own age, who was too engrossed in the menu to join in the doctor's conversation.

"Oh, he hasn't come up yet," the doctor said airily. "In

fact, if I know my cousin Grant Jarvis he'll come when, and only if, it pleases him."

"Your cousin? On the same ship? Is he an officer too?"

"Fair do's," laughed the doctor. "The other passengers have to have some gold braid at their tables. One officer to a table. No, my cousin happens to be a passenger. He's an Australian pastoralist but that's incidental to the fact he has a way of mowing down the ladies without even trying. So I'm not so fortunate after all, am I?"

"But you have exactly the same names? Isn't that confusing?"

"We only meet once in about ten years . . . and there are dozens of the family who manage to throw in a Grant in front of the Jarvis. To most of the passengers I'm just 'Doctor' anyway. And my cousin . . . to be really different from all the other members of the Jarvis family . . . carries the first name twice. Grant Grant Jarvis. How does that sound?"

The doctor was laughing and Elizabeth felt he was laughing about his cousin as well as putting her at her ease at this her first shipboard meal.

"With a name like that he ought to be an interesting table companion," Elizabeth said correctly.

This brought a whole bubble of twinkles to the doctor's eyes. He knew that Elizabeth was being a little conservative in her manner and it amused him.

"Well, what are you going to eat?" he said. "I recommend the crayfish *mornay*. Our chef makes it a speciality to win the passengers' approval from the moment of making way."

The other young woman at the table was not easy to draw into conversation so that most of the time Elizabeth and the doctor were able to have a tête-à-tête.

"Will Mrs. Morgan sit with us at this table?" Elizabeth asked. "I know she is anxious to come to meals as soon as she has got what she calls her sea legs. She had an accident, unfortunately . . ."

"Yes. I already have her on my list of patients. Not, however at my table. It's the captain's table for Mrs. Morgan. She is very well known on this line and quite an old friend of Captain Wells."

"She has travelled backwards and forwards a great deal," Elizabeth said. "You know I am her secretary?"

The doctor's eyes twinkled again.

"What she really said was 'Take care of my young friend, won't you? I want her to enjoy this voyage.'"

Elizabeth felt touched.

"Did she really? She is the kindest person I've ever met."

"Fairy godmother to everyone she knows, if you ask me. And every officer and steward on the line looks forward to her trips."

Elizabeth nibbled thoughtfully on a biscuit for a minute. Then she looked up and said quite seriously:

"That is a great tribute, isn't it?"

The doctor nodded his head.

"She's a great little lady."

"And I suspect it was she who had a hand at putting me at your table and not the chief steward at all," Elizabeth said with a smile.

"We are twin souls," the doctor replied instantly. "We think alike and exactly the same thing at the same time. Now, if Mrs. Morgan had a mind about who was to sit with whom, it was an absolute certainty that I, and the chief steward, of course, would have been in telepathic communication with her. Do you see what I mean?"

"I see all right," said Elizabeth. "But thank you for being so gallant about it. I'm glad you are twin souls, you know. I think Mrs. Morgan suffers some pain with her leg but she would never admit it to anyone . . . not even the doctor."

He was serious for the first time.

"I'll watch out for that," he said. Then to change the subject he commented again on the absence of three of their table companions.

"I'm not going to let Grant Grant Jarvis off his social commitments," he said. "I'll see that lofty young man comes to the table occasionally even if I bring him by the ear."

"Oh, he is young, is he?"

"Thirty-five . . . six. I'm not sure which. That's kindergarten age compared with an old salt like me, you know." He leaned forward and said in a shy whisper, "I think we'll play the joke of jokes on him and put him at the end of the other side, next to Miss Lovegrove there. Their conversational duet will probably make the dining-saloon resound with silence. And it'll leave you to me."

Elizabeth laughed. This ship's doctor was amusing and a good table mate even if he was a little impish. She had one more cause for feeling gratitude to Mrs. Morgan. In pulling strings, by right of being a privileged passenger, she had seen that Elizabeth would have an amusing time at the table.

And not only at the table for as they rose the doctor gave a pleasant bow and said:

"As soon as we're through the Bay of Biscay we dance on the sun deck. I'm going to be your first partner and introduce you to all the handsomest officers and the best dancers. May I have that honour?"

Elizabeth felt that her cup was full and it would be base ingratitude to the Fates to let her spirits hover sadly because Ralph might miss her to the extent of finding another girl. Wasn't she finding gay companions herself? And did that mean she deflected from her love for Ralph by one iota?

It was in a much warmer and happier mood that she found her way to Mrs. Morgan's suite and knocked gently on the door. Hetty, the maid, answered it and said:

"Oh, come in, Miss Heaton. Mrs. Morgan has had her lunch and is settled for the afternoon. But she is anxious to see you."

Elizabeth hoped she hadn't been too long away from her employer but Mrs. Morgan soon put her mind at rest.

She was stretched on a pretty chintz-covered settee against the wall of the miniature drawing-room of the suite. An equally pretty coverlet was over her legs and she was sitting up against a bank of cushions. The cabin was sweet with the odour of the many flowers that had been sent to the ship by Mrs. Morgan's friends. On the small sideboard against the inner wall was a silver bowl stacked high with fruit.

Hetty passed into the sleeping-cabin and Mrs. Morgan held out one hand eagerly to Elizabeth.

"Come and sit down and tell me all about it at once," she said eagerly. "Now whom did you see up on the decks and what are they dressed in? What are your table mates like? Do tell me, Elizabeth, are there any frightfully smart women on board and how many of the men look as if they might be millionaires or peers?"

Elizabeth could not help laughing as she sat down in a small chair beside the settee. Like the letters Mrs. Morgan had been writing to all those people in Australia her very voice was rich with her interest in other people and in the things that were happening all about her.

"I'm very sorry, I wouldn't know a millionaire from a peer," Elizabeth said. "But there are quite a lot of distinguished-looking people about. Some of the ladies look as if their coats were of mink and one man I saw wore a monocle and had another man following him with his rug and coat. I suppose it was his valet. There were two terrifically smart-looking girls leaning over the railing on the deck, but I didn't see them at lunch . . ."

"Oh, about lunch. Now tell me, who have you got at your table and did you like Dr. Jarvis?"

Elizabeth felt the questions were bubbling from Mrs. Morgan like frothy water down a mill race. It was hard to keep them in their proper order.

"I thought Dr. Jarvis was a darling," Elizabeth said promptly. "I was really very shy about going into the dining-saloon, but five minutes after I sat down I felt as if I'd been doing it all my life."

"Of course," laughed Mrs. Morgan. One of the things she liked most about Elizabeth was the girl's frank honesty about herself. "Now tell me about your other table companions. We'll see enough of Dr. Jarvis during the whole trip. I might tell you, Elizabeth, I booked our passages on the *Albany* because I was going to be certain about my ship's doctor. I've known that red-headed rascal for years. Now, tell me, dear. Have you got a lot of old fogies at the table or someone interesting?"

"There was only one other passenger present to-day. Three vacant places, I'm afraid. Dr. Jarvis introduced me to Miss Lovegrove but she's very quiet. She did not seem to wish to join in the conversation."

Mrs. Morgan helped herself to a chocolate from a dish on the shelf that was on the wall side of her settee.

"Plain or beautiful? Well dressed or just so-so?" she asked.

Elizabeth told her that Miss Lovegrove was good-looking, smart in her dressing, but as yet, not very interested in her fellow passengers. In fact, she seemed bored.

"It is the first day out," Elizabeth added with a smile. "I don't suppose anyone feels their very best after being up since about five o'clock and then making that train journey from London."

Mrs. Morgan patted her hand.

"I can guess the rest," she said with a laugh. "So you still have to wait to find out about the rest of your manger mates?"

"Dr. Grant Jarvis did tell me about a cousin of his who is to sit at the end of the table. Someone between thirty and forty, I think, he said. A pastoralist from Australia . . ." It was Elizabeth's turn to laugh. "Not very communicative, I gather. Dr. Jarvis said he was very lofty."

"Some of the Grant Jarvis family are like that," Mrs. Morgan said reminiscently. "There are dozens of them and they range from amongst the richest in the country to the poorest. The original Grant Jarvis brothers . . . there were two of them . . . went out to Australia three generations ago. One of them had fifteen children and the other eight. They spread all over the country and they're not all pastoralists. You meet them in almost every occupation. Our nice ship's doctor for instance."

"Dr. Jarvis did say this one was a pastoralist and his name is *Grant* Grant Jarvis."

"Not *the* Grant Grant Jarvis, surely?" she said. "If so we *will* have some fun!"

The maid Hetty had just come back into the room and was putting some magazines in a bedside rack near the settee.

"Hetty, bring me that passenger list that was in the cabin, will you?"

"It's here, Mrs. Morgan. I put it in the top drawer of the cabinet. I know it is always useful to have handy."

She handed Mrs. Morgan the folder of ship's passengers that was left in each cabin for the interest of all passengers. Mrs. Morgan ran her finger down the list.

"Here it is," she said. "A very modest G. Grant Jarvis. Now, I wonder . . ."

Hetty was smiling to herself and her mistress caught her eye.

"What is it, Hetty?" she asked. "I can see you've been hiding something interesting in that head of yours."

"The gentleman who has the suite next to ours, Mrs. Morgan, is called Mr. Jarvis. I heard the steward addressing him . . . and most carefully. In fact he was addressing him as if he was an Indian prince. And I must admit Mr. Jarvis sounded and looked as if he was used to it. If the doctor called him very lofty I think that must be the right word. But I must admit he is very handsome and striking looking . . ."

"That'll be him," Mrs. Morgan said with delight. "Well, we are going to have an interesting voyage with fellow passengers who behave as if they're Indian princes. Elizabeth, you must tell me all about him after dinner."

"You do not feel equal to going on deck for dinner to-night, Mrs. Morgan?"

"No, my dear. I insist on getting my sea legs first. I'm not going to appear up there like some crippled old lady who needs two helping arms as well as a walking-stick. But don't worry, child. It will only be a day or two. In the meantime, I want you to go to the ship's shop and do a little shopping for me."

"Oh, yes, certainly," Elizabeth said eagerly. "I'm most anxious to be of assistance."

"Of course you are. Well, you shall be, my dear. As soon as we're through the Bay of Biscay I want you to go through all my letters and put them in order of date . . ."

"Yes, Mrs. Morgan."

The older lady smiled.

"You see, Elizabeth, all my letter writing has a point to it. I caution all my relatives and friends they must keep my letters and hand them back to me. And from those letters I'm going to write my travel book."

This she said with a flourish and an air of triumph that made Elizabeth smile.

"I'm so glad," Elizabeth said fervently. "Those I did for you before were so interesting I thought all along they sounded like a travel book . . ." She blushed. "I couldn't help knowing what was in them, Mrs. Morgan."

Mrs. Morgan laughed her apologies away.

"And now you know why I'm so interested in people. All kinds of people. They have to go into my book. I never think a travel book is much fun myself unless it's got people as well as places in it. But you mustn't tell anyone. You must only tell me about the interesting people you see or meet. Then I'll look forward to meeting them myself. Especially the Indian prince, Elizabeth. Only, of course, we have to remember he's a millionaire pastoralist from Australia and not from India at all."

"A millionaire?" exclaimed Elizabeth.

"A wool king. If he really is *the* Grant Jarvis of Kybarrli. Near enough to a millionaire anyway, only they never use that word in Australia. They call them 'wool kings' or 'cattle kings.' But it is the same thing."

The name "Kybarrli" suddenly rang a bell for Elizabeth. Kybarrli Grade IA merino wool. The most sought-after wool by her own firm Small and Smallwoods, woolbuyers. In fact it was like a gala day in Small's when a cable came through from the buyers at the wool auctions in Australia announcing a Kybarrli buy. The competition for it was always very hard and the prices seemed in the celestial realms but the wool was so much sought after by high quality manufacturers that Small's were eager to handle it, when they could get it.

So Elizabeth was not only to see . . . but actually to sit at table with the man who grew Kybarrli merino wool. What a strange and rather wonderful world it was, after all!

The owners and growers of Kybarrli were legendary figures in a wool firm like Small and Smallwoods. No wonder Mrs. Morgan, who was the wife of one of the partners, knew all about the Grant Jarvis family.

Elizabeth felt her spirits rising very high as she went about Mrs. Morgan's shopping in the great glamour shop on the "B" deck. Mrs. Morgan had explained as a seasoned traveller she never cluttered up her luggage with the "bits and pieces" she knew could be bought on board ship.

"It's half the fun of being on board," she said. "The shop is quite the most heavenly place on the whole ship."

And so it was to Elizabeth. The showcases gleamed with every variety of small purchasable wear imaginable ranging from toilet requisites . . . every well-known make having its own glamour showcase . . . to lingerie, jewellery, tobaccos, books, magazines, children's toys, souvenirs of every kind and clothing for wear in the tropical climates. The hairdresser's shop and the barber's adjoining were equally alluring to Elizabeth. Everything was draped, decorated and arranged in a most glamorous manner; yet when Elizabeth noted the prices she perceived in astonishment that everything cost very much less than on land.

"Everything is duty free once we're three miles out," the assistant said, noticing Elizabeth's surprised expression. "Experienced travellers like Mrs. Morgan know it is much less trouble and much less expensive to leave their toilet things, their stockings, extra hankies and things until after they're on board. All you have to do for Mrs. Morgan is to sign the chit, Miss Heaton. Mrs. Morgan has informed us you are likely to do her shopping for her. She settles her account at the end of the voyage."

After Elizabeth had handed her shopping items to Hetty— Mrs. Morgan was now having an afternoon rest—her one desire was to find the writing-room and start pouring out to her mother and Ralph all the wonderful things she was discovering about a great passenger liner like the *Albany*.

Oddly enough as she tried to pen these thoughts to Ralph she found herself carefully modifying her enthusiasm, almost as if, at the bottom of her heart, she knew Ralph would not approve of her losing her head over such "trifles." He seemed so far away from her in spirit as well as in the flesh that suddenly her old anxiety came back again.

Would this journey drive an insurmountable rift between them? Oh, if only at their first port of call—Malta—there could be a reassuring letter from Ralph! How it would put the colours of the rainbow in her sky!

Suddenly, from gay, bewildered excitement, Elizabeth's feelings plunged downward and she experienced a wave of homesickness that brought the tears behind her eyes.

If only, at Malta, there would be a letter from Ralph. A letter full of love and comfort and well-wishing!

To get such a letter it would have to have been sent by air and probably within a day of her departure from Southampton. She was quite sure Ralph would not write as hastily as all that.

As she sat in the ship's writing-room, her fountain pen in her hand, her eyes staring unseeingly through the porthole, she saw in her mind's eye Ralph's face as the train had slowly moved out from Waterloo station.

His face had been a little pale, but more strikingly handsome for that very reason. He had brought her flowers, and a box of chocolates, and at the last minute he had kissed her a second time; and there had been a lingering fervour in that kiss that had caught at her heart.

Elizabeth, sitting in the *Albany*'s writing-room, felt a longing to be back, hastily running up the last steps of the Underground to see his familiar figure waiting just beyond the booking-office.

She was unaware that her eyes glistened with tears until she turned her face away from the porthole and saw that a man had sat down at the small writing-desk opposite. He was stretching his hand forward to take some ship's note-paper from the slot and he looked over the top of the desk at Elizabeth.

Through her misty eyes she saw an extremely handsome face, sunbrowned, with cold grey-blue eyes that were looking at her with a kind of intent and momentary curiosity.

Instantly the man looked down at his desk but because of his long straight back and the fact that he barely inclined his head at all Elizabeth could still see the whole of his face. He had thick, straight, dark brown hair over a square forehead with well-marked brows, a good straight nose, a jaw that was square and too firm to be kind. His mouth was a straight line. The grey-blue eyes and that mouth gave an impression of hardness . . . and indifference.

Elizabeth quickly blinked the tears from her eyes and bent her head over her own letter writing.

It was not his fault he had seen her distressed, she knew that, but she felt angry and humiliated in the face of the coldness she had read in the intense glance that dismissed her as someone of unimportance who showed her feelings in public places. Without having any idea who he was, except that he would be a fellow passenger, she hated him, not only because he had seen her with tears in her eyes but because he had shown cold humiliating dislike of those tears.

Presently, her letters unfinished, she got up and walked away. She knew that he neither lifted his head nor was aware that she had walked away. Such indifference is galling, even to a diffident and humble girl like Elizabeth Heaton.

At dinner that night a young married couple, Mr. and Mrs. Patterson, joined the doctor's table. There was still no evidence of Mr. Grant Jarvis. Neither was the doctor himself present. The married couple, who soon made themselves known and proved themselves very friendly, suggested laughingly that so many passengers already "thought" themselves seasick that the doctor had had to stay on duty.

Miss Lovegrove, who had spoken very little, looked up.

"I don't think Mr. Grant Jarvis, who will sit at the bottom of the table here, is seasick at all events. I saw him playing deck tennis with the doctor and two of the officers an hour ago."

"Perhaps he is the kind of person who doesn't eat while at sea," Mrs. Patterson said jokingly.

"Or prefers the officers' wardroom," Miss Lovegrove said. "I heard his opponents inviting him there as they finished the game."

"Let's all take up deck tennis," Mr. Patterson said. "We might get invited to the wardroom."

"It would be rather a crowd if all the passengers were invited," said Elizabeth with a smile.

"Well, let's all play deck tennis when the sports are begun after we get into the Mediterranean, anyway," persisted Mr. Patterson. "We might have a small side bet as to who gets invited into the wardroom first."

"But Mr. Grant Jarvis has already won that, hasn't he?" asked Elizabeth.

"We'll count him out," said the young husband. "From what a couple of the passengers have already told me he's first in on the privileges anyway. I suppose the only reason he's not sitting at the captain's table is because the doctor happens to be some kind of relative."

Elizabeth thought they had talked quite enough about the missing table mate who, in her private mind, she called "the Indian prince."

"I'd like to play tennis anyway," she said. "Mrs. Morgan told me they have organised sport on the decks and one has to put one's name down on the notice board outside the purser's office."

"Quite right, young lady. We'll all do it together after dinner. How about you, Miss Lovegrove?"

"I'm afraid I don't play anything. I only watch. It is just as interesting and less strenuous."

"But you can't win a trophy that way."

"No, but your time is your own."

Elizabeth wondered about how much time the organised sport would take. When she had seen Mrs. Morgan immediately before dinner she had been told to enter in the competitions and she knew Mrs. Morgan really genuinely wished her to do this. But her conscience would not rest happy if it took up too much of her employer's time.

She would be careful to enter in one or two events only.

As Elizabeth completed her meal and rose to leave the dining-saloon a tall man, extremely well dressed in a dinner jacket with a black bow tie, came in. As soon as Elizabeth saw him she knew he was the man who had sat opposite her in the writing-room. His face was just as stern and disinterested and aloof as it had been when he had seen the tears in her eyes . . . and he was not looking at her now as he walked through the room, totally unconscious that he was causing a considerable stir of interest on all sides.

Elizabeth, at the entrance, wondered if it was his good looks, his height, or his chilly air of indifference that caused the heads to turn. In her heart she already disliked him but, like the others, she could not help but turn her head to look at his receding back. She couldn't help admitting that a very unusual and striking person had just entered the dining-saloon.

To her astonishment he sat down in the vacant place at the doctor's table.

So that was Grant Grant Jarvis of Kybarrli!

She felt dismay stiffen her own backbone.

The "wool king" wasn't going to be such fun, after all. It was a good thing he did come late to meals. His cold haughty presence would spoil what otherwise promised to be a happy table. And would he remember those writing-room tears of hers?

Of course not. Neither she nor the occasion would be of much importance to a man like that.

Outside Mrs. Morgan's suite Elizabeth met Hetty, the maid.

"Miss Heaton, such fun!" Hetty whispered conspiratorially. "The Prince of India called on Mrs. Morgan and had a cocktail with her." Hetty's generally austere face flushed. "He's really quite charming and I was so excited I was afraid Mrs. Morgan would notice it."

"He's not a prince of India, he's just a wool king, Hetty," Elizabeth said. "And we're not to lose our heads over him. I've seen him and I'm quite sure too many people all his life have been losing their heads. You can see it in his manner."

"You wait till you talk to him at close quarters. Mrs. Morgan is a victim, anyway. She told me so."

With that Hetty sped away on her errand to the steward.

Elizabeth tapped on the drawing-room door and entered the suite. Mrs. Morgan was sitting in her arm-chair just finishing her coffee.

"Elizabeth dear . . . you'll never guess. I've arranged for you to play deck tennis with Mr. Grant Jarvis. You do play tennis, don't you, dear?"

"Oh, no!" Elizabeth cried. "I mean . . . yes, I do. Play tennis, I mean. But *not* with Mr. Grant Jarvis. I saw him in the writing-room and I'd be terrified of playing with him."

"Nonsense. He's utterly charming. He said he'd be only too pleased to oblige me."

"Yes," said Elizabeth soberly. "It would be to oblige you, Mrs. Morgan. You see . . . I wasn't at my best in the writing-room."

"Nobody's at their best on their first day at sea," Mrs. Morgan said firmly. "And you'll play tennis with Mr. Grant Jarvis to oblige me too, Elizabeth." Then her manner softened and the smile became gay and friendly. "Don't forget my travel book, dear. I must have a character just like him in it. Consider playing tennis with Mr. Grant Jarvis part of your secretarial duties and you're to tell me all about him afterwards."

The smile in Mrs. Morgan's eyes heartened Elizabeth to the other's sense of fun.

After all, Grant Grant Jarvis of Kybarrli was not an ogre. He could hardly eat her while throwing tennis quoits over a high net on the decks of an ocean liner.

She could match his aloofness with some of her own. There were always thoughts and dreams of Ralph to fill her waking hours without worrying about a proud rich man who would only play deck tennis with her to "oblige Mrs. Morgan."

Well, she was playing tennis with him for the same reason. Fair enough!

CHAPTER THREE

THROUGH THE Mediterranean part of the voyage Elizabeth spent her mornings going through Mrs. Morgan's accumulated letters and taking from her dictation about the people on the ship and the places they visited in Malta and Port Said. Elizabeth typed her work with carbon copies and thus Mrs. Morgan was able to send chatty copies back to her friends in England and air-mail copies on to her many "families" on the sheep station in Australia. One copy was kept for the growing file on her book of travels.

In the afternoon everyone took a rest, but after afternoon tea Elizabeth played tennis with Mr. Grant Jarvis.

The first game had shown that Elizabeth's years of tennis at the vicarage in Mereton made her very nimble and accurate with the quoits on the ship's deck. Grant Jarvis, earlier, played most of the time with the ship's officers. When the mixed doubles competition began, however, quietly and still with his remote and aloof manner, he crossed to Elizabeth, made a slight bow and requested her to be his partner for the doubles.

She knew that in the first instance it was Mrs. Morgan's suggestion and in the second instance because she played reasonably well and it preserved him from the effort of asking some other lady passenger.

Two, Elizabeth had thought, can play at the game of being aloof and indifferent. So in her manner she treated him as he treated her. They were ideal partners as the competition went on. Except for the small politenesses of the game such as "Your serve, partner," a hurried "I'll take that one," "Cross!" there was no conversation. After the game was over the four players would have a cool drink together in the glassed-in deck lounge. The conversation was always desultory because Grant Jarvis's cold manner seemed to intimidate them all.

Really, Elizabeth thought, he might make some effort to be more sociable!

Mrs. Morgan was tremendously amused and vastly interested in what she called this "very naïve situation."

She was, after a few days, able to come on deck and watch

the games. Grant Jarvis would then, at the completion of a game, sit down beside her, order a drink for her and fall quite easily into a conversation . . . always quiet and reticent . . . about their various interests in pastoral properties in Australia. He never once looked at any of the promenading passengers or evinced interest in anyone else.

Several times Elizabeth caught Mrs. Morgan chuckling about it and once she asked, rather timidly, why this cold proud man caused her entertainment.

"My dear child, that cast-iron shell of his is merely a protective barrier. People as rich and as well known as Grant Jarvis are always open to be courted, not for themselves, but for what they've got. They learn it early in life. They get a little bitter about it. I'm not being unkind when I smile, Elizabeth. I'm just amused at the deftness with which he can keep people at arm's length. It is quite an art."

"I'm only a tennis partner . . . chosen by you," Elizabeth said quietly. "A little more conversation from him wouldn't encourage me to court him, I can assure you. A person like Mr. Grant Jarvis is as remote from me, in any event, as if he was someone from Mars."

"I'm quite sure of it, my dear. That's wherein your charm for him lies." Mrs. Morgan's eyes were really laughing now. "Oh, don't look so startled! I don't mean he wishes to court you. I only mean he feels 'safe' to play tennis with you. That's why he continues to ask you. Those glamour girls over there, with their cultivated looks and their sophistication would be dynamite if they had your opportunities."

In the quietness of her own pleasant cabin Elizabeth, as she dressed for dinner, thought over Mrs. Morgan's words. She found it hard to understand why the thought of herself being "safe" was a little depressing. She didn't want to be in Mr. Grant Jarvis's company, yet it was hard to be in anyone's company on the basis that you were "safe," when beautiful and sophisticated girls were not. It meant she wasn't glamorous or sophisticated in other people's eyes. Well, she knew that. All the same . . .

Meantime, Grant Jarvis, when he did come to the dining-saloon, which was not often, always came late. Elizabeth was on time as she wished to attend to anything Mrs. Morgan wanted as soon as possible. They met only as they passed one another in the dining-room and then Grant Jarvis would give her a formal bow but no smile. Elizabeth would return the bow and offer the faintest of smiles. After a few days she was aware that other passengers, sitting at their tables, began to watch her too with curious eyes. She knew it was because she was the recipient of that cold bow as Grant Jarvis passed her.

Strangely enough that in itself began to give her a certain vicarious enjoyment. She began to see shipboard life, and the lively curiosity people had in one another . . . the speculation each had about the other, the little gossiping . . . as something interesting and fun making. She now understood Mrs. Morgan's great interest in and love of her fellow men.

Elizabeth would hasten back to Mrs. Morgan's suite to tell her all about it and had her reward in her employer's obvious enjoyment.

Mrs. Morgan always took her lunch now in the dining-saloon but she found the effort too great for dinner at night. She preferred to dress, have dinner in her own suite after asking a few friends in to cocktails and then making the slow journey to one of the drawing-rooms later in the evening to play bridge.

Elizabeth herself went to the boat deck where dancing took place every night. True to his word Dr. Jarvis had found her a host of partners amongst the officers and gradually she found herself included in a gay party each evening.

She also noticed that the two glamorous girls, both slender and expensively dressed, the one fair and the other dark, had taken much to the doctor's company. On one occasion he promenaded the deck before dinner with one on each side.

It was a glorious tropical night . . . their first night in the Red Sea. There was no sign of a breeze but a promise in the air of great heat on the morrow.

Mrs. Morgan had been a little tired.

"Go and walk the deck in the evening air, while you can, Elizabeth," she said. "If we have a following breeze in this land-locked sea to-morrow we're all going to be prostrate. You'll find that Dr. Jarvis will ban deck sports to-morrow to prevent the too strenuous from suffering from heat exhaustion and even sunstroke."

Elizabeth had already seen the notice posted outside the purser's office warning all passengers to keep their heads covered even when sitting in the shade of the awnings.

"Would you like to sit on the deck to-night?" Elizabeth asked Mrs. Morgan. "I could get the deck steward to find a cool place for you."

"Yes, Elizabeth, I would be glad if you would arrange that. Even in an air-conditioned suite the stillness of the air is oppressive."

As Elizabeth stepped into the gangway on this errand, she noticed the door into the suite next door was open. Grant Jarvis was about to emerge and the steward at that moment came into the gangway to speak to him. Elizabeth had perforce to stand still and wait the few seconds the two men took to stand back while she passed them. She could not help hearing what took place.

"Mr. Grant Jarvis?" the steward inquired politely. "There is a gentleman in Number Seventy-four. A Mr. Wallaston of Melbourne. He would like very much to see you. He inquires when you might be available to meet him."

"I'm not available to meet anyone," Grant Jarvis replied shortly. "I've given that instruction already."

The steward gave a perfunctory bow as he accepted this statement and at the same time he flattened himself against the wall in order that Elizabeth might pass freely along the short passageway.

She felt herself flinch back from that snub Grant Jarvis had handed out to the unknown Mr. Wallaston. She did not turn her head as she passed the two men to see whether Grant Jarvis was prepared to greet her or not. She felt shocked that any man could treat his fellow passengers with what sounded remarkably like contempt.

Although Mrs. Morgan had begged her faithfully to recount all the little incidents of the voyage Elizabeth could not bring herself to mention this particular one. Yet it made her so angry she could not keep her thoughts from it even when, after dinner, she sat with Mrs. Morgan on the forward part of the port deck savouring the relief given by the ship moving through the night air.

She did, however, mention she had seen the doctor promenading with the two attractive girls. They had just gone past laughing and chattering with two of the officers.

"When I'm in the tropics I always think the ship's officers look wonderful in their white uniforms," Mrs. Morgan said. "Then, when overnight we get into cooler regions, I feel thrilled to see them back in their naval blues with their gold rings and epaulettes."

"I suppose they will wear tropical whites until we get to Australia," remarked Elizabeth.

"Nearly," said Mrs. Morgan. "Don't forget that June in Australia is winter and though the sun shines and it's nothing like as cold as England it still can be fairly cold going round the southern coast. Did those two girls actually smile at us just then, Elizabeth?"

"Yes, they did. They've smiled at me several times yesterday and to-day. And they were promenading with the doctor before dinner." Elizabeth hesitated and then laughed. "He gave me an enormous wink twice as they went past."

Mrs. Morgan's laugh tinkled out.

"Don't you see, my dear? You and the doctor are the pipelines to the wool king. They want to meet him. And quite properly too, of course. Any girl who doesn't take an opportunity to meet that man is very foolish." And she laughed again.

Elizabeth was silent for a few minutes because she was thinking of Grant Jarvis's capacity for handing out a snub like a kick from a mule. At that moment he went past. He was promenading the deck, immaculate in a perfectly tailored fawn-coloured tropical dinner jacket, one hand in his pocket and the other holding a lighted cigarette. He was a shadowy figure in the half-lights of the shadowed promenade deck but his tall figure was unmistakable.

"The cat that walks by himself," Elizabeth said involuntarily.

Mrs. Morgan touched her arm gently.

"Is that how all the young people on the ship feel about him?" she inquired.

"I . . . I don't really know," Elizabeth explained. "I have been careful not to discuss him with anyone though I can't help noticing that everyone looks at him and I suppose they must be thinking something about him."

"And what do *you* think of him?"

Elizabeth would have liked to tell the truth . . . that she thought him proud and rude. She knew, however, that Mrs.

Morgan liked him and had a certain sympathy for his isola-
tion and it would be bad manners on her own part to be
critical of someone who had shown Mrs. Morgan the courtesy
of calling on her; and had seemed quite at ease in having a
conversation with her. Yet she could not stray too far from
the truth.

"He is very reserved," she said. "One cannot get to know
a person like that . . . so it isn't wise to make up one's mind
about him, is it?"

"As I said before, my dear, that reserve is a conscious barrier. It isn't there for everybody. You wait and see. We'll call
him over if he goes past us again."

Elizabeth smothered an exclamation of dismay. How dreadful it would be if Grant Jarvis rebuffed the overtures in the
same manner in which he had dismissed the unknown Mr.
Wallaston's attempt to meet him. Elizabeth felt herself quiver-
ing with anxiety and praying that Grant Jarvis would have
altered his route and gone to promenade on some other deck.
Her anxiety was all for Mrs. Morgan as she felt that any
snub directed at herself would be meaningless.

However, as Grant Jarvis turned the corner of the deck and
Mrs. Morgan called to him, he came across quite readily.

"Good evening, Mrs. Morgan," he said with a slight bow.
"I did not see you sitting there. Are you vying with everyone else for a breath of fresh air?"

As Mrs. Morgan asked him to sit down with them he
made a slight bow in Elizabeth's direction and murmured a
barely audible "Good evening." Elizabeth's reply was equally
inaudible. He sat down on Mrs. Morgan's right hand and
although there were vacant seats on Elizabeth's left she was
greatly relieved. Now he would talk to Mrs. Morgan and
leave her to her own thoughts.

However, she could not help but take an interest in their
conversation. For one thing Grant Jarvis's voice . . . so rarely
heard . . . was pleasantly modulated and Elizabeth was surprised to hear him talking about things that were of mutual
interest to both himself and Mrs. Morgan. They talked about
their pastoral properties, about the effects of seasons on certain natural pastures; or artesian bore water which kept the
sheep and cattle alive . . . and at some length about the stud
merino farm Grant Jarvis apparently owned and from which

came most of the champion rams that furthered the industry throughout Australia.

He seemed to speak of a number of different properties and Elizabeth began to comprehend just how widely spread were his land-owning interests.

Now and again Mrs. Morgan turned to Elizabeth to include her in the conversation.

"Our artesian wells are fairly shallow," she said. "But they tell me that at Kybarrli you go down almost as deep as the Persian wells at Aden."

She put out her hand and touched Elizabeth.

"By the way, my dear. When we get to Aden you must take a car and go out to Old Aden and visit the wells. They were known to be there and used two thousand years ago. I'm right, aren't I, Mr. Jarvis?"

"About two and a half thousand years, I think," Grant said. "I've got one well on the cattle run out west that could have been known to the aborigines quite as long. When I went down it for the first time I found relics and wall paintings that go further back than any other discoveries in Australia." He leaned forward slightly so as to speak across Mrs. Morgan. "If you would care to see the Wells of Aden, Miss Heaton, I shall be going up there. I would be glad to take you. I am going alone."

Before Elizabeth could speak Mrs. Morgan answered for her.

"Of course she would be delighted to go with you, Mr. Jarvis. She will be with a real authority on wells. How kind of you to think of it."

Had Mrs. Morgan not been with her Elizabeth was sure she would have declined. As it was she could only say "Thank you very much" and wish her heart didn't thump so painfully and that she didn't have a sudden longing for that engagement ring that Ralph was so long in promising her . . . and which would have protected her so much from any ideas Grant Jarvis might have as to her ready availability to accompany him.

At that moment the two girls . . . the dark and the fair . . . who had earlier been promenading with the ship's officers, strolled by. They hesitated and then came across and sat down on the deck chairs beside Elizabeth.

The fair girl spoke first.

"You're Miss Heaton, aren't you?" she said. "We've watched you play tennis. I'm Marjorie Radford and this is Sylvia Kent. Do tell us, have you travelled much that you can play deck tennis as partner to the ship's champion?"

Both girls laughed and ducked their heads forward to look past Elizabeth and Mrs. Morgan at Grant Jarvis.

Elizabeth was forced by the rule of good manners to introduce both girls to Mrs. Morgan and then to Grant Jarvis. The girls immediately edged their chairs a little forward so that the group was now sitting in a half circle. They bothered no further with Elizabeth. Having gained their end . . . which was to meet Grant Jarvis . . . they now expended their conversational charms exclusively on him.

"You play deck tennis marvellously, Mr. Jarvis," Sylvia Kent said. "The chief officer told me you were better than any of the officers . . . and that's saying something, isn't it? After all, they're at it every day of their lives whereas you spend most of your time on land, don't you?"

The question demanded an answer and Elizabeth held her breath waiting for Grant Jarvis's snub. She even felt faintly sorry for the two girls because they had so obviously laid themselves open for it. To her surprise Grant Jarvis answered quite civilly.

"I have a veranda tennis court at Kybarrli," he said. "We usually get a game in two or three times a week."

"Oh, Kybarrli" exclaimed the fair girl . . . Marjorie Radford. "I've heard of it, you know. I believe it's a fabulous place. I was at school with Gaylie Paton. She had some connection with your family. I knew her awfully well. She was always talking about you. I'm so glad to meet you. I almost feel I know you already . . . because of Gaylie, of course."

The atmosphere, in spite of the heat of the Red Sea night, froze. Elizabeth felt Mrs. Morgan stiffen beside her. It was as if Grant Jarvis sent an electric current of anger through each of them as they sat there side by side. As there was a kind of vacuum in the conversation because Grant Jarvis did not answer, Marjorie Radford hastened on.

"I've written to Gaylie from Malta and told her you were on board and we would be bound to meet you——"

She could go no further because Grant Jarvis had stood up.

"That is very kind of you, Miss . . . um . . . um." He made no attempt to pretend he remembered her name. "I'm sure that is an intelligence Gaylie, in her busy life, will have time to welcome. Now, if you will excuse me, Mrs. Morgan . . . Miss Heaton . . . I will leave you now. I have some letter writing to attend to myself."

"Yes, do go along, Mr. Jarvis," Mrs. Morgan said agreeably. "It was so kind of you to interrupt your promenade for us. Good night. And I do hope it *will* be a good night. It is getting hotter, I'm afraid."

"Good night," Grant Jarvis said twice, the first time for Mrs. Morgan and the second time probably to include the three girls sitting on the other side of Mrs. Morgan. He turned and walked abruptly away.

"Phew!" said Marjorie Radford. "Something frightened His Royal Highness off. Not very polite, is he?"

"I think it was the mention of Gaylie Paton," Sylvia Kent said. "I always thought she had her cap set at him, even when we were at school. She used to talk about his being the head of the family and everyone expecting either herself or her sister Thera to marry him just to keep all that land in the family."

"I'd forgotten that," said Marjorie Radford ruefully. "I suppose it was just one of those subjects I should not have raised."

Elizabeth felt suddenly sorry for the two girls. They had tried so hard to meet him and then having met him had tried so hard, in their own way, to establish some conversational contact . . . and had failed so dismally. Whatever this Gaylie Paton had told her school friends about Grant Jarvis she had not told them his genius for snubbing.

"He never stays in conversation very long," Elizabeth said gently. "Please don't feel offended."

"*You* seem to get on with him all right," Marjorie Radford said.

"Not in conversation. Only in tennis," Elizabeth said lightly.

"My dear child," Mrs. Morgan said firmly. "He is taking you to see the Wells of Aden. That's not playing tennis. You are much too modest, Elizabeth."

"Oh, is he?" both girls echoed in unison.

"I shall write to Gaylie Paton from Aden and tell her he's gallivanting with an English girl out on the desert . . . just to punish her for not warning us what a lofty hero he is."

Elizabeth laughed.

"Hetty calls him a prince of India," she said. "But we've decided he's just a wool king."

"Much the same thing, you'll find when you get to Australia . . . if it's your first visit there," Sylvia said. "They don't have temples and weigh themselves in jewels, but their stations, if they're big ones, are baronial estates and their stockmen are retainers in the true feudal sense of the word."

"As the wife of a station owner I must add then that feudal lords are a very kindly race as far as their stockmen are concerned," Mrs. Morgan put in gently. "And now, Elizabeth, I wonder if you would call Hetty. I think I'll go below and get some sleep before the day's heat wakes me too early in the morning, and I won't have had enough to please me."

As a little later, with Hetty's help, they went below, Mrs. Morgan laughed merrily over the evening's entertainment.

"You see, Elizabeth," she said. "It takes every kind to make a ship's complement of passengers. Those poor girls. What a fruitless approach it was, wasn't it? However, the doctor told me they were rather pushing in their attentions all round so I'm afraid they had to learn a lesson from someone."

"I was very afraid, when you mentioned the Wells of Aden, he might think *I* wished for his company," Elizabeth said uneasily.

"He invited you himself. If I did try to manœuvre it you must forgive me, Elizabeth."

They had reached the drawing-room of the suite and Mrs. Morgan straightened herself and looked at Elizabeth calmly and without a smile in her eyes this time.

"You see, my dear," she went on, "I'm very anxious to consolidate the connection between the Jarvis pastoral properties and Small and Smallwoods. You and I are on a little diplomatic mission in this matter."

Elizabeth's dismay showed in her face. Suddenly, with great illumination, she could see the truth of what Mrs. Morgan herself had said earlier . . . everyone who met Grant Jarvis wanted something from him. Even Mrs. Morgan and herself. Herself now, because the diplomatic role was exactly that which was dictated to her by the staff manager, Mr.

Ashby, when he told her of this trip abroad for Small and Smallwoods.

"Don't be too distressed, my dear," Mrs. Morgan said. "Grant Jarvis would be shrewd enough to know that. We are not deceiving him. But he must have some conversation with someone. I am the safest of all his social risks. I mean business connection with a *quid pro quo* and not a chiselling down or a taking from. He would know that. Now, good night. Hetty will look after me now. If it's not too hot to-morrow I'm going to give up this walking-stick for good. If only my wrist was a little stronger so I could lean against the rails occasionally I would be completely over that stupid accident."

CHAPTER FOUR

THE FOLLOWING EVENING only Elizabeth and the ship's doctor were at the dinner table punctually. So great had been the heat during the day many passengers disdained dinner altogether. They preferred snacks, and light salad meals served *al fresco* in the cocktail lounge or on the starboard deck. Elizabeth herself came in to dinner because Mrs. Morgan, more secure moving about because of the flat stillness of the glassy sea, had essayed to dine in the saloon.

If Elizabeth moved her head a little to the left she could see Mrs. Morgan, looking enchanting in a steel blue chiffon dinner-gown, entertaining the captain without much apparent effort. Elizabeth noticed that all the ship's officers, looking exceedingly groomed and exciting in their tropical naval dinner jackets were at the heads of their various tables. But there were many vacant passengers' chairs.

"The heat doesn't frighten the officers away from dinner," Elizabeth observed to Dr. Jarvis.

"Captain's orders," the doctor said with an impish smile. "A heat wave, a storm, a plague, or a fire . . . and we all come to dinner punctually."

"Something to do with morale, I suppose?"

"That's it. You'd be surprised how many people are afraid of heat stroke. We have to show them that life goes on normally in all climates. But you don't have to worry about morale, my dear girl. You should have plenty. You're the only girl on the ship my uncommunicative cousin has deigned to notice. Tell me, how did you manage it?"

"Charm, of course," Elizabeth said, laughing and showing her lovely white even teeth. "Didn't you notice I had any, Dr. Jarvis?"

"Indeed, I did. The best kind. Did you know I've been making a professional study of you ever since we left Southampton?"

"I'm delighted to find myself interesting." Elizabeth was still smiling. "Of course, I use the word 'interesting' in its true sense. Anything can be interesting if it's odd enough. Even toothache takes up a considerable amount of our interest, doesn't it?"

"You're not exactly toothache, nor for that matter, a pain in the neck to my cousin . . ."

"I'm lucky enough to play a reasonably good game of deck tennis."

"And you happen, quite unconsciously, to keep the other young ladies away from him. He finds that highly satisfactory."

Elizabeth was puzzled.

"But how? And why?"

"By just being you. People are so busy conjecturing why you can get close to him . . . and no one else . . . they fail to realise it is because you are natural and preoccupied with affairs other than those of Grant Grant Jarvis of Kybarrli. Is a slightly eccentric bachelor of a ship's doctor allowed to ask just what those other affairs are? A young man left behind, perhaps? A heart given very safely into someone else's keeping?"

The doctor said all this with his slightly impish smile that managed to make a joke of the whole conversation.

Elizabeth's merry smile faded a little. The doctor's upward flicking diagnostic look was quick to notice it. He reached forward and took some bread from the covered dish.

"Well, yes. I have got a young man, of course," Elizabeth said, quite unaware that a note of sadness had crept into her voice and that the doctor's carefully attuned professional ear had caught it. She looked up and said candidly, "I hated leaving him behind."

"And he hated you going away, I suppose?"

"I think so, but he didn't say so."

There was a tiny silence between them. It was the kind of silence a doctor allows to hover in the air because he knows that if the patient is not harried he or she will perhaps begin to realise the anxiety that is a burden to them. Elizabeth would never have dreamed that Dr. Jarvis thought of her in terms of a "patient." Yet he had noticed a certain tenseness in her as they had approached the ports of Malta and Port Said. He had seen her waiting for the mail at the purser's office. He had noticed the infinitesimal lowering of the spirits at mealtimes for a day or two afterwards. Above all he had noticed her polite good manners towards Grant Jarvis and a total absence of any wish to attract that highly eligible, very attractive, exceedingly rich and altogether interesting personality. Even Dr. Jarvis was not accustomed to people who did not show some kind of sharp reaction to the presence of the wool king on board a ship.

Elizabeth lifted her eyes and met the doctor's quizzical, wholly understanding glance. She flushed, then spread her hands in a little deprecating gesture.

"Yes," she said ruefully. "It's like that." She knew he understood what she meant and oddly she felt relieved in having a friend to whom she could impart that heart-gnawing uncertainty that Ralph's silence had given her throughout the voyage. There had never been anyone to whom she could unburden herself about Ralph. The little gesture she had made with her hands spoke for her and she knew it. Suddenly she found herself telling Dr. Jarvis all about her life in Mereton; about the rose-bowered bottage in which she and her mother lived. About Ralph Dalton, how amusing he could be, on *occasions*.

The doctor listened thoughtfully and kindly. The steward came and went with dishes. At last they had reached the fruit and nut stage. The doctor picked up the nutcrackers and bisected an almond with professional skill.

"Elizabeth," he said. He had not used her Christian name before but she liked him to do it, now. "I'm going to tell you what to do. You won't believe me or take notice of me for a long time. But I hope, for your sake, the time won't be too long. Drop that young man. You see, I understand his kind very well. He is completely selfish. He wants, even needs your companionship, but does not feel inclined or obliged to take on responsibility. If you did become engaged and married to him you would find yourself coupled to a very self-centred man. And the chances are that he will refrain from committing himself further until one or other of you breaks away under the strain. There you are, my dear. My advice is out. Take it."

He gave her one keen look, all his natural roguishness gone. Then he bent his glance to his plate and sorted out almond kernels from the shells.

There was something so final and authoritative in his statement that Elizabeth knew she had no argument. Nothing would change Dr. Jarvis's opinion as to what was best for her own welfare. She was a little pale and for a few minutes they said nothing.

"Shall we have our coffee in the lounge?" he asked with a sudden change of manner. "And I recommend a good liqueur. Drambuie. Do you know it?"

He had risen from his seat, stood aside as the steward drew Elizabeth's chair out for her and then, all smiles for the other people in the dining-saloon, he preceded her to the door where he stood aside for her to go through.

"Any chance of your taking my advice?" he asked.

Elizabeth shook her head. "I've loved him for such a long time," she said.

"That's what I thought," Dr. Jarvis said ruefully. "Ah, well! I wonder what Miss Lovegrove has dined on?" he went on brightly. "Shall we go and find out?"

On the day the *Albany* docked at Aden it was six o'clock in the morning when Elizabeth came on deck ready for her trip to the wells with Grant Jarvis. On the evening before she had learned from the notice board that the ship would dock at five-thirty for a three-hour stay . . . long enough to take on oil for the ship's fuel. Grant Jarvis had had delivered to Mrs. Morgan's suite a note to the effect he would be leaving the ship at six a.m. if Miss Heaton could be ready.

She had seen nothing of Grant Jarvis during the three days' voyage through the Red Sea. Because of the intense heat deck games had been forbidden by the captain and the ship's doctor. How Grant Jarvis had occupied his time Elizabeth did not know except that once, when she was promenading the deck, she had seen him sitting just inside the door of the officers' wardroom. He was sitting back in a relaxed attitude, a cigarette in one hand and a long frosted glass in the other. She had only a fleeting glimpse, yet somehow she gained the impression of a quite different man from the one she saw going in or out of his suite, and playing the odd games of deck tennis with her through the Mediterranean. One of the officers must have just said something amusing for, as Elizabeth reached the door, there was a burst of male laughter and she saw Grant Jarvis's face creased with smile wrinkles and his white teeth gleaming in his deeply tanned face. She saw what Mrs. Morgan and Hetty had meant when they spoke of his great charm. They must have seen him laughing.

He was indeed a handsome man. His polished black hair was parted impeccably, his square forehead lent a certain power to his face and when he laughed one could no longer see the cold disdainful look in his clear grey-blue eyes.

Even though Elizabeth witnessed that scene for the passing of not more than two or three seconds she saw and noticed the fine bones of his long strong hands.

On another day she knew he was entertaining some of the officers in his own suite for she could not avoid seeing the comings and goings in the short gangway that led to his own and Mrs. Morgan's suite, to her own and Hetty's single-berth cabins.

The next morning the ship's grapevine had it that the unprecedented had happened. The captain had gone to Mr. Grant Jarvis's party.

At six o'clock Elizabeth was punctually on deck. Mrs. Morgan and Hetty had insisted on having a part in advising Elizabeth what to wear and she had had to present herself for their inspection before departing.

She had chosen a pale blue flecked linen suit with the latest short coat and straight-cut skirt. With it she wore a deeper blue wide-brimmed hat with a matching handbag and shoes. She was a little excited herself, for this particular suit with its accessories had been one that had thrilled her most when she had been doing her pre-voyage shopping in the West End. She had been longing, in particular, to wear the finely tapered shoes with the delicate heels. She thought they were the loveliest shoes she was ever likely to possess; and the handbag had been made by the same firm as the shoes so that it was of the same fine polished leather and the identical shade.

"Oh, you look delightful, Elizabeth," Mrs. Morgan said. "Quite the picture to carry out your small part, my dear. Now don't forget . . . if he asks you anything about Small and Smallwoods tell him just exactly what you know . . . all the interesting little titbits about the woolbuyers coming home and any amusing little anecdotes about the office. Make it sound alive. That's all. He knows all about our business end. But your main job, my dear, is to see he is relaxed and enjoys your company. Make no demands but appreciate gracefully any small gesture he makes. We can between us render no greater service than to see that he enjoys himself."

Elizabeth understood perfectly what Mrs. Morgan meant but she could not help feeling it was ironic that a man who was so rich should have to have a small village girl such as herself to help him enjoy himself. Hetty's description of him as a prince of India was much more apt than Mrs. Morgan's. Indian princes, so Elizabeth had heard, had to have dancing girls to keep them entertained.

Well, she herself was no dancing girl, but she could play deck tennis and keep politely quiet on a long trip up into the hills behind Aden.

Hetty, at Mrs. Morgan's request, escorted Elizabeth on deck and handed her over to Grant Jarvis in the manner of the chaperons of old. Elizabeth had her first experience of the rather old-world conventions of the new world. The outback gentry of the country down under lived as their great-grand-parents had lived when they first took up their vast pastoral leases as English migrants. Mrs. Morgan had known that when she arranged Hetty's appearance with Elizabeth.

As all the passengers were on deck to get a glimpse of the brown desert port across the mooring water the little cere-monial scene performed by Hetty—delivering the goods and Grant Jarvis accepting them—was missed by none.

Elizabeth was aware of curious eyes . . . and a short way along the deck the doctor's amused ones . . . watching her. A minute later she forgot them in the sudden rising of her own spirits. Grant Jarvis was dressed in a manner that made it quite clear he was an Australian pastoralist. He wore a light fawn tropical suit, an impeccable shirt with a sober tie . . . and a fine broad-brimmed Stetson hat.

Immediately Elizabeth had said "Good morning" he indi-

cated the gangway that led down to a boat rocking in the
water below; the boatman, with eager eyes turned upwards to
the high deck, had his scull in his hand ready to cast off.

Grant Jarvis ran lightly down the gangway in front of
Elizabeth and then handed her into the boat. Several other
passengers began to descend as if they too would take this
boat inshore but Grant gave the boatman the signal to cast
off in his authoritative manner, and doubtless the look in his
eye told the boatman he would be adequately recompensed for
taking only two passengers.

The moment before they had descended the gangway the
purser's steward hurried along the deck and handed both
Elizabeth and Grant Jarvis their mail. The mail boat had come
alongside half an hour earlier.

There was only one letter for Elizabeth and a quick glance
told her it was from Ralph.

At last!

Her spirits soared. She lifted her eyes. Grant Jarvis had
been standing, one foot on the small platform at the top of
the gangway, leafing through several letters. His strong brown
hands stopped as one letter took his attention. It was a large
pink envelope with a fine flowery handwriting across it.
Obviously a woman's letter. He slipped it from the pile and
put it in the breast pocket of his coat. The others he put
negligently in the lower side pocket.

Elizabeth's mind was so preoccupied with the problem of
how and when to read her own letter she hardly noticed anything except that the special letter brought a frown to Grant
Jarvis's forehead and his eyes had a particularly steely quality
as he looked up, caught her glance and said . . .

"Shall we go? We have only three hours on shore and quite
a long way to go."

Sitting in the boat being quickly rowed towards the landing-
stage Elizabeth was still wondering when and where it would
be good manners to open her letter. Reluctantly she decided it
must wait. She would have to be alone to read that first message since she had left home. How long ago was it? Less than
two weeks! It seemed two years and as if she had been living
on board the *Albany* quite that length of time. So preoccupied
was she, she didn't notice her companion's silence. When she
realised this and that it was perhaps not very good manners

on her part, his stern face seemed to preclude all conversational advances.

What a funny pair they were going to make. Silent all the way there? And all the way back!

The happiness the letter had brought her, together with this thought, brought a bubble of laughter to her eyes and lips. She didn't realise it but her charming blue suit, the broad-brimmed hat and her smiling eyes made her a very pretty picture.

When they reached the landing stage Grant Jarvis helped her on shore. A tall, well-dressed Arab immediately stepped forward and bowed slightly, but formally.

"Mr. Jarvis?" he inquired.

"Yes," Grant replied. "You must be Sadique's agent?"

"At your service, Mr. Jarvis. I have a taxi waiting here for you. With your permission I will ride in front with the driver." He smiled slightly. "It is as well to see that the young lady is not bothered too much with the many salesmen of Aden who would wish to press their wares on her."

They left the landing-stage and approached a taxi which moved towards them from a group of others. The Arab, with a haughty scornful gesture, waved away all would-be solicitors of patronage. He rattled off a string of advice to them in his own language and then, opening the back seat of the taxi, saw Elizabeth and Grant safely inside. He shut the door, opened the one next to the driver, turned once again to the waiting vendors of a thousand wares and spoke rapidly and with high and princely dignity to them, then gave the taxi-driver orders to move off.

"What did you tell them?" Grant inquired. "The usual? I'll see one or two of their agents on the ship when I get back. I'll buy from them. But at my own leisure."

The Arab turned in his seat and still managed to convey an air of unbreakable dignity.

"I told them the Australian millionaire would buy plentifully from them in his cabin at midday."

"I'll bet you did," Grant Jarvis said with a grin.

It was the first time Elizabeth had seen him smile except on the occasion when she had glimpsed him as she had passed the officers' wardroom. It was interesting how his face changed. For a minute it was boyish and there was the fleeting warmth of a real charm which must be well hidden inside him for most of the time. His eyes met Elizabeth's and he smiled again. She found herself smiling back at him. It didn't take much imagination for her to realise that Grant Jarvis had to buy peace from the pressing salesmen, but at a price. And Sadique's agent . . . whoever Sadique was . . . would protect him ably, but also at a price. Being a wealthy pastoralist might have its rosy advantages but every rose has its thorn and Grant Jarvis had to live with the thorns as well as the roses.

"Well," Grant said, "what do you think of Aden?"

"Those brown mountains . . . Are there no trees at all?"

"Only where they're artificially grown, near water. And there's very little water in the desert. In fact, except for the wells, none."

Elizabeth found the brown colour of everything, and the utter starkness of the mountains, intimidating except for the wonder that so many human beings managed to live and even thrive in the midst of such arid heat.

The taxi passed rapidly through the lower town and climbed upward to Old Aden, the real terminus of the caravan route and the oil pipeline. Here there were a few trees standing in the bazaar and Elizabeth was amazed to see water being sold in the street.

The car did not lessen its speed and shortly after they were climbing even higher, passing through a gap in the great brown rock mountains.

"I'm afraid the only scenery to talk about is mountain and desert," Grant said. "Oddly enough, I find it has a certain fascination."

"I agree," Elizabeth said quickly. "There is something very wonderful about the solidity and endurance that one feels all around. I had never imagined anything like this . . . this . . ."

"This what?" He was looking at her with interest.

"I find it hard to explain. Just the wonder of people, animals, enduring and surviving . . . perhaps living the life of normal human beings . . . when the earth is so unkind to them"

"The very harshness you can learn to respect," he said quietly.

"Have you lived here in Aden at any time?"

"No. But I've lived in the dead heart of Australia. In fact

I've got a cattle run north of Lake Eyre. A million acres and all we have between us and extinction are the wells. Wells like these we're going to see in a few minutes."

"And you live there?" Elizabeth said wonderingly. "You live in that country?"

"Now and then. Most of the time I'm on Kybarrli. That's a sheep station. There we have regular rainfall and the picture is quite different. But I've a special feeling for Barrli itself . . . the cattle run. Wonder at the capacity for things to survive, I expect."

Elizabeth was pleased and relieved that the long silence had at last been broken.

"I know about Kybarrli wool," she said. "Triple A merino . . ."

"I know you know."

Grant Jarvis felt in his pocket for his cigarette case, took it out, opened it and presented it to Elizabeth. His eyes met her surprised eyes over the cigarette case.

"Small and Smallwoods, isn't it? I believe you are employed there," he said.

Elizabeth, who had hardly ever smoked, took a cigarette to hide her embarrassment. Perhaps she should not have mentioned Kybarrli wool. Her mission was a "diplomatic" one. Mrs. Morgan had made it quite clear. But what lay behind the need to keep up good relations with Grant Jarvis she had no idea.

The truth, she decided, was her best defence against that sabre-like scrutiny in Grant Jarvis's eyes.

"Yes," she said. "I'm a typist in the wool department of Small's. At present I'm acting as a personal secretary to Mrs. Morgan."

"A very able one I'm sure," he said dryly. "And now, tell me. Just exactly what does Small and Smallwoods want of me?"

Elizabeth flushed.

"Do you imagine, Mr. Jarvis, that a firm of great standing would discuss the policies of a higher level in the typists' room? I don't suppose you have ever been in a typists' room, Mr. Jarvis. It's a long way away from the directors' offices."

"You get angry very attractively, Miss Heaton. But you looked even more attractive when you received your mail just as we left the ship. Since your correspondence didn't seem very voluminous it must have made up for quantity in quality," he said, changing the subject.

Elizabeth was really angry now. She had to hold herself in with a tight rein for Mrs. Morgan's sake. This was a diplomatic mission. She mustn't antagonise Grant Jarvis . . . even though he deserved it. How dare he make personal comments about her mail! She would have liked to comment on his . . . especially that pink letter with the ladylike scrawl on it. How would he like that? she wondered. Perhaps no one ever spoke to Grant Jarvis on equal terms. How she longed to do so now. Yet, because of her duty to Mrs. Morgan and Mrs. Morgan's admonitions, she had to swallow her pride and her anger and pretend only pleasure in Grant Jarvis's company.

With an effort, more visible than she realised, she relaxed her tensed muscles and smiled.

"That was from my closest friend, Ralph Dalton," she said. That will just let him *know*, she thought.

She lifted the cigarette to her lips and inhaled the smoke inexpertly. It got in her eyes and she didn't know how to expel the smoke from her mouth quickly. She coughed. The smoke in her eyes prevented her from seeing quite clearly how to take her handkerchief from her bag.

Grant Jarvis took out a fresh white linen handkerchief and handed it to her.

"He must be a very close friend indeed if he makes you weep and choke at the same time," he said.

When Elizabeth had wiped her eyes she looked at him. He was smiling again but this time the smile wasn't boyish. It had an edge of cynical bitterness to it. Elizabeth had a feeling this was not the first time a girl had been in need of his handkerchief. The only difference this time was that her need had been genuine. But he wouldn't know that.

She tentatively held his handkerchief towards him.

"Perhaps I had better have this laundered before I return it to you," she said.

"Not at all," he replied, taking it from her. "It won't be the first time I've carried my handkerchief salted with a young woman's tears."

Elizabeth bit her lips and turned away to look out at the scenery. They were approaching an oasis of trees beside which stood a number of desert Arabs beside their camels. There was no reply she could make to that remark of Grant

Jarvis's without endangering the good "diplomacy" of her relationship with him.

Back on board the ship Mrs. Morgan was eager to hear all Elizabeth's adventures.

"I wish you hadn't told me about the necessity to preserve good relationships with Grant Jarvis," Elizabeth said sadly. "It made me a little self-conscious and I'm afraid I wasn't very successful. But I did try."

"I'm sure you did, my dear. Anyone as fresh and as . . . well . . . inexperienced as you are, Elizabeth, would be a pleasant change for Grant Jarvis. And that in itself would have been enough. I'm not at all worried about your proving adequate company for him."

"I think . . . I think he knows you wish to preserve the friendly atmosphere with him," Elizabeth said tentatively.

"Of course he does. The man is a very clever man. Don't worry about it, Elizabeth. The truth is . . . we of Small and Smallwoods can be of just as much service to Grant Jarvis as he can be to us. It would be to our mutual advantage if we could come in on the new pastoral company he is floating. And he knows that. Apart from all that, your presence has spared him the overtures of the other young ladies."

"Why should he wish to avoid them?" inquired Elizabeth.

"I wondered that myself. However, Dr. Jarvis whiled away one of the morning hours with me on the deck. He was really immensely pleased that you had gone with his cousin to the wells. He told me a little of Grant's past life . . . and it's quite sad, really. These big landowning families in Australia try to keep their land and their fortunes within a circle of families and to that end there is an awful lot of arranging of marriages between the young people. Not that the young people know much about what their elders are up to. Big station parties, mustering parties, race meetings on big stations . . . they're all part of the pattern of keeping the young people in touch with one another. They do a little picking and choosing and then see that Sara Ann is always about when William John is expected. That sort of thing."

"But what if Sara Ann doesn't like William John?" Elizabeth asked wonderingly.

"Oh . . . they produce Donald Dick for Sara and find Fanny

May for William John. It's quite an art . . . and quite a game.
All the grown-ups are in it."

"And did this happen to Grant Jarvis . . . when he was
young?"

Mrs. Morgan nodded her head.

"Oh, yes. That was inevitable. Dr. Jarvis told me that it
was absolutely written that he should marry one or other of
Mollie Paton's two daughters. So both girls, Thera and
Gaylie, were constantly trotted about from station to station
to be in Grant's company. Or vice versa. He did become engaged to the younger one, Thera, and this is where Dr. Jarvis
gets so annoyed . . . just in a cousinly way, of course. Mollie
Paton and her husband were cousins and both connected with
the Jarvis family. Too much intermarrying altogether for a
medical man like Doctor Jarvis to like. No, Doctor Jarvis, I'm
afraid, does not approve."

"Then Grant Jarvis is engaged to someone called Thera
Paton?"

"No, Elizabeth. That's the sad part. Thera was killed in a
motor-car accident in Italy a short time ago. Now the
families are determined that if it can't be one sister then it
must be the other. It is inevitable. So they're arranging for him
to marry Gaylie."

Elizabeth was aghast.

"Only a short time after the first girl has died? Can they
be as callous as all that?"

"According to Dr. Jarvis . . . yes."

"But what sort of a man is Grant to permit it? Surely he is
not just a pawn in a game of marriage?"

"Doctor Jarvis thinks that Grant is definitely not going to
permit it. He thinks that Grant was probably genuinely in love
with Thera and has not got over her death. Whether that is
the case or not Grant is not the type of man to discuss his
feelings with his cousin . . . even a medical cousin. But it's
quite clear he doesn't want to enjoy other female company.
He's been very aloof all through the voyage so far, as you
must have noticed. So you see, Elizabeth, you have really
served a very useful purpose in helping him preserve his
privacy."

So that is what I am, Elizabeth thought. A buffer state
between the wool empire and the female invaders.

She supposed, with a little sigh that did not escape Mrs. Morgan's notice, that this was indeed her fate in the marrying world. Ralph's letter had been friendly. He spoke of missing her but keeping very busy with his office work. He was thinking of changing his firm for one with a wider practice and more scope for conveyancing work. He had signed himself . . . *Your affectionate friend*. And he had not asked how she was enjoying herself.

She wished she could recall through the post the two letters she had written to him in which a certain amount of home-sickness had been voiced in expressing a loneliness for his company; and a longing for the old worn grey steps of the Underground which had carried her up each evening to find him waiting for her outside. She must be careful in her next letter to hold her feelings in rein a little. Ralph knew, of course, of her real love for him. It just didn't do to hurl it at him through the international post offices of the world.

The day, with the *Albany* anchored off Aden, had been more than oppressive for those who had remained on shipboard. Even the air-conditioning did not take the place of moving air in the most torrid regions of the tropical climates.

After Elizabeth had had her conversation with Mrs. Morgan she was asked to help Hetty keep all visitors away until the following day when they would be out in the Gulf of Aden and once past Cape Guardafui would get the blessing of the monsoon breezes across the Arabian Sea.

"Climate seems to have quite an effect on once broken bones," Mrs. Morgan said. "So annoying . . . but they *ache*. My bones, I mean. For the first time I am really cross with myself for having that stupid accident. So far it has let me in for a lot of amusement. But my poor broken bones refuse to feel amused to-night. Not enough of the spirit of Queen Victoria in them."

As the door of Elizabeth's cabin was opposite Mrs. Morgan's suite she left it open so that she could keep a faithful watch. She pulled out the sliding leaf from the small table by her bed and set about answering Ralph's letter, trying to match her tone with the tone of his letter.

As there was no cabin except Hetty's farther down the passage Elizabeth kept an alert ear for anyone approaching. She heard someone walking the few yards from Grant Jarvis's suite before she saw who it was. She stood up and went to her own door as she heard the footsteps approach. It was Grant Jarvis himself.

Elizabeth remembered the terrible snub he had delivered to the steward for the Mr. Wallaston of Melbourne who had wished to invade his privacy. For one moment there was the terrible temptation to use the same words in forbidding him to visit Mrs. Morgan. How would Grant Jarvis react to . . . "Mrs. Morgan is not available to visitors to-night!"

Elizabeth had never spoken to anyone like that in her life and she was astonished at the temptation. Moreover, she remembered in time that as a true employee of Small and Smallwoods she had to be very polite and civil to this man.

She smiled.

"I'm so sorry, Mr. Jarvis, but Mrs. Morgan is not really very well. I wonder if you would be kind enough to defer your visit. Actually I don't think she is receiving anyone for cocktails to-night."

He stood quite still looking at her, one eyebrow slightly flexed upward. He put his hand in the pocket of his dinner jacket and took out his cigarette case. He opened it with a kind of meticulous care as if taking time to weigh up what she was saying. She was quite sure it was a new experience for Grant Jarvis to be forbidden as a visitor to anyone.

"I hope there is no serious complaint," he said. "Has Mrs. Morgan called for my cousin, Doctor Jarvis?"

Elizabeth went on smiling.

"No, it isn't serious, Mr. Jarvis," she said gently. "In fact I'm not at all sure that she wouldn't see you." She managed to get an appealing look in her eyes. "I think it would be kinder though if we let her rest. Would you mind? You see, although she is getting well very rapidly she did have a serious accident. A trying heat like this does have some effect on her." She made a small deprecating gesture with her hand, the one that still held her fountain pen. Over her shoulder Grant Jarvis could see into the cabin, and the writing-table with the half-written letter on it. "I do hope I'm not sounding too much like the faithful watchdog, Mr. Jarvis. You see I am very attached to Mrs. Morgan. I don't like to see her looking drawn and tired at the end of the day."

Grant took out a cigarette . . . this time he did not offer one to Elizabeth . . . and struck a match and lit it.

"Watchdog, or guardian angel?" he said. "Which?" He

looked at her through the smoke of his cigarette. "As a matter of fact I was coming to ask you if you would have cocktails with me to-night. I had not intended to call on Mrs. Morgan." His eyes flicked into the cabin again. "That is, if you can drag yourself away from writing to that young man of yours. I'm sure that is what you are doing."

Elizabeth kept on smiling, even though the muscles of her face were beginning to ache a little.

"He has to wait six or eight weeks to see me again, Mr. Jarvis, so I expect his letter can wait another hour or two. Thank you for your kind invitation. I would like to come." Suddenly her smile really relaxed and became faintly mischievous. "Which do I come as? Watchdog or guardian angel?"

They stood there in the companionway in a tiny silence. There was an atmosphere of challenge in the air.

"Would you be very offended if I said watchdog?" he said. "If I use more celestial terms the young man in the letter might object."

"I'm sure he would," said Elizabeth.

As she turned into her cabin to pick up a silk stole and take a fresh handkerchief from a little table drawer she reflected ruefully that she would probably never know what Ralph would have thought or said. She was quite certain she would never dare to tell him she had been drinking cocktails with an Australian pastoralist who was a wool king and gave himself the airs and privileges of an Indian prince.

And she certainly could never explain to Ralph what a diplomatic mission was . . . and that it was very hard work.

CHAPTER FIVE

THE ARABIAN SEA, Bombay, Ceylon . . . and then the vast blue and gold reaches of the Indian Ocean. The star banner of the Southern Cross appeared on the blue velvet night sky to proclaim the ship was sailing out of one world into another.

Elizabeth and Grant Jarvis had won the deck tennis championship and were each presented with a silver cup by the captain. It was on the occasion of the farewell dinner-dance given by the ship's company to the passengers. Mrs. Morgan was walking without human aid . . . though she still leaned a little on what she called her "old faithful," a walking-stick.

There had been no thawing out in Grant Jarvis, even when he had taken Elizabeth to the main cocktail lounge before dinner on the night the *Albany* had left Aden. He had remained politely distant, his conversation slight and impersonal. Elizabeth had decided that her role was to be easily pleasant and the only way to do that successfully was to pretend he was someone else. So she pretended he was the chief clerk in Small and Smallwoods, a sensible hard-working friendly man. She chatted . . . but carefully and not too much . . . and helped preserve the distance by having her own small silences.

"Now I know what it must be like to be a member of a diplomatic corps," she said to Mrs. Morgan. "Really, it is rather fun, after a while. But very hard work."

"Good girl, Elizabeth," Mrs. Morgan said. "I think you've turned out trumps and I'll certainly make sure that Mr. Ashby back in the home office knows all about it. But tell me, dear, he's not really as hard to get on with as all that, is he? He's so utterly charming to me."

"I suppose he's on guard for fear that even I, humble and all as I am, might be trying to 'invade his privacy.' "

"No, to the contrary," said Mrs. Morgan. "He told me you were an excellent tennis player and an excellent watchdog. I don't know that I quite understand that word 'watchdog.' "

"I wouldn't let him in to see you the night we left Aden. But I barked politely."

Mrs. Morgan looked at Elizabeth curiously.

"You know, my dear," she said, "you've been of invaluable assistance to me on this trip. All my papers are in order . . . your file is a gem of tidiness and I would never have thought of an index. Now I'll know just where to look up everything as my book progresses. But apart from all that I think this trip has done you good. So does Hetty. You've got a lovely colour and that regular daily session of deck tennis has given you exercise and a really attractive liveliness."

Elizabeth smiled happily.

"I've loved every minute of it, Mrs. Morgan. I do thank you so very much for giving me the opportunity."

"Every minute? Even those spent with the ogre?"

Elizabeth laughed.

"Oh, he's not really an ogre at all. It was just that I was nervous because I knew I had to treat him with care. You know, on account of Small and Smallwoods."

"And how would you have treated him if it hadn't been for Small and Smallwoods?"

Elizabeth put her head on one side and looked pensive.

"I think I would have given him a little snub now and again so as to let him know he might be king out there on his millions of acres but not here with a suite in the same companionway as my humble cabin." She frowned. "Or would I? I wonder."

"What makes you hesitate?"

"I can't imagine why anyone has a feeling of compassion for a millionaire," Elizabeth said. "'Specially one who is so unfriendly as Mr. Jarvis . . . but somehow I do feel a little something . . . I don't know quite how to explain it . . ."

"Perhaps it is because he is alone up there on the top of his wool mountain? You have discovered that the very great and the very rich are very much alone. They are isolated by their power and their wealth and do not know who is a friend and who is there to take something from them. They can never be judged on their merits as simple human beings."

"Yes," said Elizabeth, nodding her head. "That . . . and, I think, the girl who was killed in the car crash, Thera Paton. Perhaps, under that cynical exterior of his, there is a real grief."

Mrs. Morgan nodded her head soberly.

"You could be right, Elizabeth. And of course he has to go through all the complicated trouble of either avoiding being married to Gaylie Paton . . . or of marrying her. Did you know those two girls on board who were at school with Gaylie Paton had written to her quite early in the voyage? Grant apparently was not letting his relatives in Australia know he was coming back on the *Albany* but now they'll be at Fremantle in cohorts to meet him. Doctor Jarvis says that Mollie Paton, with her daughter Gaylie, will be there to snare him."

"Does Mr. Jarvis confide everything to Doctor Jarvis?" Elizabeth asked with wonder.

Mrs. Morgan laughed.

"I think Doctor Jarvis is an adept at extricating confidences and information. He knows how to do it as a doctor so I suppose he uses his skill as a relative."

Elizabeth remembered the evening when she and Dr. Jarvis had sat alone at the dinner table and she had told him of her own anxieties about Ralph.

"Everything he hears should be confidential," Elizabeth said a trifle primly.

"Oh, I'm sure it is. But knowing Doctor Jarvis I'm sure it wouldn't prevent him acting in the interests of his patient, or should we say, confider. I think he takes a roguish delight in frustrating the activities of some of his relatives and promoting the interests of others. It must be rather fun to be a medical man in a big ambitious family like the Jarvis family."

Dr. Jarvis's "roguish sense of fun" had far greater implications for Elizabeth when the *Albany* glided through Gage Roads into Fremantle Harbour two mornings later.

The ship had let go anchor at daybreak off Rottnest Island. The immigration authorities, Commonwealth quarantine and health officers, the press and the mail had come on board by three small launches. The passengers were required to queue in alphabetical order in order to face a brief scrutiny by the health officers.

"Don't mind forming that long snake around the decks, Elizabeth," Mrs. Morgan warned her. "Australia is a country free from the dreadful pestilences of the Asian countries. It is a tropical and semi-tropical continent yet plagues like smallpox, anthrax, typhus and bubonic have never invaded it . . . all because of the strict surveillance of everyone who enters the country. As an owner of a pastoral property I'm daily thankful for the quarantine laws. They are rather wonderful when you think all of us during the last few weeks have passed through half a dozen countries where any of us might have caught a plague of some kind of other. Even if it was only measles."

Elizabeth, in the queue, found herself standing immediately in front of Grant Jarvis. There were no first-class passengers whose surnames began with an "I." So Heaton and Jarvis were two names standing one after the other in the list handed to the health officers.

Grant had said, "Good morning. I hope you're in good

health, Miss Heaton. Otherwise that bevy of doctors will soon find you out. My advice is to smile brightly and let your eyes sparkle. They look at your wrists and forearms for rashes and at your eyes to see if they're clear."

"What if my eyes are clouded and dull?" asked Elizabeth.

"You'll be sent down to the hospital bay for an examination and not be allowed off the ship at Fremantle."

"Thank goodness I feel well," said Elizabeth. "I'm not disembarking here but I would hate not to be able to see Mrs. Morgan off on her plane for her station to-night."

Grant Jarvis appeared to examine her face quite closely.

"You'll do," he said. "The pink of health, I should say."

Elizabeth put her head on one side and examined his face.

"You'll pass," she said. "Bouncing health."

Suddenly they both laughed. All the tension between them was strangely gone. Elizabeth found it hard to believe this smiling man was the cold and slightly cynical person whose presence had really bothered her throughout the long voyage. And it *had* bothered her. She would confess that to herself now that the voyage was nearly over.

Beyond the group of doctors was another group. Two men with note-books and pencils out, acutely watching the faces of the passengers as they filed past, two with small cameras and two very nonchalant young women pointing out, every now and again, some identity amongst the passengers they wanted photographed. It was not hard to tell that here was the press.

At the moment that Grant Jarvis and Elizabeth stood laughing together one of the young press women looked down the line and saw them. With some excitement she touched the arm of a photographer and pointed at Grant Jarvis. Elizabeth could not hear what she was saying but she could read the delight of a real find shining in her face.

The cameras clicked, and globes flashed and were then thrown overboard.

Really, she thought, it was too bad to be a Grant Jarvis on a ship entering a home port. He would be aware he was being photographed as royalty, and no doubt, as soon as he was past the health officer in charge, that group of press men and women would surround him. But he showed no sign. He had one hand in a pocket of his reefer jacket and the other holding a lighted cigarette. He went on talking to Elizabeth about the regulations pertaining to entering Australia and pointed out landmarks to her on the not far distant coastline. Every now and again they moved up a few paces as those in front, in their turn, moved nearer the examining group.

With a little pang Elizabeth wished her relationship with Grant Jarvis on the voyage had been as easy and natural as this. Perhaps it was because he was in his home waters. Even the press, every member of which was watching him avidly, did not worry him. Experience perhaps had taught him how to face batteries of cameras with ease, even indifference.

"You're next," he said. "Just pull up your sleeves, show your wrists, smile . . . and you'll be through."

The press woman who had first noticed Grant Jarvis now was near at hand.

"Grant Jarvis!" she said. "Just look this way and smile. We want a really good photograph. Thank you. Remember me? Dal Doone for the *West Coast Daily*. You promised me a scoop, remember?"

"If I had anything to scoop you could have it, Miss Doone," he said. "I've merely been for a trip abroad. Now I'm back. *C'est tout.*"

This conversation was going on from beyond the health officers' group to where Grant Jarvis stood in the line. Dr. Jarvis was standing beside the Chief Health Officer giving his "all clear" on each passenger that passed. He heard the press making its stir over the arrival of Grant Jarvis.

"What about Gaylie Paton?" one of the press men called out. "She's waiting for you on the wharf in the harbour. Any news there?"

Dr. Jarvis forgot his business with the passenger immediately in front of Elizabeth and turned and scowled.

Grant Jarvis shook his head.

"No comment," he said. He looked back at Dr. Jarvis and caught his eyes.

"You'll need a watchdog, Grant," Dr. Jarvis said. "Or the press will marry you off to Gaylie before we're in harbour."

Elizabeth was standing in front of the doctors now, her wrists and arms held out for examination, a real smile of amusement in her eyes and on her lips.

There was no doubt about it, she was genuinely sorry for

Grant Jarvis right now. How did a man get out of that sort of situation with gallantry?

At that moment Grant, from behind her, put his hand on her shoulder.

"She's all clear, isn't she, Doctor?" he said. "Australia ought to run up a flag of welcome for anyone as healthy as . . ."

"Say, Mr. Jarvis, who's the girl?" came the quick eager voice of another press man. "Hold it! Good, that's got it."

Cameras had blazed away at Grant with his hand on Elizabeth's shoulder, and Elizabeth with her smiling face waiting for the doctors to motion her on . . . passed all clear.

Dr. Jarvis half turned and addressed the press.

"That's his fiancée," he said. "She's there to prevent you rushing Gaylie Paton into his arms. Now run along and try for a scoop with some other passenger. Try Sir Archly Abbott. He's gone through already. He has had three wives and knows all about atom bombs. Go and get your scoops from him."

Dr. Jarvis turned back, smiled at Elizabeth and winked at Grant.

"All right . . . all clear, you two. No spots, no plague and a first-class health pass."

With a gesture he seemed to sweep Grant and Elizabeth past the health officer, into the arms of the press beyond.

Grant had his hand cupped round Elizabeth's elbow and it gripped like a vice. She could not have freed herself without a struggle. And he was working too fast for her reeling senses.

"Yes," he said to the press in mass. "Miss Heaton is my fiancée. You have the photographs. No, we don't propose to pose for another one now. Yes . . . Miss Heaton is from London. We will give you a press interview when we've landed. At the Adelphi Hotel. Excuse me, now. You heard me, Miss Doone. At the Adelphi. We'll be there sometime around noon."

With sheer physical force Grant steered Elizabeth through the press group along the deck in through the open way to the lounge.

"Mr. Jarvis . . ."

"Not now. We'll get down to my suite." His face, absolutely implacable, looked down into hers. "A hundred pounds to go through with it, Miss Heaton. I've hired you."

She tried to shake herself free, but his grip tightened.

"Two hundred?" he said as he guided her rapidly towards the lift. "Done! That's the fastest commission Small and Smallwoods have earned since the wool boom in 1949."

They were in the lift now and he released her. He put up his hand and pressed the right button.

"Excuse me, Mr. Jarvis," Elizabeth began again with great dignity. "I'm not for sale."

He didn't smile.

"I didn't suggest you were. I am buying your services. Not you. Any objections? You sell your labour and time to Small and Smallwoods, don't you?"

"That's different. I work."

"You're going to work now, don't make any mistake about that. Ask any actress."

The lift had stopped and the gates opened automatically. He stood aside and then as Elizabeth left the lift his hand closed on her elbow again.

"I'm not a prisoner, Mr. Jarvis. And I don't know what an actress has to do with it."

"She plays a part. And you are a prisoner till I get you out of the way of the pursuing press. I'm not paying you to give the show away at this stage."

Grant Jarvis did not release Elizabeth as they went along the corridor to the turn-off to his suite. He walked with the utmost composure and purpose. Yet, because of the purposefulness of that walk, and the iron grip on her arm, she had a feeling of being hustled. All she needed now, she thought, was a film stage set-up and a man with a gun stuck in the small of her back to feel what film stars are supposed to be feeling when they are in the process of being kidnapped.

Just how far did he think he was going with this act?

There you are! Thinking already in terms of actresses, film stars and acts, she thought. Even though she was dismayed at the physical way Grant Jarvis was at this moment bullying her as he ushered her into his suite . . . his hand still on her arm . . . she could not help something inside her standing aside, appraising the scene and finding it quite interesting.

Once his suite door was shut Grant Jarvis released her. He indicated an arm-chair in the small drawing-room and, leaning his back against the door, took out his cigarette case.

"Well?" he said, looking up at her as he lit his cigarette.

He flicked the match out and tossed it into a tray on the table near him. He leaned back against the door in a half reclining attitude. "Is it a deal? Two hundred pounds for your services. Have you ever earned that much before?"

There was an odd smile in his eyes. It was not unkind.

"I'm sorry to appear to manhandle you. I didn't want to argue it out in front of the press," he added.

Elizabeth was speechless. All she could do was look at Grant Jarvis with big puzzled eyes.

He was asking her to do something for him. He was employing her to play a part. But what a part! Was it strictly honest? And just what would Small and Smallwoods think of it?

The ship was in this port for one day. Was she actually being offered two hundred pounds to play a part for one day? Or while the *Albany* was in Australian waters? It was incredible and somehow wrong. The sum was too much, anyway, and she was sure Small and Smallwoods would not permit her to accept it.

"Well, what do you say?" asked Grant Jarvis. His eyes had not left her face.

Still Elizabeth hesitated.

"I'm in a fix," she said helplessly at length. She simply didn't know what to say. She didn't know what was the right thing to do.

Grant moved over to the telephone table. He lifted the telephone from its cradle, then looking at the door put it back with a bang that made Elizabeth wince, crossed quickly to the door and locked it. He caught the look of fleeting anxiety in Elizabeth's eyes.

"I'm not locking you in, Miss Heaton," he said. "I'm locking the press out."

He went back to the telephone.

"Give me Mrs. Morgan's suite, will you?" he asked.

As he waited the few minutes for the connection to be made he flicked his cigarette ash into a tray on the telephone table and stood looking, his eyes narrowed, out of the porthole at the port of Fremantle lying across the water on the starboard side.

"Oh . . . Grant Jarvis, Mrs. Morgan. Good morning. I believe you're one of the lucky ones who get a personal visit

from the medical officers and don't have to queue up. . . .
Yes, I'm through the line. And so is Miss Heaton. She is with
me now. I wonder if you would be good enough to come in
for a few minutes. Miss Heaton and I would like your advice
. . . Yes . . . Thank you very much. I'm most grateful."

He put the telephone back on the cradle, then lifted it again.

"Give me cabin sixty-three in the second class, please . . .
Thank you."

This time while he waited for the connection he turned his
head and looked at Elizabeth. Her puzzled expression brought
a slight smile to his eyes.

"My staff," he said. "They like to travel independently."
Then, turning to the mouthpiece, "Is that you, Mrs. Bolton?
. . . Is Tim there? . . . Good. Both of you come up to my
suite, will you? I think you'll find the communicating door
open now we're in port . . . Yes, right away, please."

He put the telephone back. At that moment there was a tap
on the door and he turned the handle and the key in the lock
simultaneously so that the visitor would not know the door
had been locked.

"Good morning, Mrs. Morgan. Very good of you to come.
Come in, please."

*

CHAPTER SIX

MRS. MORGAN stood in the doorway, leaning slightly on her
stick. She had on a pretty blue jersey dress of fine wool and
wore her string of pearls. She had her habitual happy smile
and the blue of her dress added colour to her expressive eyes.
Elizabeth felt a wave of affection sweep over her as she saw
Mrs. Morgan standing there. It wasn't only that Mrs. Morgan
had, perhaps, come to her rescue, but that suddenly Elizabeth
realised that they would part in a few hours. Mrs. Morgan's
life . . . as much because of all those letters as anything else
. . . had become part of her own. With a pang, Elizabeth
realised there would be henceforward a gap in her life.

Something of the expression on her face reached out towards Mrs. Morgan for the latter came into the room and

straight over to the girl. Elizabeth had stood up and Mrs. Morgan put her hand on the girl's arm.

"Well, my dear. You didn't have any difficulty with the health officers, did you?"

Elizabeth shook her head.

"All clear," she said.

"Of course. Dr. Jarvis would have told me if you had any complaint coming on." She turned to Grant Jarvis. "What is this rather sombre atmosphere about, Mr. Jarvis?"

"Sit down, Mrs. Morgan. Please do. I have a proposition to make to you."

"To me?"

Mrs. Morgan sat down in the small chintz-covered arm-chair. Elizabeth sank back into her own chair. Grant sat down on an upright chair on the other side of the room and spoke across the intervening space to Mrs. Morgan.

"My cousin, the doctor . . ." there was a cynical edge to Grant's voice, "had the generous idea of presenting me with Miss Heaton as a fiancée, to get me past the press. He doesn't realise I've been handling press interviews since my father died twelve years ago. However, there it is. The thing is, I've decided to go through with it."

"Marry Elizabeth?" said Mrs. Morgan, startled. Her eyes turned quickly towards the girl.

"Oh, no," said Grant coldly. "Only make an announcement to that effect. The thing is to make it a paying job for Miss Heaton for the duration of her stay in Australia. I presume she is staying until the *Albany* leaves for the United Kingdom sometime early next month."

Elizabeth gasped.

"You mean for more than the one day the *Albany* is in this port?" she exclaimed.

"So you had been thinking of it as possible?" Grant cut in quickly.

Elizabeth flushed. She opened her lips as if to say more but as quickly closed them. She was trapped. She could not tell Grant that if she had actually been considering it, it had been because of her instruction to handle Grant Jarvis diplomatically. What had been bothering her was the two hundred pounds. She had not comprehended that though this was a vast, and therefore an uneasy sum, to her, it was chicken feed to Grant Jarvis. And she had thought he had meant *one day*. She was booked to sail round the coast of Australia on the *Albany*. Not stay in the country.

Mrs. Morgan saw the dismay on Elizabeth's face. She put out her hand and touched the girl's arm.

"You shall not do anything you do not wish to do, my dear child. Rest assured on that. But let us hear what Mr. Jarvis has in mind." She turned to Grant. "Go on, please. You know that I am not only a wife of a director of Small and Smallwoods but I sit on the Board myself. At the present moment Miss Heaton's services can only be used at the discretion of the firm."

Grant Jarvis smiled. In that smile Elizabeth read all that he knew about the firm's policy of being "diplomatic" with him. It was a worldly, knowledgeable smile with the faintest edge of cynicism to it.

"That is why I asked you to come in, Mrs. Morgan."

In that smile Mrs. Morgan also read what was in Grant's mind just as he read what was in hers by her hesitation.

"Please, explain." Mrs. Morgan said.

Grant Jarvis did, at length.

"I propose to leave the ship here and cross the continent to Melbourne by plane. I would like Miss Heaton to accompany me. My head stockman from Barrli, the cattle station, is on board with his wife. Miss Heaton will be placed in Mrs. Bolton's care until we reach Melbourne. At Melbourne my mother will meet us. It simply means that Miss Heaton will stay a few days with my mother in Melbourne, proceed with us to Kybarrli where I have some duties to perform. I may possibly go on to Barrli to look at the cattle. At Kybarrli Miss Heaton will be required to play an important part. The State Governor is to be our guest for two days during his annual tour of the state. It will mean full scale activities for several days before and after his visit.

"I am aware the *Albany* sails on from Melbourne to Sydney and Brisbane but Miss Heaton can pick it up at Melbourne on its return voyage."

"You have thought a great deal in a very short time, Mr. Jarvis," Mrs. Morgan said slowly.

"It took me exactly the three minutes it took the health officers to examine my wrists on deck a quarter of an hour ago. The fee for Miss Heaton's services is two hundred pounds, Mrs. Morgan."

"Unthinkable," Mrs. Morgan retorted at once.

"The fee? Or Miss Heaton accompanying me in the role of fiancée?"

"The fee, of course. The girl is not to be bought. Do you realise you are dealing in human beings and not sheep, Mr. Jarvis?"

He smiled that grim, slightly bitter smile again.

"Anyone or any firm that employs labour employs human beings, Mrs. Morgan. I propose to use Miss Heaton's services —not Miss Heaton. You can rest assured she will be safe-guarded in every way."

Elizabeth felt as if she was only now coming up for air. She had been completely taken aback by Grant Jarvis's pro-posal but more than this she was suddenly aware that Mrs. Morgan herself was in a plight. She would like Elizabeth to perform this service for Grant Jarvis . . . for the sake of the firm. But her kindness, and goodness, prevented her from making use of the girl for purely business reasons. It was Mrs. Morgan who could not bring herself to deal in human beings. Not Grant Jarvis. Whatever he said, and whichever way he put it, this was exactly what he was doing. Mrs. Morgan, on the other hand, was on the point of refusing on Elizabeth's behalf, because she would not have the girl do something distasteful to her. Yet that refusal would neces-sarily be reluctant. It meant a great deal to Small and Small-woods to come in with the new pastoral company being launched by Grant Jarvis.

"I will go, Mrs. Morgan," Elizabeth said quietly. "I would like to see Australia from the inside . . . and this way I could do that." She turned to Grant. "I'm glad to be of service to you, Mr. Jarvis, and I think the opportunity to see something of the country and particularly your two stations will be adequate reward if you will see that my travelling expenses are met."

Her statement was received with a tiny silence. It was Mrs. Morgan who spoke first.

"Elizabeth . . . if . . ."

"You've no idea how much I would like to go, Mrs. Morgan," Elizabeth said with a smile. " 'Specially travelling in an entourage like royalty. Think of the wonderful time I'll have."

If she was convincing Mrs. Morgan that she *wished* to

undertake the project, she was not convincing Grant Jarvis. He looked at her sharply.

"You accept the bargain?" he said. "You undertake not to disclose the fact you are not my fiancée?"

"I do," said Elizabeth. "But not the two hundred pounds. I am adequately paid by Small's while I am abroad and there is more dignity in not being bought."

She put the faintest emphasis on the last word. Grant Jarvis pulled in the corners of his mouth.

"You have no idea how expensive the Jarvis women like to appear," he said abruptly. "They're quite capable of looking like two hundred pounds in one dress. I'm afraid I'll have to ask you to dress up to my relatives." He softened his manner a little. "Actresses, especially good ones, generally have their wardrobes for the play provided, I'm sure."

It was Elizabeth's turn to hesitate. The clothes she had bought to accompany Mrs. Morgan were good ones. The firm had arranged for that. But there were not many of them and certainly not one of them cost fifty pounds, let alone two hundred pounds. In fact Elizabeth thought she had been something of a wizard in the way she had managed to get the best by cutting down the number of clothes she bought. She would indeed be at a grave disadvantage if she didn't have the right things . . .

At that moment there was a discreet tap at the door. Grant Jarvis went to the door quickly. When he opened it, it was to disclose a tall, pleasant-looking woman dressed in a smart suit of grey wool with a rust-red hat and a matching handbag. Beside her stood one of the tallest and thinnest of men Elizabeth had ever seen. His head would have touched the door frame if he had not ducked as he came in. He was sunburned a deep brown and weather wrinkles all over his face declared him a man who spent his life out of doors. He looked as if he might be in his late forties . . . five or six years older than his wife.

" 'Morning, Maria, 'morning, Tim," Grant Jarvis said without ceremony. "Come in, will you?"

This time he did not lock the door but he closed it firmly.

"Mrs. Morgan," he said, "may I introduce Tim Bolton and his wife? Head stockman on Barrli."

Mrs. Morgan inclined her head as she returned the Boltons' greeting.

"Miss Elizabeth Heaton," Grant added, then looked at her with that faintly derisive smile in his eyes and added, "my fiancée."

Both the Boltons looked first at Grant, then at Elizabeth. It was plain they were startled. The man bowed to Elizabeth.

"Pleased to meet you, ma'am," he said. He turned to his wife. "The future mistress of Barrli," he added.

Elizabeth opened her lips again but Grant spoke first.

"Miss Heaton is making her first voyage to Australia. Maria, will you be kind enough to help her in any way? You might for instance give her some idea of station life . . . on Kybarrli, of course. Tim, if it's okay with you, I propose we should all leave the *Albany* to-day and get bookings, if possible on the Trans plane . . . there are two of them I think . . . to-night. Right?"

"You're the boss, Grant," Tim Bolton replied. "What you say goes. Have you tried for plane bookings yet?"

"No, that's your job. See the shipping agent in the purser's office right away. They'll probably pull a few strings for me. If we can't get bookings then hire a small plane through the Aero Club at Maylands, will you?"

Tim Bolton immediately excused himself and left the suite.

"Sit down, Maria," Grant said a shade irritably. "Or do you have to go and pack?"

"Yes, I'll have to pack, Grant," the woman said quietly. "We didn't anticipate leaving the ship at Fremantle."

"And you, Elizabeth?" Grant asked.

Elizabeth started. She was busy thinking how dictatorial Grant was about other people's lives and being somewhat surprised by the fact that the Boltons called him by his given name. Also her own Christian name coming so easily from his tongue that way made her start. Oddly enough it had the effect of making her feel the tightening of the frail strings that now held her to him. It almost made her feel as if she belonged, and again for a strange reason it warmed her heart a little. It was as if he had put out his hand and touched her. She didn't feel so isolated, sitting there on the far side of Mrs. Morgan. It drew her into the warm circle of the known people in the orbit of Grant Jarvis's world.

If she was leaving the ship at Fremantle she would have to pack, of course. She looked at Mrs. Morgan for direction.

There was a faint frown of worry on Mrs. Morgan's forehead.

"Elizabeth, are you sure you wish . . ." She stopped, remembering Mrs. Bolton's presence and that that woman knew Elizabeth only as Grant had announced her. His fiancée.

Strange, Elizabeth thought, how Grant using her Christian name had given her confidence. It was her cue to go on the stage. It was stranger still how she felt herself rising to it . . . walking on before the footlights as it were, and unexpectedly finding all nervousness falling away from her like an unnecessary cloak. . . .

She smiled serenely at Mrs. Morgan.

"I wouldn't dream of letting Grant go by plane without me," she said. "Nor, since he is in such a hurry to get back, would I press him to continue the voyage by sea."

She stood up, smoothed down her dress and then smiled directly at Mrs. Bolton.

"Would you come and advise me what to wear when we land, Mrs. Bolton. I believe the press is interviewing us at midday and, of course, I haven't the faintest idea what the weather or temperature in Perth is likely to be."

She held herself erect and her head at a proud little angle.

How am I doing? she asked herself, and could hardly hide the fun-making smile that was edging itself on to her lips. She avoided looking at Grant as she walked to the door. As she turned her head away from him she met Mrs. Morgan's eyes. Suddenly she bent impulsively forward and kissed that lady on the forehead.

"It's going to be grand," she said.

She smiled again at Mrs. Bolton and walked calmly from the suite. At a nod from Grant Mrs. Bolton followed her.

Mrs. Morgan and Grant were left looking into one another's eyes. He sat down on the upright chair opposite her and took out a cigarette.

"Do you mind if I smoke, Mrs. Morgan?" he asked.

"Mr. Jarvis," she said quietly and firmly, "that girl is my charge. She is one of the nicest girls I've ever had anything to do with. She is very inexperienced and this is a strange country to her."

"I thought her manner when she made her exit polished in

the extreme. I am surprised to hear you say she is in-experienced."

"She has been well trained in her career in Smallwood's. She has had little or no experience of worldly people such as ourselves."

There was a sardonic gleam in his eye.

"Would you be cautioning me to preserve her innocence, by any chance?"

Mrs. Morgan allowed a gleam of anger to show in her eyes.

"You know very well what I mean, Mr. Jarvis. I am think-ing of her emotional inexperience. It will be a great strain per-forming this particular . . . particular . . ."

"Line of work?" he prompted her.

"Call it that, if you like." Then suddenly and firmly she added, "Don't tamper with her feelings, Mr. Jarvis."

He looked down the line of his cigarette at the ash-tray. When he looked up his eyes were a cold iron grey.

"There's not the slightest likelihood of that happening," he said with finality.

Elizabeth, sitting opposite Miss Dal Doone of the *West Coast Daily*, with Grant Jarvis beside her and camera flashes occasionally dazzling her eyes, felt as if she had been doing this all her life. She was amazed at herself.

They were in the Adelphi, one of the luxury hotels of Perth, and true to his word Grant Jarvis was giving Miss Doone her scoop.

On the other side of the room, with Mrs. Morgan, sat Mrs. Paton, a very smart matron looking quite *chic* and at least half her age in the only "sack look" suit Elizabeth had seen and really fallen for. Her daughter, Gaylie, was not in a sack. She wore a lovely bunchy soft biscuit-coloured wool jacket above a slim short tapered skirt of a deeper shade. She was of medium height, slender as a willow, as golden as a prim-rose, her skin was smooth like that of a china doll and her great blue eyes had a bewitching way of looking both innocent and sophisticated at the same time. How she managed it Elizabeth could not guess. Mrs. Paton and Gaylie did not look like two hundred pounds apiece. They looked like two million-dollar bills. When Grant had introduced Elizabeth to them after the *Albany* had berthed they had, in turn, leaned for-ward and kissed Elizabeth perfunctorily on the cheek and they had each smelt like a whole garden of flowers. Very exotic flowers, too.

Elizabeth's spirits had unaccountably sunk. No one, in all the world, she felt, could match these two women . . . the older and the younger . . , for *chic*, natural beauty, and the absolute know-how of making the most of it. And the know-how of conveying to her that she, Elizabeth, was unaccountable.

Perhaps that was why her spirits had sunk. Her status of bufferstate-cum-watchdog on the voyage out had hardly been a compliment but the quick all-seeing glance that Mrs. Paton and Gaylie had given her had dismissed her as not even being equal to those onerous tasks.

Then from momentary depression Elizabeth's spirits had lifted again.

After all, Grant had chosen her to pose as his fiancée . . , not Gaylie Paton. She did have something, whatever it was, that he needed. And so far the only evidence of his feelings for Gaylie was that of wishing to be beyond her reach.

The reason was, without a doubt, Gaylie's sister Thera. Had she been as beautiful and willowy and golden as Gaylie? Elizabeth would probably never know.

The only thing she was genuinely sorry about was that for Grant's sake she did not look the part a man of his standing and station in this country would be expected to claim in his fiancée. Quite suddenly she saw the wisdom of accepting that two hundred pounds in the form of a wardrobe to be bought, with Mrs. Bolton's help, in Melbourne.

Meantime, to-day, she wore the blue linen suit she had worn at Aden and over it a lightweight wool tailored coat with the new belted back that had just reached display status as Elizabeth was buying her voyage clothes in London. She had on her head a small white head-hugging hat that was what the saleslady had called "a pet" and she carried a handbag to match. Her shoes, the same colour as her near navy blue coat, were taper-toed and the welt was stitched in white to match her hat and bag.

She knew she did not look like a million-dollar bill but she hoped she looked over the pass line. Just!

Of all that Gaylie Paton wore the things that captured Elizabeth's heart most were Gaylie's shoes. The heels were tiny, shaped, and not very high but the beautiful fawn-coloured suède leather, the finely tapered toes and the moc-

casin stitching made of them things of beauty and a joy
for ever.

To bolster up her own ego Elizabeth decided it was a
mistake on Gaylie's part to wear such heavenly shoes. They
took the beholder's eyes away from the near-perfect beauty
of Gaylie's face to dwell on the impeccable beauty of what
was on her feet.

Later, as they all sat in the hotel drawing-room, sipping
morning tea and facing Miss Dal Doone of the *West Coast
Daily*, Elizabeth found that Gaylie's shoes were a magnet
from which it was hard to tear her own eyes.

The one comforting thought was Mrs. Bolton's whispered
words of cheer as the whole party had moved through the
customs sheds on the wharf to the waiting cars on the road
beyond.

"She's beautiful, isn't she?" she said, referring to Gaylie.
"But nothing can match that English complexion of yours,
you know. You'll be the envy of everyone you meet . . . so
take care of it, won't you?"

Elizabeth was used to her complexion, so there, stepping
into a car the size of a battleship, she found it hard to con-
jure up in memory just what it was like in comparison with
Gaylie's smooth, carefully made-up golden skin.

Elizabeth seemed to remember she did have roses in her
own cheeks. And she hardly ever needed much lipstick because her lips were a natural red. She did not remember or
see what Mrs. Bolton could see, that her skin was soft and
warm and had a bloom on it that was as natural as the bloom
on peaches.

She told herself she was anxious to compare not too un-
favourably with Gaylie Paton and her mother because she had
a job of work to do, and it was her duty to look the part.

While Gaylie chatted across the room of her own recent
return from England, Miss Doone asked the kind of searching
questions Elizabeth was relieved to leave Grant Jarvis to
answer.

Were there any plans for an immediate wedding? No.
This was Miss Heaton's first visit to Australia. She would
see something of it first.

Would they make their future home in the Melbourne
home, the Sydney home or on one or other of the Jarvis

stations? Four homes were always maintained in the Jarvis family.

Had the English end of the Jarvis family . . . those living in England . . . met Miss Heaton yet? No.

Oh. So Miss Heaton's family was not known to the Jarvis family? Oh, yes, it was. A cousin of Grant Jarvis . . . Doctor Jarvis . . . had first introduced them.

Then it was something more than a "shipboard" romance? Certainly. Shipboard romances were ephemeral affairs at the best.

When Grant had made this reply Elizabeth had caught his eyes. There was a touch of whimsical humour in them. What a strange man he was! And not easy to interview, she decided. His replies to Miss Doone were very bald. But then what could they be and remain somewhere near the realms of truth?

They were leaving for the Eastern States to-night? Yes. It was desirable for Miss Heaton and his mother to meet as soon as possible. Yes, his mother would meet them at Melbourne. Miss Heaton was at the moment being accompanied by Mrs. Bolton. She had travelled out from England with Mrs. Seaton Morgan of Caramanda Station, North-West. Mrs. Morgan was leaving by air for the north-west on the M.M.A. plane late to-night or in the early hours to-morrow.

Mrs. Paton and Gaylie were already staying in the Adelphi and Grant had booked a private suite for Mrs. Morgan, the Boltons, Elizabeth and himself for the day.

When at last Mrs. Morgan, catching Elizabeth's eye, put a period to the press interview by suggesting she and Elizabeth would like an opportunity to wash and a few minutes' rest before lunch, it was Gaylie who made it easy for them to retire.

She stood up gracefully.

"Come and interview me, Miss Doone," she said. "If you put Grant's photograph in the paper you ought to put mine too." She laughed. "I'm very photogenic, you know." She paused, head on one side. "I'm not sure about Elizabeth. Her features . . . now, let me see! Oh, well, if she smiles her charm will show through, that's something at any rate."

She said all this with a teasing laugh and Elizabeth wasn't sure whether there was a touch of satire in her manner, or not.

"Run along, Elizabeth," Gaylie added, waving her hand. "I'll entertain Grant in your absence. But mind you . . . I warn you . . . you'll be lucky if you find him still here when you come back. Finds keeps, and he was mine first. At least he belonged to the Jarvis family first. And you do know there's as much Jarvis blood in me as there is Paton?"

All this was said with a tinkling bell-like laugh.

At that moment Dr. Jarvis came into the drawing-room. He had had to wait until the formalities of docking had been completed before he left the ship. He heard Gaylie's words and stood, a smile of wisdom on his humorous face, and watched her making a very graceful and sophisticated gesture of farewell to Elizabeth . . . as if she was seeing her off for ever instead of into another room for half an hour.

"My dear cousin Gaylie," Dr. Jarvis said. "Anyone as beautiful and expensive as you does not have to compete, surely."

"Oh, there you are," said Gaylie's mother to the doctor. "Now just you come here and confess what you've been up to. I can't believe you were not in this affair."

Mrs. Morgan had risen and crossed the room with Elizabeth.

"What affair?" she asked quietly, turning to look at the Jarvis family. She spoke with an unassuming dignity.

"The affair of Grant's heart, of course," Dr. Jarvis put in quickly. "According to the evidence of his conduct on board ship he couldn't bear that young lady over there out of his sight. Deck tennis every day. Trips abroad while in port . . . You're not letting her go just when I arrive, are you, Grant?"

"Ask Elizabeth." Grant returned the doctor's look with something that was sardonic.

Elizabeth smiled across the room at the doctor.

"I'm not used to press interviews, Doctor Jarvis. Besides, you are all one family. Mrs. Morgan and I would like to leave you together for a little while. I will be back soon."

"Oh, not too soon," said Gaylie with her tinkling laugh. "We want to talk about you behind your back, you know. We'll promise to say only the nice things."

For that, thought Elizabeth, I'll earn my first ten of the two hundred pounds. She walked across to Grant, bent down and kissed him on the forehead lightly.

"See you later," she said lightly.

His eyes met hers and there was a look of smouldering anger in them. He got up and accompanied her to the door. Mrs. Morgan went through first. Behind them Dr. Jarvis was explaining himself and his very existence to Mrs. Paton and Gaylie. Amidst a clatter and chatter Miss Doone and the camera men were leaving the suite.

"You don't have to go too far with your act, Miss Heaton," Grant said quietly. "It's not wise to overplay a part."

It was on Elizabeth's lips to ask him to give that advice to Gaylie but she remembered in time she herself was only playing a part. She wasn't really engaged to Grant, and he didn't really belong to her. For one stupid moment Gaylie had made her feel as if he did, and that she had to fight to keep him.

"I'm very sorry," she said, looking down. Then looking up at him quickly she added contritely, "Of course, I'll need an awful lot of coaching."

Inside the bedroom she closed the door and leaned her back against it, her hands holding the door knob. Mrs. Morgan looked with curiosity at Elizabeth.

"My dear," she said. "That look you just gave Grant. Eyes down and then up. You're sure you're not falling in love with him yourself, Elizabeth?"

"I couldn't possibly fall in love with him. I'm in love with someone else. Someone in England whom I've been in love with for years. It was just a sort of imp in me that made me want to . . . draw fire, as it were. He's so very fire-proof, isn't he?"

"Absolutely. Don't make any mistake about that, or you'll get hurt. And that I can't allow. Elizabeth . . . you will be careful, won't you? I feel so very responsible . . ."

Elizabeth smiled and shook her head gently.

"Don't worry, dear Mrs. Morgan. I have a kind of feeling that Gaylie will win him in the end. She's quite superb, isn't she? The very person to stand beside him at the head of the Jarvis empire. All I'll turn out to be is a delaying action. I wonder why Grant wastes his time . . ."

"Getting over Thera's death takes time. But time does cure . . . I know that. It is one of the great consoling lessons of life. I think he was just tired of being followed, badgered and schemed over by designing women. You gave him a rest from that."

"I wonder what she was like," said Elizabeth.

"Thera? Don't wonder, my dear. The less you wonder about Grant Jarvis the safer is your peace of mind. Now come and put cold cream on your face and soak cotton pads for your eyes. You've got to look the part for at least another six hours before that plane departs to-night."

Elizabeth left the door and came into the middle of the room.

"Do you know what?" she said. "I'm beginning to enjoy myself. I very nearly feel I *am* a beautiful, charming and wealthy lady, about to marry a millionaire. Do you suppose all actresses feel like this when they're playing a role?"

"Of course they do . . . otherwise they wouldn't be a success. But dear girl . . . I must advise you. You must be wise in your relations with Grant Jarvis. You do not know anything about the world of wealth and power . . . or the people who inhabit it."

Elizabeth put her handbag on the bed and drew off her "pet" of a hat. She shook out her hair before the mirror.

"Please don't worry," she said with a smile. "Remember I spent a morning with him in Aden. It was like receiving attentions from the North Pole. Only as we are in southern latitudes I'd better call him the South Pole. And his behaviour was absolutely above reproach." She looked at Mrs. Morgan's reflection in the mirror and added mischievously, "You're not afraid he will make unfair overtures to me, I hope?"

"That," said Mrs. Morgan firmly, "is one thing we do not have to fear. He won't make advances, fair or unfair, to anyone . . . of that I'm sure. They, unfortunately, all get made to him."

CHAPTER SEVEN

THE ONLY THING that disappointed Elizabeth about the air plane trip across the vast continent was that it was taken at night time and she was not able to see the thousand miles of Nullarbor desert beneath them.

At the last minute of parting Mrs. Morgan had given Elizabeth her fur coat.

"I have three fur coats, Elizabeth," she said when the girl

protested. "To make you happier I would say you can return it to me when this venture is over. But I'm afraid the fear of losing it might worry you. So I am giving it to you."

"I shall return it," said Elizabeth firmly. "It's . . . it's just heavenly but I'm afraid it would look out of place on me back home in England. You see, everybody would know I could never afford to buy anything like this."

She did not add that Ralph's amused reaction to anything so costly and glamorous would have worried her. She could just imagine Ralph's smile, seeing her arrayed as she now was. In two hours of shopping with Mrs. Bolton in Perth she had bought a most charming cherry-red air travelling hat, a pair of cherry-red moccasin type taper-toed shoes that exactly matched the little hat; a pair of gloves and a bag to go with the tawny brown travelling suit which she had bought in England. The suit, at least, she thought proudly, was one to catch even Gaylie's quick appraising eye. The gloves and bag also matched the fur coat, which fitted Elizabeth beautifully, as she was exactly Mrs. Morgan's height.

"If anything happens to the coat console yourself that the firm would replace it," Mrs. Morgan said. "You are to play the part . . . dressed for the part, Elizabeth. Imagine yourself a mannequin or model . . . and feel at home in the things you are to buy in Melbourne, as well as in that coat."

She had leaned forward and kissed Elizabeth and her hand had lingered on the girl's arm.

"Beauty and fine dressing is armour, child," she said. "A knowledge that you are at least equal to all others in that respect will carry you through many difficult situations. I do not know what other advice I can give you except to carry yourself with dignity on all occasions. Be proud of yourself . . . then you'll never be humbled by the awkwardnesses of a strange country, and a strange life which you are now entering. It won't be for long. And Elizabeth . . ."

"Yes, Mrs. Morgan?"

"Get some fun out of it."

Elizabeth caught the knowing twinkle in Mrs. Morgan's eye and her own eyes responded.

"I shall," she promised.

Mrs. Morgan, with Hetty, had insisted on accompanying the party to the airport, as the trans-Australia plane left earlier than her own north-west one. At the gate on to the tarmac she and Elizabeth shook hands. She tucked a piece of paper in Elizabeth's hand.

"I copied that out for you," she said. "The bishop said it to me, many years ago. Now good luck and God-speed."

She turned to Grant Jarvis.

"Take care of that girl," she said in an undertone. "I have grown very fond of her."

Grant had allowed himself a slight smile.

"Something seems to have transformed her in the last few hours," he said. "She looks very capable of looking after herself." Through half-closed eyes he watched Elizabeth cross the short distance to the Viscount aircraft. "I'm only too thankful the air company couldn't find berths for my aunt and Gaylie. Two such striking young women might have taken the pilots' minds off their jobs."

"I understand Mrs. Paton and Gaylie are staying two days longer in Perth. I've no doubt you'll meet up with them again in Melbourne or at Kybarrli."

"I've no doubt, either," said Grant dryly. He turned and shook hands with Mrs. Morgan. "Thank you for lending me your secretary," he said. "And as a matter of interest I'm instructing my agent to get in touch with Small and Smallwoods about the Kybarrli and Paton Pastoral Company which I'm just underwriting. Are they likely to be interested?"

Mrs. Morgan did not have the slightest doubt as to the meaning of the sudden glint in Grant Jarvis's eyes and the knowledgeable smile that accompanied his words.

"Let's not beat about the bush, Grant," she said. "This is the *quid pro quo*, isn't it?"

"Unless that girl lets me down," he said calmly, "your firm has the first offer."

"Rather a ruthless way of doing things, isn't it?" she asked sadly. "The girl doesn't know how much she is carrying on her shoulders."

"That is your affair," he said. "I'm afraid I'm a business man, Mrs. Morgan, just as you are a very astute business woman. You also have put a load on that girl's shoulders. In fact, you put it there first, I think."

Their eyes met in a battle. Elizabeth was already mounting the steps to the open door of the aircraft where the hostess, in her well-tailored blue uniform, stood awaiting her. For

one moment Mrs. Morgan was tempted to call Elizabeth back.
In fact her hand went up and she actually opened her mouth
to call. But in that crucial instant Elizabeth turned and lifted
her hand in a last farewell wave. She was smiling. In her
cherry-red hat and the fur coat she looked elegant and yes,
quite beautiful. Her smile was confident. Mrs. Morgan
dropped her hand and turned again to Grant Jarvis.

"I think I will leave you in Elizabeth's hands," she said.
"I have a feeling there might be a few surprises in store for
you, Mr. Grant Jarvis."

"I have reached the age when nothing would surprise me,"
he said shortly.

With a polite bow he turned and went through the gate,
across the tarmac and up the steps of the plane. Mrs. Morgan
noticed that the hostess nearly fell over herself greeting him.
And beyond the hostess's shoulder could be seen the captain's
peaked cap where he stood waiting to greet this Very Important Person.

The air company's agent went out on to the tarmac, stood
at attention, then saluted the captain. This was the signal that
the company had handed the plane over to the captain of the
craft. It was now all his.

Mrs. Morgan turned away and Hetty took her arm.

In the plane Elizabeth found her seat had been allocated
with Mrs. Bolton on the port side. Grant Jarvis sat with Tim
Bolton on the starboard side across the aisle. While Mrs.
Bolton was arranging the small hand luggage on the rack overhead Elizabeth glanced at the piece of paper Mrs. Morgan had
pressed into her hand. She read:

"Go forth into the world; be of good courage; hold fast
that which is good; honour all men."

The tears suddenly smarted behind Elizabeth's eyes, and
there was a lump in her throat.

In that two and a half weeks' voyage from Southampton
to Fremantle she had learned to love and understand Mrs.
Morgan. Oddly enough, for all her inexperience, Elizabeth
knew that Mrs. Morgan had sent her, Elizabeth, out on to
this mission for Small and Smallwoods as much for her own

sake as for Mrs. Morgan's and the firm's sake. It was shaking her out of herself. It was making her go into the world on her own steam. And it showed trust in her.

Sitting there in the plane, saying "Yes" and "No" at the right times to Mrs. Bolton and the air hostess; completely ignoring the two men in the seats across the aisle, Elizabeth was looking at herself as Mrs. Morgan had looked at her first in London and then in the first week on the ship. A shy girl who beat a two-way track between her office and the outer suburb of Mereton; knowing no one in her heart but Ralph Dalton and her mother and aunt. Not good enough, had been Mrs. Morgan's verdict. So she had taken Cinderella, waved a wand and sent her travelling in an aeroplane across Australia in the smartest little red hat any girl ever wore out of the very best fashion magazine; and sitting over the way from the handsome wealthy man whose destiny had seemed to be to turn the head of every woman he met and plumb the depths of every pocket of the men he met.

Ah, well! Now we shall see what we shall see, thought Elizabeth, and she leaned her head back on the back rest, closed her eyes and presently fell asleep.

The plane touched down at Adelaide in the small hours of the morning. They all got out to stretch their legs and go to the airport restaurant for refreshment.

Grant Jarvis was as aloof as when Elizabeth had first met him on the ship. Looking at him she could hardly imagine him ever unbending enough to play a game of deck tennis, let alone a good one. She wondered what the Boltons were thinking. They must think it was a very odd engaged couple with whom they were travelling . . . that is, unless Grant had taken them into his confidence and they knew what was the real situation.

They sat at a table by a window in the restaurant and Grant Jarvis ordered the breakfast without any reference to Elizabeth or the Boltons. She wondered how he knew, or if he knew, just what everyone would like. In any event he was indifferent to their likes or dislikes.

He ordered grapefruit, steak and eggs, tea and toast. Elizabeth was to learn this was the standard breakfast of Australians. The steak, medium rare, was of the melt-in-your-mouth variety and the tea very hot and very strong. When she saw how easily the other three drank theirs she decided she had better learn to drink it easily and like it too. This was probably one of the social graces she must quickly adopt. Hot, very strong tea.

"Good enough for a blackfellow," Tim Bolton said appreciatively as he drank his second cup. Elizabeth gathered that this was a compliment from the expression of pleasure and satisfaction on the waitress's face.

Grant Jarvis and Tim Bolton talked about sheep, cattle and wool. Elizabeth and Mrs. Bolton talked about clothes.

They had had a quick wash and brush up in the rear lounge compartment of the plane but she was now delighted to find she could have a real bath and change in the facilities provided by the air company at the airport. Melbourne . . . and Grant Jarvis's mother . . . were only two flying hours away so she was glad to avail herself of the chance of making herself look her best.

When she later rejoined Grant and the Boltons on the plane she saw Grant give her a quick appraising glance. She read satisfaction in the fact that he did not frown.

Just as Mrs. Morgan had said . . . fine clothes were an armour. She knew she carried her head higher and had walked across the tarmac and into the plane with confidence. Already she was beginning to feel the part and live it. In fact, every now and again, when she did remember who she really was, she experienced a little falling of spirits. She wasn't then so very sure that what she was doing was right. The whole thing was a deception. She was even, at moments, deceiving herself. Was that a good thing?

In those moments she longed to be back home . . . running up the Underground steps to find safety in the customary presence of Ralph standing just beyond the ticket office. With a sharp pang she would remember the warm comfort of Ralph's arms, the occasional smile in his eyes.

Then she would remember she was doing a job of work for her firm. All work was honourable, and Mrs. Morgan had said Grant Jarvis was no fool. He knew well enough that Small and Smallwoods wished to please him.

How sad, she thought, always to have to *buy* one's pleasures.

When she leaned forward to replace a magazine in the rack on the back of the seat in front of her she stole a glance sideways across the aisle at Grant's face. He was leaning back against the back rest, his eyes half closed and looking straight in front of him. He had a very good, if a severe, profile. His nose was straight and his jaw firm. If his lips were a fine line it was because of the way he held them. At that moment he looked completely cut off from everyone around him. He was isolated in his own thoughts, and from the hooded expression in his eyes they were not gentle thoughts.

He was a hard man, and a cold man, she thought. But a lonely man.

Silly, as she had remarked once to Mrs. Morgan, to feel compassion for a millionaire. Yet something about his loneliness touched her. If his silence hadn't been so forbidding she would have spoken to him.

Mrs. Bolton noticed Elizabeth's questing glance and touched her hand.

"He is always like that when he is travelling," she said as if to reassure Elizabeth.

Elizabeth decided Mrs. Bolton did not after all know of the true situation between herself and Grant. She was so obviously sympathetic and trying to comfort her. Perhaps she thought Elizabeth was suffering because of her "fiancé's" apparent lack of attention . . . and certainly lack of affection.

Elizabeth smiled readily.

"Oh, yes, I know. I've travelled across the world with him, haven't I? But under that silence there is a lot of sterling worth. That is what really matters, isn't it?"

Mrs. Bolton looked at Elizabeth closely.

"I'm so glad you realise that," she said quietly. "So few people do realise it. My husband says he's the finest man he knows. Only you've got to know him."

"That is a fine tribute," Elizabeth said. "I'm glad you told me."

"But you knew it yourself, surely?"

"Of course," Elizabeth answered warmly. She didn't know what to add. She could hardly say "That is why I love him" or "That is why I became engaged to him"! She couldn't bring her lips to express the lie she had, more or less, to live for the next week or two.

"Tell me," she said, hastily changing the subject. "What is Mrs. Jarvis, his mother, like? Grant says so very little . . ."

She couldn't, of course, confess Grant had said nothing. Elizabeth hadn't the faintest idea what to expect and she was quite certain Mrs. Jarvis would be the toughest of the problems to be faced.

"Mrs. Jarvis is a great lady," Mrs. Bolton said in a tone approximating awe. "She is the matriarch of a great family. She never forgets it and never forgets her duty to that family. And to all the dependants of the family. She is a very *good* woman, if you know what I mean. And very, very *correct*."

"Do you mean correct about the way people dress, and behave?"

"Oh, yes. You wait and see. Everything is done by the book of etiquette as laid down by some very grand personage generations ago before the Jarvis brothers first came to Australia. Everything is done at Kybarrli the way it was done by Victorian great-grandmothers. You will find quite a lot of the station owners, and the older families, are like that. It's a mixture of the formal county house type of life . . . on the inside of the homestead . . . and the freedom and independence of the outback out on the station run. But don't let me frighten you. It's a lovely life. I've been in England and I've lived both kinds of life, so I know. My husband was brought out here as a young man by Grant's father. He has never regretted coming."

"I'm sure I shan't either," said Elizabeth. "I hope I please Mrs. Jarvis."

For the moment she had forgotten again that she was playing a part. She actually felt the necessity of pleasing Grant's mother and of being taken, without difficulty, into the fold. She put out her hand impulsively and touched Mrs. Bolton's arm.

"Grant calls you Maria so I'm sure that you and I can use our Christian names. Please call me Elizabeth."

Maria Bolton smiled.

"That's one big surprise in store for you," she said. "In Melbourne people are very conservative about the use of names but on the station only Christian names are used. That is because the natives use only Christian names. They don't understand the two names and they even call Grant by his given name. The stockmen, rouseabouts, jackaroos . . . everyone does it. Though I think you'll find the outback stockmen . . . those who never come near the homestead . . . will be shy of using any name at all. They'll just call you 'Miss.' Even when you're married."

Married? That brought Elizabeth back to earth with a jolt. But she and Grant weren't going to be married! She felt that the momentary descent of her spirits was due to the fact that this other life, this station life, was beginning to assume the charm of a fairy tale. As usual, rather than sink into the void of being nobody belonging nowhere, she thought of Ralph and the fifty-two steps up from the Underground. She took refuge from disappointment in the memory of Ralph's arms and his flippant way of dismissing anything that he didn't regard as important.

She closed her eyes as if on some inner pain. It was really to hide from the light the sudden need of a pair of strong arms to enfold her. She didn't really want to be gallivanting round the world and living in the unreality of somebody else's fairy tale. She wanted her man, and love, and security.

When she opened her eyes it was to see Grant Jarvis leaning forward and looking across at her.

"Are you all right, Elizabeth?" he asked. "Do you feel air sick?"

Air sick! Elizabeth felt a sudden welling up of anger. And if she had been air sick just how much would Mr. Grant Jarvis, alleged fiancé, have cared? He hadn't uttered ten sentences to her since they had landed at Adelaide. And any moment now they would be arriving in Melbourne. It would be amusing to see how much and how well he played *his* part, when they came face to face with the matriarch of clan Jarvis and had to account for themselves before *her* questing eye.

"I'm quite well, thank you," Elizabeth said briefly. She leaned her head back on the head rest and looked straight in front of her as he had been doing for the last hour and a half.

Now he can look at my profile, she thought. Then with a sudden quirk of nervousness she fell to wondering just what her profile was like anyway. She wished she had examined it more minutely in all the years of her existence before she had been crazy enough to go afloat at Southampton. One thing was certain, her nose wasn't as straight as Grant's nose. And nothing about her was comparable with Gaylie.

At Melbourne their party was the last, by Grant's instructions, to leave the plane.

As Elizabeth emerged, dressed in her pretty red hat and red shoes, the fur coat wrapped elegantly around her, she felt

Grant standing beside her at the top of the steps. He took her arm. It was unexpected and a tiny shiver of surprise went through her. He looked down at her quickly.

Perhaps he thinks I'm going to make a mess of it, she thought. She straightened her shoulders, lifted her head and looked up at him confidently.

"For two hundred pounds," she said with an even smile, "a job must be very well done. I am ready, Grant, if you are."

There was a hint of surprise in his eyes. Then something like a shutter came down over his face and except for the cold aloof look it was expressionless.

"Good," he said. "My mother will probably be waiting for us in her car on the other side of the airline offices. She does not wait in crowds. However, there will probably be press photographers beyond that gate . . ." He pointed across the tarmac. "And even now they may be photographing us through the distance lens. Be so kind as to keep smiling and talking to me."

His words brought a genuine smile to Elizabeth's lips.

"You sound like the director of a film," she said. "And I feel like the leading lady."

Grant turned his head towards hers as, together, they descended the steps leading to the ground.

There was a shout from beyond the fence that kept the public from the disembarking passengers.

"Look up, Grant Jarvis!" a man's voice called. "Come across slowly, will you? We want a sequence."

"More than the press," said Grant quietly to Elizabeth as they walked forward. "The newsreel, no less. And tell me, how come you know a director talks and how a leading lady feels?"

Elizabeth went on smiling, first at the crowd where that photographer must be and then up into Grant's face.

"I've read all about it in books," she said.

"A vicarious way of leading somebody else's glamour life," he said. "That's very good, Miss Heaton. When we get to the gate we needn't keep this up any longer. I shall drop your arm and turn to the reporters. You should wait for Maria Bolton and if anyone interviews you don't say anything more than that you've had a good journey, that you are going directly to stay on Kybarrli. There is no need to let the press know we will be a few days in Melbourne."

He dropped his hand from her arm. Elizabeth kept her face upturned to his face.

"Don't forget to call me Elizabeth and not Miss Heaton. You missed a cue there," she said.

Her impish smile was real. Again there was a look of startled surprise, quickly veiled, in his eyes.

He held out his right arm as if to make a way for her through the press of people in the gateway and standing about in the entrance to the airline reception rooms. Cameras were clicking but Elizabeth tried not to blink. In less than a minute Grant had two young men bailing him up . . . note-books and pencils held out like six-shooters; and Elizabeth found three exceedingly well-dressed and charming women doing the same to her.

She wanted to reach out behind her for Maria Bolton. Fortunately Maria was so close on her heels she took Elizabeth's arm in time to give her confidence.

It was twenty minutes before the four of them, Elizabeth, Grant, and the Boltons, were able to escape through a side door.

"Over there, Grant," Tim Bolton said, pointing.

Parked in a line of cars was a black liner of a car. It was long, streamlined and had shining chromium fittings. The driver was standing beside it in the act of opening a door. In the centre of the back seat, with a very regal air, sat a tiny little lady in a black astrakhan coat with a diminutive violet flowered toque on her white hair. The matriarch of the Jarvis family could be, surely, no taller than Queen Victoria.

Elizabeth gave Maria Bolton a surprised look. Maria nodded her head and smiled.

"But every inch of her is a ruler," she said in a whisper.

As Grant, again taking Elizabeth's arm, advanced to the car, the tiny straight-backed lady turned her head, lifted a pair of lorgnettes to her eyes and examined Elizabeth. She lowered them to look at her son.

The driver had the car door open now and Mrs. Jarvis leaned slightly forward to address them.

"Well, Grant," she said, "you have done very well. I suppose the newspapers were waiting for you?"

"Both at Fremantle and here," he said dryly. "Heading a trade commission to the United Kingdom has its price."

"A successful one has its price, my dear," said the little lady in firm but very modulated tones. "Well, you've probably done great things towards saving the wool industry. That is news to a country that lives on the sheep's back. I hope the pastoralists of Australia will be properly grateful to you."

Elizabeth felt bewildered. This was something about which she knew absolutely nothing. Grant had not just been taking a holiday to England then? He had been on some kind of official business that had proved successful. This was the major reason why he was so fêted and photographed. In a sense she felt relief. She had almost suffered for him that he had to spend his life in this white glare of publicity. It was a thing of the moment, apparently, and moments, like all other moments, pass on, giving place to others.

Grant made no attempt to kiss his mother nor did she, sitting so upright in the back of the car, make any gesture that would make that act of love possible.

Perhaps they are all a cold, unaffectionate family, Elizabeth thought.

She stood beside Grant while he and his mother exchanged these few remarks, and so interested was she in the small woman with her perfect grooming and irreproachable manner of correct public deportment, that she forgot to be nervous. Forgot, in fact, she was playing a part. She was both fascinated and delighted with Mrs. Jarvis. The regal little lady sitting alone in the back of the enormous car was like someone out of a book.

"Mother," said Grant, "this is my fiancée, Elizabeth Heaton. You received my telegram from Perth?"

Mrs. Jarvis lifted the lorgnettes and looked at Elizabeth again.

"How do you do?" she said with a polite smile.

Elizabeth almost bobbed a curtsy. Inside herself a little imp of delight, whose existence she had only discovered in the last few days, twinkled with laughter at this very near gaffe. What, she wondered, had nearly inspired her to bob a curtsy?

"How do you do?" Elizabeth said, and she too inclined her head but added a charming smile to the salutation.

"Will you get in, Elizabeth and Grant," Mrs. Jarvis said. "Sit one on either side of me, please. Grant, you had better

go round to the other door. How are you, Maria and Tim
Bolton? Will you please sit in the dicky seats when Elizabeth
and Grant are in."

Maria Bolton stood smiling politely at the little lady and
Tim Bolton stood, hat in hand, feet together at attention,
and made a slight bow.

"Very well indeed, thank you, Mrs. Jarvis," they both
said together.

Elizabeth got into the car and the driver settled her coat
away from the danger of being caught in the door.

"You were born in London, Elizabeth?" said Mrs. Jarvis
as the car moved off.

"Out of London, Mrs. Jarvis. A village, now a suburb
really, called Mereton."

"I know London very well," said Mrs. Jarvis. "My grand-
mother had a home there. In Kensington." She turned to
Grant. "Has Elizabeth an engagement ring?"

Elizabeth took in a deep breath.

Grant said, "No. We have only just become engaged."

Mrs. Jarvis drew off the black kid glove from her left hand.
Her fingers were almost weighed down with rings. She slipped
a ring from her third finger and handed it to Elizabeth.

"Put it on," she said. "It will look better until you make
up your minds if you're really going to be married at all."

As if mesmerised, Elizabeth took the ring in her hand. She
dared not lean forward to see what Grant wished her to do.
When she looked towards him she met Mrs. Jarvis's eyes instead. They were a cold proud grey, yet deep in them was a
knowledge of the ways of young women with Grant. Or was
it the other way round? Elizabeth took in a deep breath, and
then suddenly smiled. Somehow . . . she would probably
never know how . . . but this stern little lady *knew*.

CHAPTER EIGHT

AFTERWARDS, when they were having lunch in the beautiful
old-world morning room at Jarvis House in Toorak, it occur-
red to Elizabeth that Mrs. Jarvis had known this was an impossible engagement as soon as she had looked through her
lorgnettes at Elizabeth. She had known that this little girl

. . . very nicely, even elegantly got up in a cherry-red hat and a very expensive fur coat . . . was just not the type that a Grant Jarvis would marry. The thought was sobering . . . even a little depressing. Mrs. Jarvis would probably have had an entirely different reaction if it had been a counterpart of Gaylie Paton walking across the road on her son's arm instead of Elizabeth.

When they had arrived at the Toorak house a maid in a black frock and white cap and apron had been directed to take Elizabeth to her room. Mrs. Jarvis and Grant had gone at once into a small drawing-room off the vast hall. Tim and Maria Bolton had simply disappeared into nothing.

Elizabeth had followed the maid up the staircase along a thick-piled carpeted hall to a room overlooking a most beautiful lawn and garden at the side of the house. It had been a cold, frosty morning, but the sun was now shining through the trees, making diamond dancing patterns on the lawn. The shrubs, evergreen, stood in a thick cluster round the garden beds. In the very centre blazed an enormous group of crimson poinsettias.

The room was big, and beautifully furnished with heavy old polished mahogany furniture. The four-poster bed stood, a memorial to the early pioneers who had brought it to the country, the centre piece of the room. A full length wall mirror was behind a Regency table on which stood a powder bowl of cut crystal, and cut glass scent bottles and pin trays.

Elizabeth's suitcases, last seen at the airport, were by some miracle of transport already there.

"The door on your right leads to your bathroom, Miss Heaton," the maid said. "If you need anything will you please ring?"

Noiselessly she went out and closed the door.

Elizabeth took in a deep breath and then moved across the room and sat on the bed.

She shook her head.

"I hadn't any idea . . ." she said to herself. What she hadn't any idea of was the noiseless perfection of arrival and disposal of a guest; of the comfort and evidence of solid, timeless wealth.

No wonder Grant was so aloof: no wonder Mrs. Jarvis so regal. No wonder Gaylie Paton and her mother would not let a prize as rich as Grant Jarvis escape their net!

She looked around the room; at the chairs, the wardrobe—big enough to house the clothes of an entire family—at the thick flower-patterned carpet, at the beautiful old mantelshelf with its bowl of flowers on it. Then she held out her left hand, the back of it towards herself, and looked at the large diamond ring flashing on the fourth finger.

"I must never tell Ralph about any of this," she said with a sigh. "He would laugh and be witty about it in a not very kind way."

The following day Maria Bolton took Elizabeth shopping. With the discretion of absolute good manners Mrs. Jarvis had said over the grapefruit, steak and eggs, hot strong tea breakfast:

"Mrs. Bolton will show you something of Melbourne this morning. We will be going to Kybarrli on Friday. Mrs. Bolton will know if there is anything you need on the station."

On the previous day Mrs. Jarvis had asked Elizabeth nothing personal of herself, her home or her parents. She had talked of trivial things such as the weather, the advantages of air travel and the cultivation of indoor growing pot plants. Grant had treated Elizabeth with engaging but distant good manners. Elizabeth wondered if he had taken his mother into his confidence or whether he thought she was in ignorance of the true situation. Of what had they talked when they had gone into that little drawing-room and Elizabeth had been taken upstairs by the maid?

Their treatment of one another was so considerate, good-mannered yet distant, that it was possible this mode of social intercourse between members of the family was customary. Therefore Grant's distant but carefully polite treatment of herself would not appear unusual to Mrs. Jarvis or her household.

It was all a riddle. Elizabeth was thankful it was one she didn't have to solve. She had just to appear in public as Grant's fiancée until the *Albany* was due to sail back to England from the Eastern Pacific ports of Australia.

How the broken engagement would be explained to Grant's public was Grant's business.

On the first evening, the day before she went shopping with Maria Bolton, Elizabeth, Grant and Mrs. Jarvis had had dinner at the immense mahogany table in the big dining-

room. After dinner several people of Mrs. Jarvis's age came
in for coffee. They sat on the Regency chairs in the spacious
drawing-room and talked pleasantly and lightly of subjects as
irrelevant and trivial as ships and shoes and sealing wax. To
each Elizabeth had been presented as Grant's fiancée, and
each had shaken hands politely, bowed politely and asked
after her health and the state of the weather in London.

Their cars called and took them away at an early hour and
immediately afterwards Mrs. Jarvis retired.

Grant escorted Elizabeth to the head of the staircase.

"The light is left burning in the passage all night," he said.

Elizabeth hesitated, looking at him.

"How am I doing, Grant?" she said curiously. "Do I pass
muster?"

"As my fiancée? Admirably."

"I have a feeling nobody believes it."

He looked surprised.

"Why not?" he said. He sounded annoyed.

"Well . . . they're not very interested, are they? I mean
. . . There was such a fuss made over your arrival by the
press. They . . . I mean your mother and those people here
to-night . . . would surely be interested in how you came to
meet and be engaged to me. The fiancée of such a potentate
ought to mean something to them."

"They've read all about you in the papers," Grant said
coldly. "It would be bad manners on their part to dilate on
the details."

"Oh, the papers!" said Elizabeth. "I had forgotten I would
be in them too."

"You haven't seen the evening papers? Come into this
small sitting-room and I'll get them for you at once."

He turned on a light and showed her into a small den-like
room furnished in bright chintz-covered furniture. He walked
rapidly down the passage past Elizabeth's room to one at the
far end. A few minutes later Elizabeth heard him coming
back. He came in with two papers in his hand. He handed
them to her. Elizabeth unfolded them and then stared
astounded. A large photograph of herself and Grant occupied
the centre of the front page of each. Grant looked even more
handsome than he really was. And that smiling girl? Could
that really be herself? Yes, it was. She recognised the likeness.
But that girl was beautiful. And smart. Elegant. What was the

word for it? Why, glamorous! Oh, of course. They had touched it up in the newspaper office. It was the *news* that had to be glamorous.

"We don't really look like that, do we?" she said.

"Don't we?" said Grant.

He was watching her with a curious smile on his lips. He took one paper from her and examined the photograph.

"Don't we really look like that?" he said.

Over the edge of the paper his eyes met Elizabeth's. A flush mounted her cheeks. There was something quizzical in the way he asked that question. Had her question sounded like that? Almost as if they had a right to be coupled together in that "we" of whom they both spoke. Or was she imagining it all?

She wasn't imagining Grant's smile as, his head a little on one side, he examined the photograph again.

"A very handsome couple, I would say," he said. "We ought to have it framed and kept for our grandchildren."

The surprises that were in store for Elizabeth, she thought, were without end. Who would have thought that Grant himself had the capacity to enter into the "joke" of the whole affair.

He folded the paper and put it on a table. He took the other paper from Elizabeth's hand and placed it on top of the other.

"Come along," he said. His voice was almost friendly. "I will show you to your room. Breakfast is at eight downstairs. I'm afraid my mother is a stickler for eating in the dining-room. Punctually."

He walked along the hall with her and opened her bedroom door. Then he stood aside.

"Good night, Elizabeth," he said. Then quite seriously, "And thank you very much. You're doing fine."

For the second time in ten minutes Elizabeth flushed. Grant's words of satisfaction gave her real pleasure.

"I've instructed Maria Bolton to take you to Madame René to-morrow. She will fit you in something outstanding in evening wear. There is to be an evening reception at Kybarrli on the night of the Governor's visit. The secretary at Government House in that State has sent me a note to that effect. His Excellency will wear full dress and decorations."

With that he turned abruptly away and walked rapidly down the hall.

The most astonishing revelation of all the day's events had been this wall of good manners, or Jarvis social usage, which had prevented anyone from expressing too obvious an interest in the girl who, they thought, was to marry the scion of their circle.

On Friday morning the party, which included Mrs. Jarvis and Tim and Marie Bolton, went to the airport to take a plane on a feeder line from the main airline to a town some hundreds of miles inland which Elizabeth overheard someone call Endall.

On the previous day, after her shopping spree with Maria Bolton, Elizabeth had returned to the great house in Toorak and to the strange walled silence which on her first day she had thought was due to the odd social customs of the Jarvis family. After a really interesting walk through the great stores of Melbourne and afterwards through the fabulous Botanical Gardens which were to Melbourne what Hyde Park was to London, Elizabeth found the correctness and minutiæ of the day's routine in the big house oppressive. Maria Bolton had been an excellent guide and had given Elizabeth a really happy and interesting morning. In contrast the Jarvis House seemed sombre and even intimidating. Elizabeth was suddenly fervently glad they were going inland to the sheep station. At least she would be in the open air. Kybarrli could not be a second Jarvis House, surely!

Throughout Thursday there had been no sign of Grant. Elizabeth realised that if he had been abroad on a Trade Commission for the Government he must have important business matters to attend to before he left Melbourne for the outback. Already, from the interesting things Maria Bolton had told her, the word "outback" had become in Elizabeth's mind synonymous with open air, sunlight and wide spaces.

She was disappointed, however, when they returned to Jarvis House that morning to find Grant absent. She told herself that Grant near at hand made her feel more secure in her role. Yesterday, while he had been here, she had had no worries about what to do and what to say. Mrs. Jarvis had by no means ignored Elizabeth but her conversation had been formal and required only trivial answers. On this second day, sitting alone at lunch with the little lady, Elizabeth felt different.

There was no way of feeling or behaving naturally. Mrs. Jarvis's stiff manner and stiff back forbade it.

Quite suddenly Elizabeth, enjoying some beautiful grilled fish and pineapple salad in spite of herself, decided this atmosphere was not habitual at all. Mrs. Jarvis had simply and utterly disposed of Elizabeth as of no consequence.

As Mrs. Jarvis made light inconsequential remarks without ever once looking at the girl Elizabeth had time both to follow the current of her own thoughts and make suitable replies to Mrs. Jarvis at the same time.

Well, after all, she thought, I am not of any consequence to these people. My existence, as far as they are concerned, is temporary. If Mrs. Jarvis doesn't know the whole thing is a fake then she does at least know I'm no competition for any other plans she has in store for Grant. She is letting time dispose of me. And that is just exactly what time will do.

She wondered why she felt deflated. Perhaps it was because of the beautiful glamorous clothes she had tried on this morning and the tremendous impression made on the sales girls, and Madame René, when they discovered she was the Miss Heaton of yesterday's newspaper photographs, and that she was to marry into the Jarvis family.

Strange how Mrs. Jarvis, without saying a word, reminded her of just who she was, and more important still, who she was *not*. Yet Elizabeth, though a little afraid of her, could not help admiring the stiff little lady. Not one impolite word did she utter. Not by a gesture or a glance did she imply that Elizabeth was strange company for Grant to be keeping.

Elizabeth wished vainly that Grant would come in. Grant sitting at the end of the table would have given her reassurance.

The small Dove plane that took the Jarvis party to Endall was very diminutive compared with the Viscount that brought Elizabeth and Grant across Australia. Nevertheless it was comfortable. Each person sat in a single seat and Grant, who wanted to talk over station matters with Tim Bolton, had to turn in his seat and talk to Tim sitting behind him. Tim leaned forward. Elizabeth could not hear, over the hum of

the engines, what they talked of but as she sat in a seat farther
to the rear on the other side she could watch their faces.

Both men had appeared that morning almost identically
dressed, except that when one looked closely one could see
that Grant's clothes were of better, finer and probably more
expensive materials. They both wore dark brown trousers with
flecked Donegal tweed sports coats, light tan shirts with a plain
khaki brown tie, and wide-brimmed Stetson hats. Grant wore
highly polished brown leather shoes with a moccasin finish but
Tim Bolton had light leather elastic-sided stock boots. The
Dove carried two other passengers who were dropped at a
country town two hours later, and two more came on board.
They too were dressed as were Grant and Tim. Elizabeth
realised that this, particularly the tan coloured shirt and brown
tie and wide-brimmed hat, was a kind of uniform of the outback. As a soldier's uniform will proclaim his profession so
did this dressing of the men proclaim pastoral pursuits.

Elizabeth sat watching Grant's face as he, turned about,
talked to Tim. The coldness was gone from his face and in
its place was a certain keenness. He had a habit of half-
closing his eyes as if looking through shutters. This made his
eyes seem hard and keen. His mouth rarely smiled so he
seldom showed his teeth but when he did Elizabeth was
surprised to see how they flashed in his brown face and how
there was a sudden shining quality as if there was somewhere
in him a bright light that only occasionally shone through.
But the laugh was so short it was like a light turning off
and so rare that Elizabeth found herself watching him and
waiting for it . . . almost as if she was waiting for the
revelation of a treasure.

Once he raised his eyes and caught Elizabeth's intent gaze.
The quick flick in his eyes told her he observed that she was
watching him and that there was something curious and inquiring in her scrutiny.

She turned away and thereafter did not dare to look back
at him. Yet all the time she had to fight a compulsion to do so.

At Endall they found a fleet of cars waiting for them. The
only cargo the Dove was carrying was for Kybarrli Station
and a tall stockman took charge of it, together with the luggage, and proceeded to help the airline man unload the plane
and load up the station wagon.

A second car, a shabby big American tourer driven by an aboriginal stockman, was for the Boltons. Two other stockmen were standing beside two other cars. As Mrs. Jarvis with Grant and Elizabeth approached them they took off their wide-brimmed stockmen's hats and grinned shyly and awkwardly.

"G'day, Missis Jarvis. 'Day, Grant," they both said. They averted their eyes from Elizabeth as if afraid to see her.

Mrs. Jarvis nodded her head and to Elizabeth's surprise held out her hand and shook hands with both stockmen. Elizabeth hadn't thought Mrs. Jarvis likely to shake hands with anyone on earth but a Jarvis. She remained a stiff, regal little lady but she smiled as she spoke to both men, and further to Elizabeth's surprise these two men, obviously too shy to look at her, found no difficulty at all in talking to Mrs. Jarvis. They talked through tight half-closed lips and Elizabeth could not understand them but quite clearly Mrs. Jarvis could and was interested in what they had to say.

After a few minutes Mrs. Jarvis turned to Elizabeth, made a small gesture with her hand and said:

"Well, Elizabeth, you had better meet Bill Smith and Peter Smith." She smiled. "They are no relation to one another. Every second stockman in the outback is named Smith and every second Smith is named John. Bill and Peter are Kybarrli variations." She turned again to the two men. "Bill . . . Peter," she said firmly and clearly, "this is Elizabeth Heaton. My future daughter-in-law."

Elizabeth was so taken aback by this announcement she was as self-conscious as the two stockmen. They kicked dust with the toes of their boots, looked up quickly and then looked away quickly and said, "G'day, miss." Elizabeth intuitively followed Mrs. Jarvis's example and held out her hand.

First one horny hand went into hers and then another. The men dropped their hands as if something had stung them.

At that moment Grant, who had been speaking to Tim Bolton by the other car, came across.

"'Day, Grant. How you doin'? How's old Blighty?" asked one.

"Weather cold over there, Grant?" asked the other.

They seemed to be relieved to be able to address their attentions to Grant and so remove them from Elizabeth.

Grant shook hands with both men.

"Just the same as it always is, Peter. I saw your old grand-

mother, as you asked me. She's still alive though your grand-
father has been dead about ten years."

"You don't say," said Peter, pleased and astonished at
Grant seeing his people. "So there's still some relations over
there?"

"Yes. But not by the name of Smith," Grant said with a
grin. "Everything going all right on Barrli?"

"Yeah. We just got in here to Kybarrli two days ago. Everything fine and dandy then. You comin' out there this trip,
Grant?"

"Yes. I want to get across to Barrli after the week-end. You
two fellows take charge of my mother, will you. No speeding,
Bill."

"Not with Missis Jarvis on board," said Bill with a grin.
"There isn't the stockman living who'd dare."

Both men grinned and Bill turned to hold the rear door of
the big streamlined Customline for Mrs. Jarvis. Elizabeth
looked inquiringly at Grant.

"You come with me, Elizabeth," he said crisply. "I'll drive
my own car and I want to go round by the out-camp. Mother
will go straight up to the homestead."

Grant spoke as if they were going for a five mile drive.
Elizabeth found it was a hundred and twenty miles to Kybarrli
Station homestead. At the speed with which Grant drove . . .
another battleship of a modern streamlined car . . . it didn't
seem like a hundred and twenty miles either.

Elizabeth was puzzled as to why Grant had not sent her
with his mother. Perhaps Mrs. Jarvis had made the arrangements.

Elizabeth, sitting beside Grant in the big car, found the
easiest topic of conversation to be the scenery.

"Is . . . is the whole country like this?" she asked, looking
out at the vast undulating country, very sparsely clad with
trees.

"Australia stretches from the tropics in the north to the
south temperates in Tasmania," Grant said, watching the
winding gravel road in front of him. "That's a pretty wide
stretch of earth you know."

Elizabeth felt rebuffed. If she had ever looked at the map
properly she would have realised that, but somehow the vastness of this continent was something one knew theoretically
but found hard to believe when one was looking at it in reality.

A three-wire fence ran along on either side of the road, but beyond, on either side, were unlimited paddocks which flowered away over the horizons without any evidence of human habitation.

"Frightening to be lost in it," Grant said, turning his eyes off the road for a minute and looking down at her. One eyebrow seemed to flick upwards as if enjoying her astonishment . . . or was it her discomfiture?

"The car is not likely to break down, is it?"

"We could always walk."

"Over a hundred miles?"

"There've been many hundred stockmen and drovers walk far greater distances than that in their week's work."

"I hope you're only teasing me," Elizabeth said. The incredible loneliness of the land, the emptiness of the gravel track seemed eerie to her.

"Briefly," Grant said as if explaining elementary arithmetic to a dull child, "every station man is his own mechanic these days. So if the car broke down I could fix it up."

"Oh!"

"And that goes for Bill and Peter driving my mother to the homestead."

"I see," said Elizabeth contritely.

"And it goes for the humblest rouseabout and the cheekiest jackaroo."

"What are they?"

"A rouseabout is the odd job man. A jackaroo is a young man learning the business of running a station. Generally another station owner's son. A sort of apprenticeship. The jackaroo on Sandor Downs is a son of Lord Angell. The family intends to buy into a station lease when young Ronald has got enough experience."

"Were you a jackaroo before you took over the ownership of your stations?"

Again he turned his eyes away from the road and looked down at Elizabeth. His look was clearly scornful.

"I was not," he said shortly.

Oh, thought Elizabeth. Too high and mighty. Too wealthy. Born with a silver spoon in his mouth.

If she felt unkind at these thoughts she felt he merited them. Perhaps that was why Grant was so cut off. He had not had to follow his career the hard way. He had not had to battle his way to the top.

Yet he could act as mechanic to his own car. That was something in his favour. All the same it might have done him good to have had, some time or other in his life, to work for someone else.

They drove on for many miles in silence. Not once in a whole hour did the landscape change. They might have been driving through the same stretch of country they had driven through when they left the airfield outside the small country town.

A quarter of an hour later Grant pulled in at the side of the road. He pushed his hat on to the back of his head and leaning back in his seat took out a cigarette and lit it. He appeared suddenly to remember that Elizabeth was with him.

"Would you like a cigarette?" he asked.

Elizabeth shook her head.

"No, thank you," she said.

"No! I seem to remember they are not exactly successful with you."

He was thinking of the occasion when the smoke had got in her eyes and caught in her throat. His manner was faintly derisive and Elizabeth wondered if he wanted to make her feel small. It made her feel angry and subdued. She had no weapons with which to fight back at this man.

"When I've finished this cigarette we'll have lunch," he said. "There's a hamper in the back. I'll spare you smoke in your eyes and give you tea from a Thermos flask instead."

So he *was* thinking of the time she had choked and cried over that cigarette. Without a doubt he was accustomed to girls like Gaylie Paton who could smoke a cigarette as if born handling one. It was probably regarded as a social grace like being able to play the piano and golf.

He put his gold cigarette case on the ledge in the dashboard and in the smooth circle in the middle of it Elizabeth could read his initials. G.G.J. from T.P.

T.P. would be Thera Paton . . . the girl he had loved and who had died. Suddenly Elizabeth didn't feel angry with him any more.

"I will have a cigarette after all," she said gently. "Maybe, if I learn to smoke one now and again, I won't feel nervous when I'm carrying out my part amongst your relatives and friends."

He looked at her for a moment, then leaned forward and took up the cigarette case. He opened it and held it towards her. When she had taken a cigarette he snapped the case shut, put it back on the ledge, then struck a match. He leaned towards her.

"Draw back very slowly and very gently when I put the match to the end of your cigarette."

The match was still an inch away from the end of the cigarette. Elizabeth had a frown of concentration on her forehead and was nearly squinting down the length of the cigarette, waiting for Grant to put the match to its end.

For a brief moment he held the match there, looking at her face and its concentrated expression intently. Then suddenly he flicked out the match, put up his hand and took the cigarette out of her mouth. He broke it in two between his fingers and threw it out the window.

"There are other things you will have to learn without bothering about cigarettes," he said.

Elizabeth was looking up at him, her blue eyes wide with surprise. He did not move his position, his hard flint-like eyes were looking into her.

"Such as . . ." he said.

"Yes?" said Elizabeth. "Such as?"

His eyes held hers. Intuitively she knew what was coming. His arm, unaccountably, was along the back rest behind her. His body seemed to loom over her. His eyes held hers, mesmerised.

"Such as kissing me in public," he said. "The occasion might arise. Could you carry it off with ease?"

"You think we should practise now?" Elizabeth almost whispered. "In the middle of nowhere?" She felt as if her very heart was standing still.

"I thought of it," said Grant.

Elizabeth sat as if carved in stone, unable to drag her eyes away or move her head.

"Are you afraid of kissing me?" he asked, his eyebrows flexed and his mouth just a little bitter.

"No," she said gravely.

He bent his head and kissed her on the lips.

"Quite puritanical," he said. "You'll have to show a little

more warmth in public. I hope for your sake the occasion
does not arise!" He reached across her and opened the door.
"Get out," he commanded. "We'll have lunch."

A little shiver passed through Elizabeth. She wondered if
he knew he had been cruel. Then she decided he had been
that many times. It made her want to hit him.

Instead she got out of the car and walked across the
rutted verge to the wire fence. She stood leaning on it and
looking out across the great undulating land. When she had
composed herself she turned round.

She would never forgive him.

Then suddenly she knew she would forgive him. The act
of kissing would have reminded him of Thera, as it had
reminded her of Ralph. It would be bitter to him too.

CHAPTER NINE

GRANT JARVIS took the picnic hamper from the boot of the
car and brought it over to the tall blue gum tree that stood
by the fence where Elizabeth was now waiting. Ordinarily it
would have been her instinct to go forward and ask if she
could help. The scene a few minutes earlier in the car had
filled her with a kind of reticence. She was at a loss as to
how to react to his distant yet oddly magnetic personality.

If he was determined on appearing as a safely engaged
man before his relatives and friends . . . if he was going to
take cover, as it were, behind a relationship with herself
it was only reasonable that he should take the precautions
of making all the appearances true to life. An engaged couple
did kiss sometimes in public. A greeting, or a farewell.

Standing stiffly by the fence Elizabeth watched Grant lift
the cover of the basket, take out a plastic box and open it to
reveal neatly cut sandwiches and small cakes, and finally a
Thermos flask and some coloured plastic mugs.

She wondered why her knees felt stiff. She wondered
what Grant Jarvis would say to break this silence that had
long become something more than accidental.

She didn't bargain with the fact he wasn't going to break
it at all. In fact, except for setting her sandwiches on a small
plate, and pouring out tea for her without reference to

whether she did or did not take milk, he didn't appear to be aware that she existed. He took his own sandwiches and a mug of tea over to the car, set them on a stump nearby, lifted the bonnet of the car and began tinkering with the engine. Every now and again he would lift his head, reach for a sandwich, take a gulp of tea, and put his head back in amongst the engine parts.

Elizabeth couldn't stand by the fence all day, waiting for this intractable man to persuade or cajole her to take a little refreshment. The scene was rapidly getting near the ridiculous.

Elizabeth moved over to the grass patch under the tree and sat down by the lunch basket. She put out her hand and took the cup of tea. Its warmth encouraged her and she took a sandwich.

She hadn't realised she was so hungry. The excitement of the early morning departure from Melbourne had prevented her from taking much breakfast. In fact she had forgotten she hadn't eaten and that her stomach was empty and that for quite a long time she had been feeling hollow.

She took another sandwich. At that moment Grant Jarvis lifted his head and turned round. Then she realised she was behaving like a foolish child at some other child's tea-party. She was waiting to be persuaded.

She immediately poured herself another cup of tea. She got up and carried the Thermos over to Grant's mug and filled it up. The Thermos was now empty so she put back the stopper and repacked the basket except for the remaining sandwiches. She ate her own sandwiches and watched Grant. He used a spanner with one hand and ate with the other.

When he had finished doing whatever he was doing with the car he put away the tools, wiped his hands on a piece of waste and took the empty mug and plate back to Elizabeth. She finished packing the basket. He picked it up, put it in the boot of the car, then held the car door open for Elizabeth.

She glanced at his face. He had a faraway, thoughtful look and she realised that his thoughts were a long way away from this scene. While she had been feeling first hurt and indignant and finally angry, and with a return of common sense, just a little contrite because she had attached so much importance to a meaningless kiss, he had simply been unaware of her existence. He had not uttered a word because when something else seized his imagination she had ceased to exist. He was as remote from her as if he lived on another planet.

She leaned back in the corner of the car and closed her eyes. She might as well sleep as do anything else. She wasn't expected to make conversation the way she had been making it before their picnic. Like all good paid servants she was expected to be seen and not heard.

Elizabeth actually did doze and the car pulling up to a halt about an hour and a half later woke her up with a start.

They had stopped in front of a gate stretching right across the road. Grant got out of the car, opened the gate, got back in and drove the car through. He got out again, closed the gate, got in and drove on.

"I'm sorry," Elizabeth said, still in a daze of sleep. "I could have saved you time by opening and shutting the gate for you."

"You can do it at the next gate. About ten miles on."

"Are we inside Kybarrli now?" she asked. "Have we arrived?"

His eyes were half closed as he looked into the westering sun. Elizabeth realised he must be very tired. But he said nothing of that.

"We're at the out station," he said. "I'm going the long way round to Kybarrli because I want to call in on an old-timer who acts as boundary rider for me at the wells here." He gave no further explanation. Elizabeth, remembering her newly discovered "place," did not ask for one.

At the speed with which Grant drove the big car over the stubbly track . . . for it was now more of a grass track than a road . . . they seemed to be at the next gate in a very short time.

Elizabeth got out and opened it while Grant drove through. When she had closed the gate and got back in the car he did not attempt to start it up. He sat leaning forward, both hands on the steering wheel and looking through slitted eyes into the distance. Quite clearly he was looking at something that struck a note of concern in him. Elizabeth could feel his tensed body and the sharp concentrated probing of his eyes.

"Is something wrong?" she asked.

His mouth was drawn in a straight line.

"Those crows," he said. "And the eagle."

Beyond the rise, a quarter of a mile away, Elizabeth could see black dots rise and fall in the air. Overhead a larger dot hovered as if stationary.

"What does it mean?" she asked.

"Could be something dead," he said as he let out the clutch and put his foot down on the accelerator. "Could be something still alive. That eagle is waiting. It hasn't grounded yet."

"An animal, do you think?"

"Not with Old Flinty on the job. He clears up and burns any dead stock around. And there's no smoke in the air."

The car seemed to rocket over the tussock grass. Elizabeth had to hold on to the door strap to keep herself steady in her seat.

The land fell away in a long slow decline to a shallow valley. There was no river or creek but at the bottom, immediately in front of them, was a small wood and iron hut, an open iron shed that seemed to be no more than a roof on four posts over a plant of machinery; and beside it a windmill. The fan of the windmill was racing round in the breeze. There was no smoke emerging from the hut and no sign of any human being about. Three horses, one of them saddled, were drinking at a trough under the iron shed.

Grant pulled up the car with a skid of brakes at the fence of the small enclosure that surrounded the hut and windmill plant. For a minute he made no attempt to get out. He sat leaning forward as before, his hands on the wheel and his eyes a mere slit between his lids. His head was turned slightly as if he both listened and looked.

The sun was going down beyond the low hill and a penetrating coldness was settling over the wide saucer-like valley.

Grant moved suddenly.

"Stay here," he said. His voice was sharp and commanding.

He got out, shut the car door behind him and moved across the ground, through the wicket gate of the enclosure towards the shed. Elizabeth could now see that water was flowing over the trough walls and there was a quagmire of water everywhere around it. Grant was moving with great speed now. He went over to the mill; appeared to loosen a chain of sorts, heave on something and, then obviously using his strength, elevate a big lever which he slipped into a slot on the main column of the mill. He walked past the three horses. They tossed their heads and whistled through their noses. Grant pulled a small rod out of the side of an enormous bin and threw back the lid. The horses had their noses in it before he could get clear of them. For a frightening moment Elizabeth thought he would be crushed between them.

Then, eyes on the ground as if he was looking for something, Grant moved over to the open door of the hut. In the doorway he stooped, put his hand on something, then stood up looking at his hand. In another minute he had disappeared into the inner darkness of the hut.

Elizabeth seemed to wait in the car for a long time. The only time she took her eyes off the door was when the horses began throwing chaff and food out of the bin with their noses. The darkening night air seemed to be full of flying particles.

Supposing there was something wrong in the hut . . . and that Grant needed help . . .

Elizabeth swung open the door and got out. She went through the open wicket gate towards the hut.

It took her eyes a minute to get used to the darker light inside the hut. Then she saw that Grant was sitting on the side of a low bunk on which a man's legs, fully clothed including stockboots, could be seen. Grant was leaning over the man and holding something to his mouth.

When Elizabeth's dark shadow appeared in the doorway he turned his head.

"Can you drive that car?" he said abruptly.

"No, I'm sorry, Grant. I can't drive any car."

He turned back to the man whose head and upper part was hidden from Elizabeth by Grant's broad shoulders.

"You wouldn't," he said quite savagely.

Elizabeth went forward to the bunk.

"Can I help you?" she asked quietly.

"Only by driving that raking car," Grant said through half-closed lips, his eyes on the face of a very old man with an enormous Saint Nicholas beard.

Grant held the mug of water again to the old man's lips and let a little water trickle through. Some of it trickled down the beard. The old man opened his eyes, said something that was only a croaking sound to Elizabeth, and then closed his eyes again.

"Give me that mug," said Elizabeth quietly. "And you drive the car."

Grant turned his head sharply and looked up at her.

"Each to his own work," Elizabeth said in a low voice. "I'll look after the old man while you go for help . . . if that is why you want the car driven."

Grant turned back to the man, gave him a little more water, put the mug down on the wooden uncovered floor beside the bunk and then stood up.

He stood looking down at the old man, deep in thought. Then he turned to Elizabeth.

"Light the fire in that stove over there, will you please?" he said. "Get the billies all full of water first. Then look on those shelves and see if you can find a tin of clear soup of some kind. In those bins against the wall you'll find flour and powdered milk. Use powdered milk in the soup. Failing the soup, use powdered milk in some warm water. Don't touch Flinty. He's injured his back. Just keep him alive. I'm going to take that saddle horse and ride up the telephone line and see if I can find the break, or where the line has come down."

It was almost dark inside the hut.

"Where can I find a light?" Elizabeth began.

Grant nodded at two storm lanterns hanging on the wall.

"Make do with those," he said. "Get the fire going first. That will give you some light. Are you sure you can manage?" He looked at her keenly.

Elizabeth nodded.

"You go. I'll stay," she said simply.

Except at the cinema Elizabeth had never seen a storm lantern in her life, but nothing would induce her to ask Grant how they might be lighted. Her stocks were already rock bottom because she couldn't drive a car.

"Don't give him anything more to drink till you've got that soup ready," said Grant. "Then give him a spoonful at a time up to half a cup. Then stop."

He didn't tell her how to light the stove without kindling. All her life Elizabeth had lit coal fires with pine kindling.

She went outside and began to gather up damp gum leaves and small pieces of bark from under the handful of thin straggly trees that stood at the side of the hut. Except for this small outpost of civilisation, and the great liner of a car, there was nothing all around Elizabeth but the vast, silent almost treeless earth and the great hood of sky that was purple in the east and livid with streaks of crimson in the west. Even as Elizabeth stooped . . . her coat dangling in the dust . . . to pick up the kindling the crimson streaks to the west dulled and died and the darkness was coming down like a blind being drawn slowly but inexorably.

Grant came out of the hut door.

"There are matches by Old Flinty's bed," he said. "Can you manage?"

Elizabeth nodded.

Grant had bound something . . . pieces of sacking . . . round his legs, he carried a small satchel-like bag which Elizabeth guessed contained tools; and an axe. He went over to the horses and caught the saddled horse by the bridle.

In the very last minute of daylight Elizabeth saw him swing himself up in the saddle, wheel the horse and, digging his heels into its flanks, head it through the gate and out across the grass wastes. It seemed as if he had ridden away into a vast nothingness.

Inside the hut it would be pitch dark. And she did not know how to light a storm lantern.

Then she looked up and saw that the car was faced towards the hut. Cars had headlights.

Elizabeth put down her kindling and went through the gate and got into the car. She had an idea that when Grant had started the car he pulled out knobs. She pulled all the knobs one after another. With the first four nothing happened but with the fifth the light went on on the dashboard. Well, that was something. Grant had left his keys in the lock. Elizabeth turned them but nothing happened. Then she turned the knob that held the keys. The headlights went on.

Elizabeth felt she had been as flukey as if she had won football pools. Luck was with one sometimes, she thought. The lights shone to the left of the hut door. She pulled with all her strength on the steering wheel. She inched the car wheels round, released the handbrake . . . that, at least, she knew about . . . then got out and pushed the car.

She couldn't move it more than a foot but it was enough. The lights streamed straight in the hut doorway. From this distance she could pick out the outline of the iron stove that she was to light and which stood against the wall opposite the door.

Yes, she breathed with delight, luck can really be with one, *sometimes*. Just imagine that stove being built there, in the very right spot for me to see it.

She pulled on the handbrake, got out of the car, regathered her kindling and went back into the hut.

The old man had not moved.

Using old leaves instead of paper and then stacking about them small twigs, Elizabeth built a humble fire pile. Then she lit it. There seemed no flare of the leaves catching on. Little lights danced along the edge of the leaves, leaving a dust of black charcoal but there was nothing to catch the twigs.

"Blow on 'em," said a voice from the bed. "Use your lungs, girl."

Elizabeth could have cried with relief that the old man was still alive. But she didn't waste breath saying so. She blew on the leaves and kept on blowing until the twigs had caught. Soon there was an adventurous blaze and to that Elizabeth added larger and larger twigs until she had put on quite large pieces of wood.

She filled the billies outside from the overflowing trough and only then did she turn to the old man. In addition to the stream of car lights coming through the doorway there was now a dancing, flickering light shifting shadows in the corners of the room from the fire.

"That's pretty good goin'," said the old man's croaking voice. "Takes some city folks a lifetime to learn how to light a fire of bush leaves. Half damp, they only smoulder."

"What can I do for you now Mr. . . . er . . . Flinty? . . ." Elizabeth said, going to him. "I must wait for the water to warm a little before I give you something to eat."

"Just fill up me pipe, will you, miss. Roll the bacca kinda in the palm of yer hand and stuff it in."

"You shouldn't smoke, you know."

"Shouldn't I? Just try me. You'll have to put the pipe in me mouth. I can't use me hands. Paralysed they are. So's me toes. I've jiggered me back. I know that. So I might as well have a pipe or two before I go out."

"You're not going out," Elizabeth said firmly. "Mr. Jarvis has gone for help. I'll give you a pipe when you've had a little soup. I'm afraid you will have to be patient and wait."

"And who's Mr. Jarvis? You don't mean Grant, do you?"

"Of course."

"Swelp me bob, 'e must 'ave got swelled head since he went home to England. Well, if I live long enough I'll take that outa 'im. Now, miss, you go and turn them headlights off. If Grant, or any other bloke's goin' to drive upta the homestead before mornin' they're going to need that there battery. It's a raking awful road from here to Kybarrli homestead."

"Will the fire give us enough light?" Elizabeth asked doubtfully.

"You bring them two lanterns off the wall and I'll tell you how to light 'em. They've got no kerosene in them because I didn't fill 'em before I went out and fell down off that windmill and hurt me back. Serves me right, of course. Well, now, you got to go out to that shed and you'll find a big barrel marked 'Kerosene.' Now for lummy's sake don't go to the barrel what's got petrol in. You'll like as not blow us all up. You got to get a syphon . . ."

How Elizabeth got the kerosene, brought it in in a tin can, filled the lamps, juggled with the levers and double wicks and got those lamps alight she never afterwards knew. All the time she was beset with the terror of blowing up the petrol barrels or setting on fire the acetylene. She was, of course, working in the dark outside.

Instead she got the lamps alight, trimmed the wicks as Flinty told her to do, polished up the glass funnels so that the light was clearer, and put the lamps on the table to light up the whole hut. In the meantime she had turned off the headlights of the car to save the battery.

By this time the water was warm but remembering the horses had been drinking out of the troughs from which she had drawn the water, Elizabeth waited until a cupful in one billy had boiled, then she added the soup and a little milk powder, and cooled it down by tossing it from tin mug to tin mug until it was fit for the old man to take. Then she sat down on the side of his bunk and fed him half a cup of it.

"That's all," she admonished as Flinty looked longingly towards the stove. "Grant's orders."

"How much spunk you got to lie down under orders from Grant?" the old man asked derisively. "Well, give us that pipe."

Elizabeth, travelling in the Underground, had seen men

pummelling tobacco in the palm of their hand. She made a fairly good job of filling Flinty's pipe. She put it in his mouth and held a match to it. He drew on it.

Elizabeth burst out laughing. Never had she seen such an expression of beatific joy lighten the face of anyone . . . child or man.

Really, she thought, all he needs is a harp to look like St. Peter, with that great white flowing beard and his benign blue eyes.

"I don't know whether I should have given you that pipe," she said doubtfully. "Grant might be very angry."

"So what!" said Flinty. "I've seen him mad plenty of times but it never made no difference to me."

"You know him very well?"

"When you've travelled across the Northern Territory with a man the way Grant and me've travelled you know him like he was your twin. Where's he gone? Up the telephone line?"

Elizabeth nodded.

"I think so. He didn't say very much. He just seemed very business-like, and had a sack of tools with him."

"Did he take the axe and a whopping big thick pair 'uv leather gloves I keep on the shelf alongside them tools?"

"Yes, he did."

"Stout feller. He's gone to fix that line. An' it won't be easy. We had a bonza cock-eyed bob the day before yesterday an' the telephone line and the light line both came down. I was going to fix 'em. Saddled old Rastus and then went up the windmill to fix one of the vanes what was bent. Three horses out there all right?"

Elizabeth nodded.

"There were three. One of them was saddled. Grant took that one."

"I knew they was all right for water. It was feed I was worrying about. I was just hopin' one of them 'ud have sass enough to break down the fence and get out."

"How did you get back in here, Flinty?" Elizabeth asked.

"Dunno. Just dragged meself. Took me all morning, I think. Only I forgot to pick meself up some food and water on the way. Thought I was a goner then. You think I could have a drop more of that soup, miss?"

"Grant said you were only to have half a cup."

"To hell with Grant," said the old man. "It's me what's starving. Not him."

Elizabeth laughed. Somehow she loved the way Old Flinty said "To hell with Grant." Odd, but she felt delighted there was someone in the world who had the nerve, or the authority, to say that. The Grant Jarvis she knew was someone who looked and sounded as if no one had ever dared say anything so impertinent either in his presence or his absence.

She didn't know what was the extent of Old Flinty's injuries but she was beginning to feel sure they couldn't be fatal. He had so much spirit, and so much courage shining in those bright audacious blue eyes. No man near death could be looking and talking the way Flinty was.

Every now and again she took the pipe from his mouth so that he could take in a deep breath of air and expel all the smoke from his lungs. She took it now and put it on a chair by the bunk.

"All right?" she said. "A little more soup but no more pipe for a while."

"Can't have everything, I suppose."

She cooled some more of the soup and tipped the mug to pour about two tablespoons into the old man's throat. By some quick dexterous movement of the head and, by opening his mouth very wide, he had swallowed all the contents of the mug before she had time to see what had happened.

"Now you'll have to wipe me beard," said Flinty. "You sure made a mess of me that time."

"That was very naughty of you," said Elizabeth anxiously.

"Baloney!" Then as she wiped his beard he looked at her closely. "Say, I've never seen a girl as pretty as you except those Paton girls, Gaylie and Thera. My, they were pretty girls. But you're prettier b'cos you got a kind face along with it."

Elizabeth delicately dabbed the piece of towelling around Flinty's lips.

"Was Thera as pretty as Gaylie?" she asked.

She took her eyes off what she was doing and looked into Flinty's eyes. His eyes were wide open and searching hers.

"Now, that's a mighty funny question for you to be askin'," he said. "Does it matter how pretty Thera Paton was . . . now she's gone and joined her Maker?"

"Yes, it does, rather . . ."

Elizabeth dropped her hands to her lap and turned her gaze towards the fire now blazing, an orange eye, brightly in the stove. She wondered why she had said that. Did it matter? Could it possibly matter to anyone but Gaylie? And of course it must matter to Gaylie, otherwise she would always feel her sister's shadow lay between herself and Grant.

It was very patent to Elizabeth that Gaylie must in the end win Grant . . . unless there were other very beautiful expensive young women who had an equal claim to assist keep the Jarvis acres and Jarvis money within the tight circle of approved landed families.

Whoever it was who ended up by standing at Grant's side as the bride of Kybarrli would be concerned about how beautiful Thera Paton had been. And what kind of person Thera had been. Her shadow, surely, would always lie across Grant Jarvis's doorstep.

Even if it had been she herself who was really, instead of phonily, engaged to Grant . . .

Surprised and a little upset at the drift of her thoughts, Elizabeth shook herself. She stood up.

"I feel I ought to straighten your bed for you, Flinty."

"Don't you touch nothing," he said, suddenly fiercely angry. "You leave that to Grant. . . ."

CHAPTER TEN

ELIZABETH WENT to the hut door to see if there was any sign of Grant's return. The fire had warmed the hut and she had forgotten how clear and sharply cold the night was outside. Even the white moon and the white stars had the edge of cutting cold in their sharp brilliance.

A terrible wailing howl suddenly filled the night air. Elizabeth stepped back into the hut and closed the door. She stood leaning against it.

"What . . . what was that?"

"That's Red," he said. "Old man dingo. I been hunting him two years and last night he knew I'd got the bomb. Came right in close to the hut and kep' up that sing-song all night.

Like tellin' me the game was up an' I wasn't goin' to hunt him any more."

"It sounded a long way away to-night."

"Yeah. He's a cunning one, that. He can see the light. He's jes' let out that howl to let me know he's still around. Can you use a gun, miss? If you just kinda sent a shot off into the dark he'd kinda know I wasn't so far gone as maybe he thought. It 'ud give him something to think about."

"No," Elizabeth said hastily. "I wouldn't know which end of a gun to hold."

"Well, never mind. Say, what was that!"

Elizabeth bent her head and listened. A long way off there was a faint thrumming. Gradually it became louder.

"That's ol' Rastus," said Flinty. "That's Grant comin' back."

Elizabeth was so relieved she could have cried. The dingo and the talk about guns had unnerved her. She opened the hut door and ran out to the enclosure gate. She opened it as Grant came galloping up.

He threw his leg over the saddle and slid off.

"Old Flinty all right?"

"Yes," Elizabeth said breathlessly. "But there was a dingo——"

"Oh, was there? Did you get some food into the old man?"

"Of course I did," said Elizabeth with some asperity. "Have you ever heard a dingo howl, Grant?"

"Have I *what*?"

He halted on his way to the hut door.

"Listen," he said. "A dingo is a wild dog. It doesn't eat human beings." He turned again to the hut. "Unsaddle Rastus, will you, and throw the saddle over the . . ." Again he stopped and then turned to Elizabeth. "Oh," he said shortly. "I forgot. I'm sorry. You wouldn't know anything about unsaddling a horse, would you?"

"No, I wouldn't," said Elizabeth. "But I did know how to look after Flinty. He's had food and drink and he's very much alive and talkative."

Even in the moonlight Elizabeth could see the tenseness go out of Grant's tall broad-shouldered body.

"Good," he said.

He did not wait for Elizabeth to go into the hut but

strode inside, leaving her out in the moonlight cold. She went gingerly over to the horse which stood, head down, the bridle trailing on the ground. Elizabeth had seen horses being handled in films. Otherwise she had no idea what now to do with Rastus. She picked up the reins from the ground and to her relief and surprise the horse lifted his head and began following Elizabeth towards the troughs. Somewhere she had read that a blown horse mustn't drink too much. When she thought Rastus had taken one long drink she pulled on the reins to lift his head. Obediently the horse turned aside from the trough. He then went quickly to the food bin. As he stood munching some chaff she examined the girth to see how one went about loosening it and removing the saddle. She had no idea her powers of observation in films was so good. And she had no idea that taking a saddle from a horse, except for its weight, was so easy.

As the saddle slid over the horse's side its weight carried Elizabeth with it and before she knew what had happened she was on the ground, the saddle on top of her.

She scrambled up again. The saddle was nearly too heavy to lift. Old Flinty used an old iron-framed type of saddle famous for its comfort over day-long stretches of boundary riding, and the pride and joy of Old Flinty's life had been to decorate his saddle with every known kind of brass and silver ornament that he could lay his hands on. Furthermore there were a multitude of heavy brass hooks, pockets and flaps that he used for carrying gear. In trying to lift Old Flinty's saddle she was trying to lift a very heavy weight . . . even for a man.

She dragged it to the fence and let it lie there. She surveyed Rastus.

"I don't know how to get that thing out of your mouth," she said. "So I guess your bridle can stay on. But I'll tie it behind your head . . . just so. Then you won't trip on it, or get it caught."

She felt she had done all she could do and only then did she realise she was bitterly cold. She had taken off her coat as soon as she had got the fire going; and when she had heard Grant galloping up had run out without thinking to put it on.

Inside the hut Grant Jarvis was sitting on a small three-legged stool by a telephone hand set. He was talking.

"Okay," he said. "Bring Peter and Bill with you . . . and the litter. I think the station wagon will be a better go than my car. We can try them both. Get through to Endall and catch the doctor. Someone can go in for him if necessary."

He hung up and turned and looked at Elizabeth as she came in the door.

"That will bring some assistance from the homestead," he said. He stopped short. "Come in and shut that door. There'll be ten degrees of frost by morning."

He stood up, put his hands in his belt.

"What in the name of fortune have you been doing?"

"Nothing," said Elizabeth. "Why?"

She saw Grant's eyes travelling down her dress. She looked down. The skirt was wet and covered in black smears. Where she had fallen under the horse's saddle had been a quagmire from the overflowing water and the trampling of the three horses in the last two days.

"I fell over," she said. "But I am not hurt. If I stand in front of the fire this mud will dry . . . and then scrape off. But hadn't you better attend to Flinty? And there's some soup for you too. I found some tinned butter and a rather hard scone loaf but it's not too hard to eat. And there's tea."

"I'll wash Flinty first."

Flinty who had been lying as if asleep now let his eyes fly open.

"No raking fear you don't, Grant," he said. "I've seen cracked backs before. You don't touch 'em. No matter how high they get. If you're that keen on getting someone undressed get that dress off that girl. It's a terrible pretty dress and she's sure made a mess of it. An' it's wet too. Mighty uncomfortable . . ."

Grant looked at Elizabeth as if this was a reasonable suggestion from the old man. He turned his head this way and that not only to examine how much damage had been done to her dress but possibly the ramifications of how it came off.

Elizabeth hastily put her hands on her chest as if hugging her dress to herself.

"No, you don't . . ." she said.

"No, I don't what?" asked Grant.

"You don't take my dress off."

"What made you think I would? You've got two hands, haven't you?"

"There's no need for me to take it off at all."

"There's every need and if you think Old Flinty and I are at all interested in the process you are quite mistaken. There's that coat hanging up there behind the door. It's long enough to cover two of you. Take off your dress and put on the coat while I wash Flinty's face and hands. He might have some more soup now."

He turned to the stove to take a billy of hot water from it.

"I'd rather stay in my dress, thank you," said Elizabeth primly.

"Take it off," said Grant, lifting the billy with a piece of leather. He looked up for a fleeting moment. "Or I will take it off for you. They won't be down from the homestead for three hours. That'll make it nearly morning. You're not going to stay in a wet dress all that time."

He carried the billy over to the chair by Flinty's bunk and poured some of the hot water into a basin. He sat on the edge of the bunk, his back to Elizabeth. She felt like a child behaving like a prig.

Three hours? Nearly morning? What time was it now, she wondered, as obediently she took the coat from the door, stood so she was exactly behind Grant and his body was between herself and the old man lying on the bed.

As she stepped out of the dress Grant said, without turning round:

"Hang it across the front of the stove. It'll dry quickly. Now if you'd bring me that soup again . . . Maybe then we'll have time for a cup of tea ourselves."

Elizabeth had taken off her dress so she felt she might as well take off her shoes too. They were much wetter than the dress. In the darkness she had stepped right into four inches of water when she first went to the trough for the billy water. Her feet had been steadily getting colder and colder ever since.

She put on the big coat and put her shoes on the hob beside the stove, then began to make the tea for herself and Grant. She noticed there was no teapot but the tannin stains of two of the billies told her how Old Flinty was used to making tea for himself. She made tea in two small billycans and stirred powdered milk into one for herself. At their picnic lunch Grant had taken his tea black.

She sliced the stale scone bread and toasted it in the fire coals, then buttered the toast and put it in the oven. She found another small enamel bowl in which to put some soup for Grant.

As she padded around barefooted she realised the wisdom of Grant's order to put on the big coat from behind the door. It was heavy, a kind of military coat, and made of wool so thick, no cold, surely, could seep through it. Her own coat would have been spoiled, and it barely covered her, as it was a shaped coat and the lapels met but did not overlap. She wondered if Grant had noticed the fashion of her own coat that he had told her to put on the other.

What a strange day it had been! After the luxury of Jarvis House in Toorak the clean, almost sterile bareness of the lonely little hut in the middle of a lonely moonlit plain seemed fantastic.

What was the time? She was so intimidated by Grant's former brusqueness and present silence she did not like to ask him. There was no evidence of Old Flinty having a watch or a clock. It must be nearly midnight surely.

What were the things that had happened to her in the last sixteen hours? She had awoken in the luxury mansion. She had taken an aeroplane flight. She had set out across a vast lonely stretch of treeless plain country with her intimidating pseudo fiancé. She had discovered that for all he had been reared in the lap of luxury and could order about a retinue of fifty people with the snap of his fingers, he could attend to the inner workings of a motor engine, turn off a windmill, repair a telephone and electric light line, ride off pell-mell into the night on a strange horse and, thank God, ride back again. He could administer to an injured old man and he was as much at home in this bare humble little shack as he had been in the suite on the *Albany* or in the big house in Toorak.

And, yes. She had been kissed. She hadn't forgotten that. She just didn't want to attach any importance to it.

She wasn't thinking about Grant Jarvis. She was thinking about herself and the things that had happened to her.

Here she was alone in the middle of the night with these two men of whom, four weeks ago, she had never heard. A

dingo had howled and made her think of churchyards yawn-
ing; and the old bearded man lying there on the bed had
suggested she pick up that enormous gun standing in the
corner and take a pot-shot at the dingo.

Really . . . if she were to write and tell her mother, or
Ralph . . .

Suddenly Elizabeth began to laugh. Actually she was
crying tired. The laughter had tears in it for there were tears
in her eyes but all the same it was pure laughter. Just imagine,
she said to herself. Mother's face. And Ralph's!

And the saddle! Taking that saddle off that big horse and
falling down in the mud and water by the bins and trough!
And her feet being wet and cold. And herself standing here
in front of a wood stove stirring powdered milk into a billycan of black tea, with no dress on and an old military coat
over her slip, barefooted!

There was a queer little choking noise in the back of her
throat.

Grant Jarvis stood up, put the soup mug on the wooden
table in the middle of the room and came over to Elizabeth
standing in front of the stove. He spun her round as he
grasped her shoulders.

"What is the matter?" he asked.

Elizabeth's eyes were swimming. But she was laughing. She
had to make him see she was laughing and not just ready to
drop down there on the floor and pass out from sheer exhaustion.

"So this is Kybarrli!" she said weakly. "World famous triple
A merino wool at the world's top prices. I am on Kybarrli
Station, aren't I, Grant? Don't look as if you're going to slap
me. I'm not hysterical, you know."

For a long deadly minute he did look as if he would slap
her. Then suddenly he dropped his hands from her shoulders,
pulled up a chair before the stove and pushed her into it. He
opened the lid of the oven and put a heavy leather strap across
it. He bent down and lifted Elizabeth's feet so that they rested
on the oven lid and the warmth came out tenderly and made
them tingle with returning life.

He took the billy of tea she had been stirring, poured some
of it into a mug and then taking a black bottle from a shelf
poured some liquid into it.

He held it towards her.

"Drink this, Elizabeth," he said. "There's rum in it. It will warm you."

Elizabeth did not know what hour it was when she woke. She had a feeling of being cramped, but not cold. The floor under her was hard but there was warmth on either side of her. She opened her eyes and looked straight into the stove fire. It was burning as brightly as ever. Perhaps she had been asleep a few minutes, after all. But how did she get down here on the floor. And this thing over her? What was it? A tarpaulin, or something? And beside her? On the other side?

Then she knew what it was that had wakened her. Noise. There was the sound of heavy footsteps outside and the door behind her was thrown open. She turned, to discover that Grant was lying full length on the floor beside her, keeping warm the side that was farthest from the fire.

The door was wide open and two or three men crowded in. Elizabeth's first thought was that it was funny to see men in the middle of the night with their hats on. She recognised immediately Peter Smith and John Smith, the stockmen who had driven Mrs. Jarvis from the airport.

The three men stood hands on hips and surveyed the couple before the fire.

"For crying out loud, Grant," one man . . . the stranger in the trio . . . said. "You sure look a pretty sight." He shook his head from side to side. "Too bad you couldn't give the little lady a comfortable bed on her first night on Kybarrli."

Grant got slowly to his feet. He extended his body several inches more when he stretched.

"Bring the litter?" he said. "And the dope?"

"Everything. How's Old Flinty?"

Grant looked at the watch on his wrist.

"He was all right twenty minutes ago."

The whole group converged on the bunk and looked down on the old man. He was very silent lying there. Elizabeth hoped he was only asleep.

She got up, less steadily than Grant had done.

"Is he . . . is he all right?" she asked as she wrapped the big coat farther round herself and kicked aside the tarpaulin. The stockman Peter Smith leaned over Old Flinty.

"Say, Grant," he said, "you haven't been pulling our legs? He smells more drunk than sick to me."

"That's about what he is," said Grant. "I gave him a snorter of rum when I was sure enough he could take it. It put him to sleep."

Elizabeth put her hand over her mouth. Whatever would the men think if they came near her? She found herself backing away to the wall, keeping the greatest possible distance the tiny hut would allow.

Grant, having bent over Old Flinty, now straightened himself. He turned to Elizabeth.

"Could you brew these men some tea, Elizabeth?" he said. "We'll get Old Flinty transferred to the litter. It's going to be quite a job."

One of the stockmen crossed over to the stove.

"Water's boilin'," he said. "Golly, we could do with that tea. It's taken us four hours twenty minutes to get down here over those raking tracks. Say, Grant, you'd better build a decent road this away next wool clip."

He went back to the bunkside and the other two men went outside and brought in a litter similar to those used in an ambulance. Grant had taken a leather pouch from the stranger and Elizabeth saw him take out a hypodermic syringe. He came over to the stove and took some boiling water from the big can, and a small bowl. He looked down at Elizabeth as he did this.

"When we've got Flinty stowed away in the station wagon, and had tea, go and get in my car, Elizabeth. It will be more comfortable travelling up to the homestead."

"Who . . . who will drive it, Grant?" she asked, looking up at him.

A smile flickered in his eyes.

"I will," he said. "Old Flinty will be just as safe with the boys as with me. They'll look after him with their lives."

"I didn't mean that. I mean . . . I'd be quite all right, of course." She couldn't say she was afraid of the odour of rum on her breath.

"Of course you would. The safest place in the world for any woman is in the trusted care of a man's best friends," he said. "All the same I'll take you up."

"I'd better put on my dress . . . somehow."

With sudden dismay she realised all the men must have seen her dress hanging there in front of the stove.

This time Grant really smiled.

"I shouldn't worry about your dress, in front of the fire or on your back," he said. "When you've been outback a bit longer you'll see, or hear of, many worse predicaments for young ladies than being caught in the middle of the night without a dress on." He looked down at her obliquely. "You were in very safe company, you know," he added.

Elizabeth flushed. She turned quickly back to the business of tea-making. Once again she felt that anger against him welling up. He managed always to place her at the disadvantage. It amused him that she should attach importance to something about which he didn't care a fig. He had conveyed his indifference very clearly.

She wondered how he would like it if he found himself unexpectedly sitting on the North Pole with a bunch of Eskimo women around him. As she poured the tea into a line of pint-sized mugs she reflected that all the Eskimo women would probably fall in love with him. And that would take all the strangeness out of Grant Jarvis's predicament.

With the billycan of tea held tipped for the last drop she wondered why she should be so certain the Eskimo women would fall in love with him. She hadn't.

When she turned round they had taken Old Flinty, still inert, and reeking of rum, out of the door. Old Flinty's mouth had been very wide open, when last she glanced his way, and he showed his not very handsome toothless gums.

Elizabeth swallowed some tea and ate a little of the toasted scone loaf. What had *she* looked like when Grant had lowered her to the floor and put that tarpaulin over her? Well, if her mouth had been open at least it was full of her own teeth. But those rum fumes!

If he had ever seen the beloved Thera, or even Gaylie, asleep it would have been the story of Prince Charming and the Sleeping Beauty. With herself it was more a case of Raggle-Taggle-Gipsy-O.

Immediately after they had finished tea the party left the hut, Grant folding Elizabeth's dress under his arm and then throwing it unceremoniously on the back seat of the car. He installed her comfortably enough in the front seat beside him, switched on the engine and the headlights and unexpectedly said:

"Thank you for your help, Elizabeth."

"Please don't thank me," Elizabeth said, embarrassed. "It wasn't anything very much at all."

"Oh, yes, it was," Grant said. In the half light from the dashboard Elizabeth could see his mouth curving in a faintly sardonic smile. "I'm afraid I wasn't on ceremony myself . . . but then I was afraid of losing time for Old Flinty's sake."

In some unaccountable way Elizabeth felt her heart warmed. The praise was wrung from a man who rarely gave it since in the general run of his life he always was able to buy service. There was no occasion to thank and praise people who were adequately paid for what they did. He was acknowledging that Elizabeth's services, such as they were, were extra and given as a matter of course, not of expediency.

Yes, her heart warmed to a feeing that was nearly companionship. If only he would soften . . . and be *human*.

The next minute he poured a little cold air on the growing warmth that might have been temporarily between them.

"Five or six weeks hence, when you are back in England, you'll find nobody will know of your dressless antics in the middle of an Australian night," he said. "Now, I suggest you get some more sleep, if possible. It is a long and not very interesting drive to the homestead."

CHAPTER ELEVEN

ELIZABETH DID NOT see what the approaches to Kybarrli homestead were like. She didn't wake up until the car stopped, doors opened and shut, and voices were heard all around.

Grant was helping her from the car, she was pretending not to be too stiff and hoped she didn't look too awful.

A large-boned cheerful woman with a heavenly Lancashire accent was saying:

"Bring her right in, the poor duck. What a way to bring your bride home, Mr. Grant. You ought to be downright ashamed of yourself. And her all night out in that awful out-camp. The poor lamb."

Elizabeth could have cried on that broad Lancashire bosom. She felt as if she had come home.

"Look, luv, I've got a nice hot bath for you. Then there's a fire blazing in your room. I'm going to put you right to bed and bring you breakfast there. Then off you go to sleep for the day."

"But I've slept and slept and slept . . ." Elizabeth said weakly. "And I'm not even sick. Poor Flinty, now . . ."

"The boys 'ull look after him. Us women'll stick together. Of course you're not sick. But you're tired and you're grubby and you've come a long way. You need that bath and bed."

"Do I look grubby?"

"Well, you've got mud on your face, but it's what you feel more'n what you look that matters. A bath, and breakfast and bed for you."

Elizabeth was taken in through a wire screen door, across a wide veranda into a narrow side passage in what looked, in the dim light, to be a big stone house. She meekly followed where she was bidden. Already the hot water was flowing freely into the bath and Mrs. Wheeler, as the large woman was called, was helping her out of Old Flinty's great heavy coat.

"For goodness' sake, where's your dress, luv? You haven't had an accident, have you?"

"No, it got wet and Grant made me take it off. Then he wouldn't let me put it on."

"The bully."

Elizabeth had never had a lady's maid but Mrs. Wheeler didn't seem to think Elizabeth was capable of attending to herself. In a few minutes she was put in the bath and its warmth not only comforted her but it brought life back to her stiff limbs.

She washed her hair as well as herself and when she stepped out of the bath there was a warm nightgown and a bathrobe lying on the chair ready.

There was a tap at the door and the kind Mrs. Wheeler was ready to show her down another long narrow passage to her room.

"What time is it?" asked Elizabeth.

"Just six o'clock, dear."

"In Melbourne Mrs. Jarvis always had breakfast punctually at eight o'clock. Does she observe the same custom here?"

"Oh, yes, my dear. The heavens would fall down if Mrs. Jarvis, dressed to the very last detail, didn't have her grape-

fruit put in front of her, in the dining-room, at exactly one
minute past eight."

"Then I've got an hour and a half to rest," said Elizabeth.
"Will you promise to call me at half-past seven?"

"My dear child, after the night you've had you're entitled
to stay in bed until after lunch."

Elizabeth gave Mrs. Wheeler a small firm smile.

"You said the heavens would fall if Mrs. Jarvis didn't put
in an appearance. The heavens didn't fall on me last night,
and I must follow Mrs. Jarvis's example, you know. What a
lady of sixty can stand up to, a young woman of twenty-two
can attempt."

Mrs. Wheeler's eyes met Elizabeth's. Surprise turned to
thoughtfulness and finally to agreement.

"You are right, Miss Elizabeth," she said. "You will one
day be walking in her shoes. Better begin as you intend to go
on."

"Yes," said Elizabeth soberly, wondering what she ought
in all truthfulness to reply to that remark.

When Elizabeth appeared at the breakfast table she was
relieved she had obeyed her instinct in doing as Mrs. Jarvis
would have done in the same circumstances. Grant was
present, bathed, shaved and well-dressed in clothes that belonged to the station life rather than Melbourne or cosmo-
politan circles. Mrs. Jarvis, upright back, hair impeccably
dressed and her face delicately made up, was sitting in her
place in a large upright chair of ancient but beautiful structure.
She wore a fine grey woollen dress with a wisp of pink silk
tucked in at the neckline and folded in cravat fashion.

Mrs. Jarvis looked up at Elizabeth as she came in.

"Good morning, Elizabeth," she said as if absolutely nothing had happened since they last met and as if they had not
been transported from the Melbourne breakfast table six
hundred miles away to the Kybarrli breakfast table in the
heart of the sheep country. In fact except for the appoint-
ments of the room it might have been another breakfast in
Jarvis House, Toorak.

Elizabeth found Mrs. Jarvis's correctness so intimidating
she did not dare to look round too obviously at the heavy old
colonial furniture, the huge mantel and chimney piece, the
framed pictures of stud rams that decorated the high papered
walls.

"Good morning, Mrs. Jarvis," she said pleasantly and went to the place on the older lady's right hand . . . just as she had been disposed at the table in Melbourne. Grant, as in Melbourne, sat at the end of the table. Quite a long way away.

"Did you sleep well?" Mrs. Jarvis asked.

"Very well, thank you," Elizabeth said.

She didn't ask if her hostess slept well. She imagined Mrs. Jarvis would have replied, "Of course. I do everything properly. As it ought to be done." Neither did Elizabeth dare remark on the fact that though she had slept well it had been in three different geographical settings . . . the floor of Old Flinty's hut, the front seat of Grant's car, and the lovely big four-poster bed of Kybarrli's guest room. She thought Mrs. Jarvis either didn't want to know these facts or knew them already and would comment in her own time . . . if she commented at all.

Elizabeth would have liked to inquire after Old Flinty but she didn't dare do that either. Fortunately she had her curiosity and compassion on that score satisfied when Grant, having said "Good morning" very formally to her, turned to his mother.

"I found Old Flinty on his bunk with a back injury," he said as he dug his spoon . . . a beautiful hand-beaten silver spoon like those Elizabeth and his mother were using . . . in the grapefruit. "I don't know how serious the injury is but he's easier this morning. I've got Dr. Baker coming out from Endall."

Mrs. Jarvis nodded her head.

"The station wagon's going in to Endall in any event," she said. "It had better wait until after Dr. Baker's visit in case he prescribes something we can't provide in the sick quarters."

"I'm afraid Old Flinty is for hospital," Grant said.

"In that case the station wagon can go in before lunch. Your Aunt Mollie was on the morning flight from Melbourne. She'll have to be picked up. It is a pity she didn't come with us yesterday. It would have saved two trips with the wagon."

There was a tiny silence after this pronouncement. Elizabeth dug her own hand-beaten silver spoon in her own grapefruit. Goodness, she thought. That was pretty fast following. She'd had a feeling all along that Gaylie and her mother wouldn't be far behind Grant.

It was Grant himself who asked the great question.

"Has Gaylie come with her?"

Mrs. Grant shook her head.

"I understand Gaylie is staying in Melbourne another day or two. But she will be here for the Governor's visit." She turned to Elizabeth. "Grant has told you His Excellency will be staying here during his visit to the district?"

"Yes," Elizabeth replied quietly. "If there is anything I can do to help you, Mrs. Jarvis, I hope you will allow me."

This offer, which was quite natural to Elizabeth, brought a strange reaction. Both Grant and Mrs. Jarvis lifted their heads and looked at her. They looked as if they were examining her. Elizabeth flushed. Had she said something wrong? Was this an indelicate offering of hers?

"Thank you," Mrs. Jarvis said at length.

The steak and eggs were now being served by a lubra and there was a silence at the table. Suddenly Elizabeth found it a little silly. It was as if the three of them were playing parts in a shadow play or dumb charade. Surely the Jarvis household didn't always run on these oiled wheels of silence.

"Did you sleep well, Grant?" she asked, looking directly at him. He lifted his head and his eyes met hers. She knew hers were challenging. "It wouldn't have been long, but was it good?" she asked.

"I didn't sleep at all," he replied. "I had to settle things with Old Flinty down at the sick quarters. I'll make up for it after we get him away to hospital."

Elizabeth felt a little sick that she had asked the question that way. She had meant to shake them out of the stilted silence. She realised that though Mrs. Wheeler had politely suggested that she, Elizabeth, had had an exhausting and uncomfortable night, she had in fact had a very easy time in comparison with Grant who had mended communication lines, attended to Old Flinty, driven miles, looked after herself and finally kept the latest watch with the sick man.

Elizabeth would have apologised if she had known how to confess she really did understand and appreciate all that Grant had done since early morning yesterday. Was it yesterday or a year ago?

"Of course," she murmured instead.

Grant was still watching her.

"After breakfast," he said, "I will show you the immediate surroundings of the homestead. There are a number of stockmen's cottages on the creek slope. You should meet their wives." There was the faintest glimmer of a smile in his eyes. "At least their wives are very anxious to meet you. Incidentally Maria and Tim Bolton have a cottage here as well as at Barrli. They will remain here for the Governor's visit."

That hint of a smile eased things for Elizabeth for she felt it opened the door of conversation between them on the subject of her presence at Kybarrli.

"My visit will be very short, Grant," she said. "Perhaps it is early days for anyone on the station to take too much interest in me."

Elizabeth expected this to draw some kind of reaction from either Grant or Mrs. Jarvis. Oddly enough neither made any sign. They were progressing with their breakfast. Grant leaned forward and took another piece of toast from the toast rack. Mrs. Jarvis delicately and precisely put another small portion of steak on the end of her fork and then in her mouth. There seemed to be a conspiracy of reticence between them.

As an opening gambit Elizabeth realised her remark was not very successful. After a minute's silence Mrs. Jarvis looked down the long table at Grant.

"Elizabeth should wear a hat," she said. "The sun can get warm enough to spoil her complexion."

This was not a bare statement. Buried deep in it was a compliment. From a person so icebound as Mrs. Jarvis Elizabeth felt it was the gift of a bouquet. Although there was no particular warmth in the words they were said in a way that implied that Elizabeth's complexion *mattered*. It was a beautiful complexion and should be cherished.

Some little thing about Elizabeth had won Mrs. Jarvis's attention and admiration. Elizabeth did not know how she intuitively knew this, and she was a girl without a vestige of personal vanity, but she did know it. She would have liked to thank Mrs. Jarvis, but again she did not dare. And she wondered why the words had had such a heart-warming effect on herself. It was as if a tiny thread of contact had been put out and it now, fragile and invisible though it was, bound her to the older woman.

"Yes, wear a hat, Elizabeth," Grant said. "And don't mind

that the other women and all of the children will be bare-
headed. They are used to this climate and they won't find the
sun very hot to-day."

"It is still winter, surely . . ." Elizabeth ventured.

"Very much so. Icy cold at night but warm in the day if
the sun is shining." He buttered his toast with consideration.
"In fact hot enough to wear cotton clothes between ten and
four, at any event. After that you have to rug up." Now he
looked up at her. "As you well know. The thicker the coat
the better."

He was, of course, referring to Old Flinty's army coat which
she had worn last night in preference to her own lighter coat.
Grant's grey eyes looked into hers and though they showed
no expression she knew he was thinking of her in that "petticoat scene" and being slightly amused by it. Well, Elizabeth
was not amused but at least she was grateful to him for focus-
ing his attention on her. That was an achievement in itself.

At the conclusion of the meal, and as they stood up to leave
the table, Grant turned again to her.

"When you are ready, Elizabeth, will you come to the
office door? It is the last door in the passage leading to the
west veranda. There is a veranda door if you come around
that way. You may use either door."

She wanted to bob a curtsy. When had she felt like that
before? When she had first seen Mrs. Jarvis, of course. How
very royal were these Jarvises when at home in their own
castle! And how cynical she was getting herself. Oh, dear!
Please . . . she asked an invisible God . . . don't let that happen
Not *that* kind of armour!

When Grant later escorted her out through the homestead
garden to the big square beyond she forgot the awkwardnesses
of the breakfast table.

For a moment she had forgotten everything about her curious position in the wonder and pleasure that the garden gave
her. From her own bedroom window she had seen a huge area
of lawn shaded here and there with immensely tall gum trees.
Beyond that had been a cyclone fence sparkling with the
morning dew on it and beyond that the same vast undulating,
untroubled endless plain, over which they had travelled yesterday. There had been absolutely nothing and no one in sight.

She now learned her bedroom was at the east side of the

house. The great square which was made up of a wide space of hard red-brown gravel closed on three sides by a host of buildings and cottages stemmed out like an elongated village from the west side of the homestead. Masses of trees and shrubs screened the main entrance to the homestead from this village.

The square sloped away gently down a hill to the creek about four hundred yards away. Though Elizabeth could not see the water in the creek she could see the line of trees that marked its course. From the air the homestead, the garden and the village would probably look like a rectangle, the longer sides of which were parallel with the creek.

Beyond the square and its minor houses, down to the creek and up the slight rise that led away into the illimitable dis tances, was the same vast treeless plain. It was only broken by several red-brown tracks wavering here and there across it, and two diverging lines of high poles carrying wires. Doubt-less the telephone lines. Over one of these tracks they must have come to the homestead in the early hours of the morning.

So curious, beautiful and lonely was this scene before Elizabeth that it took her mind from the conversation she had meant to have with Grant on their way to the "inspec-tion." She had intended to make it her opportunity to try and find out her exact role with Mrs. Jarvis, and the house-hold.

First the breathtaking, sweet-scented garden, thick with flowering shrubs, then the vast canvas of the countryside . . . and the almost apocryphal loneliness of the station homestead and out-buildings made her feel as if she was struggling to orientate herself. She could be dreaming. The civilisation and the luxury of the house, the cultivated beauty of the garden . . . then, it seemed, the whole planet beyond the square empty of any form of life whatever. The contrast was unbelievable.

"Oh!" Elizabeth said as Grant held open the small garden gate for her. "Where . . . where are the sheep?"

What she had meant, of course, was "Where is the rest of the world?" But she said "sheep" because it was the first thing that came into her head.

"They're out round the bores," Grant said casually. "We've had nothing but drought this season. There's not enough water for them in the home paddocks. We need rain badly."

He'd been home only a few hours but he knew about the state of his station already, apparently.

As they walked across the square past several of the galvanised iron out-houses that looked like big well-constructed sheds, towards the cottages that formed the farthest side of the square, she found herself adding up Grant's personality. He was ambassador, pastoralist, medicine man, telephone linesman, electrician, motor mechanic, horseman. And, of course, tennis player. He was indeed a man of many parts. She wondered why, since he was so proficient in the trades as well as the arts, he had scorned the work of a jackaroo as something beneath him. Strange he should have that little streak of snobbery.

As they traversed the square Grant was pointing out several of the buildings to her.

"That's the store, centre of station life," he said. "Over there is the tool house. The next is the smithy and beyond that the garages. This building on this side houses all the windmill parts and beyond that is the saddlery and the welding shop. That open shed is the specimen woolshed. The big woolsheds are on the other side of the creek. The trees hide them from here. The meat house is, of course, back there behind the homestead. Also the main refrigeration plant and engine house. That place on your right is the carpenter's shop. The plumbing is, of course, all done from the windmill shed. The big open place there is where all major engineering jobs are done."

"And do you ... do you own all these activities, Grant?"

As soon as she asked the question she knew it was naïve. This was what a station was. She hadn't realised it before. She had imagined a big farm house with very big sheep paddocks. Perhaps some stables. As it was, it was a whole industry with all the modern equipment and ramifications of a major industry.

There was a slightly sardonic smile on Grant's lips as he nodded.

"Quite a responsibility," he said. "Now, just before we reach Tim Bolton's cottage, that big one over there with the small garden around it, is the school."

"The school?"

"Of course. We've close on fifty children on the place."

Elizabeth felt her heart suddenly lift.

"Children!" she said. "Where are they all?"

"In school. Probably dressed and shined up awaiting our arrival." This Grant said now with a cynical edge to his voice. "The small ones not yet school age are being kept inside, probably under compulsion. Their mothers are trying to keep them clean for the inspection."

"Why do you use that word inspection, Grant? It seems so remote, and just a little unfriendly."

"Because that is what it is. Nine o'clock boat-drill, if you like to call it that. Every house and every building on the place is inspected every morning by my mother, myself, or in our absence our deputies. A return of the 'Boss' . . ." He looked sideways and down at Elizabeth. "That's me, you know . . . means an extra polish up. They're probably all inside their cottages on tenterhooks for fear something boils over or one of the children gets dirty hands before we arrive."

Elizabeth looked at Grant gravely.

"You sound as if it amuses you to think of everyone being nervous."

"They've nothing to be nervous about if everything is in order."

"And if it is not?"

Grant was silent a minute.

"It always is," he said at length. There was something final in that short clipped statement.

He is a hard man, Elizabeth thought. And just a little cruel. I wouldn't like to be in a defaulter's shoes.

She began to feel that she herself did not like very much this new role in which she found herself.

There had been plenty of noise and activity in the various work sheds they had passed but she could not help feeling there was a strange silence about the cottages they were approaching. Yet Elizabeth remembered Grant's easy and friendly manner with Tim and Maria Bolton. All the same the Boltons had travelled second class while he himself had travelled *de luxe* in a suite on the same ship.

"Why did Mr. and Mrs. Bolton travel in a different class from you coming out from England, Grant?"

"Because they wanted to. Probably to escape me." He was actually smiling. Then he looked at Elizabeth and was serious once again. "I make everyone, black or white, pay for what they get on this place. I give nothing away. I accept no

Government grant for the natives on Kybarrli and I make every native buy everything he wants. It gives him self-respect. And I make him work for his money. It gives him self-respect too. Tim and Maria Bolton probably felt they had other things on which to spend their money than travelling first class. I wouldn't know."

Elizabeth was still regaining her poise from this blunt breathtaking statement when Maria Bolton herself came out of one of the cottages. Though it was still early and a little chilly she was in a sleeveless cotton dress.

She, at least, did not show any of the strain of waiting. Then, of course, the Boltons were privileged. Maria was smiling her welcome.

"Good morning to you both," she said cheerfully. "Grant, you don't expect me to have everything in order yet, do you? All our boxes haven't arrived."

"You have to pass muster, Maria. You know me." He was smiling. "Where's Lalla?" he asked.

"Here she is."

A stout aboriginal woman, impeccably clean in a snow-white cotton dress but with bare feet came out of the cottage. Her face was one vast smile, a new moon of snowy teeth.

"G'day, Grant," she said. "You ready for inspection, hey?"

Grant loked at his watch.

"Nine o'clock," he said.

"Okay, Boss. We'll start here."

"You must meet my fiancée, Miss Elizabeth Heaton. Lalla." He turned to Elizabeth. "Lalla is the head woman on inspection duty, Elizabeth."

Elizabeth shook hands with Lalla.

"I'm very glad to meet you, Lalla," Elizabeth said.

'I'm pleased to meet you, missus," Lalla said, beaming. "You ready, Boss? Okay, let's go."

Then started the strangest hour for Elizabeth. All four of them—Grant, Maria, Lalla and herself—proceeded from cottage to cottage. Women and children were introduced, every room was entered and occasionally a cupboard was opened and once or twice a drawer.

From the cottages of the white stockmen they passed beyond the schoolhouse to the natives' cottages. They too were inspected in the same manner. The chief difference between their cottages and those of the white stockmen was that their cooking was done under a galvanised roof outside the house and the washing in a communal open shed around a tap in the ground. There was a row of huge coppers.

"Blackfella like to talk plenty when he work," Lalla said with a wide grin. "Blackfella like outside best always!"

Everyone shook hands and smiled on Elizabeth and as they left each cottage the inhabitants remained outside chatting to one another and looking after the departing quartette.

"I feel exactly like royalty," thought Elizabeth. "Only there is something wrong about this kind of royalty. What is it?" In the end she decided it was because it was a daily routine and no one on Kybarrli station would have any real privacy. What right had Grant to have access to every woman's kitchen?

In the schoolroom sat rows of children of every age range —and yes, of every colour. Somehow this scene was rather fun. Elizabeth had never seen so many clean and shining faces, such clean hands, and such tidy desks. And such smiles. The teacher, Mr. Rolfe, had been trained in a teachers' college for this particular work.

"I started school there myself," said Grant. "And so did Lalla."

Elizabeth loked at Lalla. She was all smiles.

"He was top of the class, that one," she said.

"How's the singing, Bill?" Grant asked the teacher.

"We'll sing you out the door," the teacher replied with a smile. "If you stay much longer, Grant, I'll lose control. Mrs. Good is away sick to-day and I've got all the little ones on my hands too."

"That'll keep you busy. Well, we'll leave you to it."

As they went out of the door the teacher gave the signal to stand. Suddenly the children broke out into the most beautiful part singing.

> "Will ye no come back again?
> Will ye no come back again?
> Better lo'ed ye canna be.
> Will ye no come back again?"

Elizabeth walked quietly away with the others to the strains of the childish voices on the air. They sang as if they meant it. Indeed Elizabeth was certain they meant it. Grant couldn't be such a very big ogre after all.

· Finally the quartette, still including Maria and Lalla, went up to the homestead. They were met at the side door by Mrs. Jarvis and, now a quintette, they inspected every room in the homestead. Three lubras in the kitchen stood, spotlessly aproned, their hands behind their backs but rocking backwards and forwards on their bare feet and breaking out every now and again into giggles.

To everyone Grant spoke. In every nook and corner of the kitchen did Lalla and Maria look. Grant's smile, as usual, was rare.

When they emerged through the front door Lalla said, "Thas all ri', Grant. See you some more," smiled her new moon smile and waddled happily away down across the red gravel square.

"You'll stay and have morning tea with us, Maria?" Mrs. Jarvis asked.

"I've a great deal to do this morning, Mrs. Jarvis," she said. "Please excuse me. But may I take Elizabeth with me? I'm sure she would like to know something of the life of a head stockman's wife and she can boil my kettle for me while I go on unpacking."

Elizabeth could have fallen on Maria's shoulder with relief. If there was anything on earth she wanted most to do it was get away from Grant and Mrs. Jarvis and find out just what it was all about.

Grant was so hard, always aloof, and sometimes grim. Yet these people all smiled on him. They seemed to *like* him. Why?

"I think that would be a splendid idea," Mrs. Jarvis said.

Grant hesitated. He looked at Elizabeth, then at Maria.

"Very well," he said. "Elizabeth, I do want to talk to you. Will you come to the office when you come back?"

Elizabeth wondered if Maria noticed that this request was not exactly framed in the manner of one lover to another. No one, Elizabeth thought, could surely be in any doubt as to the "phoniness" of this engagement. She herself felt she was what she *was*—another employee of Kybarrli Pastoral Proprietary Limited.

CHAPTER TWELVE

As ELIZABETH walked away with Maria, she found herself thinking of Thera Paton. It was almost impossible to imagine Grant Jarvis in any lover-like attitudes to anyone.

And yet . . .

Elizabeth thought of the fragile spun-gold look of Gaylie Paton. Her mental picture of Grant changed. Yes, oddly enough, she could imagine him . . . leaning over someone like Gaylie, encompassing her with his great frame, his strong arms, his head bending towards the polished gold of that perfectly groomed head . . .

She shook her head and blinked.

"The sun is bright," she said weakly.

"If you haven't any sunglasses you could get them from the store," Maria said. "Gaylie and Thera Paton always wore sunglasses when they came to Kybarrli."

So Maria Bolton too was thinking of the sisters in connection with Grant. She must be wondering what she, Elizabeth, was doing here . . . wearing Thera Paton's shoes.

Keeping them warm for Gaylie, Elizabeth thought and was astounded at the touch of bitterness in her own thoughts. In Maria's cottage Elizabeth relaxed for the first time since the *Albany* had let go anchor in Gage Roads outside the port of Fremantle. Was it possible that was only five days ago, two thousand miles away?

Maria waved Elizabeth into a seagrass cane chair in a corner of the kitchen and took another by the window. Elizabeth had taken off her hat and now let it rest in her lap.

"Take your shoes off too, if you like," said Maria with a smile. "Mine are coming off." She shook her feet and let her flatties clatter to the floor. With one stockinged foot she thrust them aside.

"How understanding you are," said Elizabeth and followed her example. The inspection had taken quite a lot of walking and the ground was hard.

"It's the heat that does that to one's feet," Maria said.

"I can't get over how warm it is compared with the real cold in the night."

139

"I wondered how you got on down there in Old Flinty's hut during the night. Grant lit a fire in the stove, of course?"

"I did," said Elizabeth proudly. Then she caught Maria's inquiring glance. They both laughed.

"It's quite a feat to light a fire of frost-wet gum leaves. I suppose Old Flinty didn't have anything inside? He never does. Those old bushmen can light a fire with sodden wood two inches thick. It's all in the art of when, where and how you blow."

"I blew all right," said Elizabeth. "And how!"

While Maria's lubra got them some morning tea Elizabeth found herself telling Maria of her experiences during the night. To her own astonishment she found herself recounting them all as if they had been humorous and as if, throughout all, she had had an entertaining time. Only over the petticoat incident did she falter.

Maria perceived the hesitation and as she passed Elizabeth her cup of tea she came to the rescue.

"For heaven's sake," she said. "You didn't mind a small thing like appearing in a slip before Grant and Old Flinty, did you? It's easily seen you know nothing of station life. When a lot of people live in a very remote, isolated place like the outback, there are incidents occurring daily that occasion a great many odder things than taking off a wet dress in the middle of the night. A baby piccaninny gets born in the creek bed . . . with only Grant within earshot; a mad steer rips a stockman off his saddle and his clothes off his back. A child hanging by his pants in the redgums . . . and some stockman's wife with such shocking lumbago that two men take it in turns to do the massaging . . ."

"And all sorts of impromptu medical attentions, I suppose," Elizabeth said, remembering Grant's ministrations to Old Flinty in the night. She sipped her tea soberly.

"Tell me," she said, looking up. "Is there anything that Grant can't do? I have been amazed at his resourcefulness in the last twenty-four hours. Yet some of it seems so out of character."

"For instance?"

"Motor mechanics. Mending the telephone line. Giving Old Flinty the right kind of injection."

"My dear child, you do have a lot to learn. Every stockman

on the place can and must be able to do those things. Some
with lesser degrees of skill than others, of course."

"But Grant is not a stockman. He's the 'Boss.' Oh, I don't
mean the man should never soil his hands. I mean Grant, as I
first knew him on shipboard, is a man who has absolutely the
simplest things done for him by stewards or servants. I even
wonder if he picks up his own clothes as he steps out of
them."

"You don't know Grant very well," Maria said. She smiled
to soften her words. "I shouldn't say that to you . . . who
are engaged to him. But then I suppose you've only seen the
lover-like side of him."

Elizabeth felt a sudden unexpected pang, like a painful
regret. She had thought that Maria must guess the real
relationship that existed between herself and Grant. Maria's
next words explained her blindness.

"As a matter of fact when I said a little while ago . . . or
rather implied it . . . that Grant as well as stockmen could
do everything, I nearly added . . . 'except make love to a
woman.' Being the Boss he often gets talked about by the
staff and the one thing we can never imagine is Grant making
love . . ." Maria laughed, then went on: "You don't know
about the other things he can do but you're the authority on
that one intriguing secret."

Fortunately Maria had turned to the small table to re-
plenish her own cup with tea. She did not see the uncertainty
and fleeting embarrassment in Elizabeth's eyes. For an instant
Elizabeth was tempted to break down and confess the truth
to this woman who, she sensed, was friend and confidante.
But for the sake of Grant's dignity she felt she must not do
this, no matter how much it would ease herself. Her first
duty . . . *paid* duty, she mustn't forget . . . was to Grant.

"Didn't he ever have Thera Paton here with him on
Kybarrli?" she asked instead. She wanted Maria to understand that this was not a delicate subject and as Grant's
current fiancée she felt no jealousy of her predecessor.

To Elizabeth's surprise this question brought a long silence
from Maria. At length she looked up and said soberly:

"Grant became engaged to Thera when they were abroad
some time before Thera was killed."

"Oh." Elizabeth blinked as she sipped her tea. It was very
hot.

"She was killed in a motor car accident," Maria said quietly. "Grant was driving the car. Didn't you know?"

There was a stunned silence in the room. Grant was driving the car! Elizabeth felt as if the roof had dropped on her head. Her immediate reaction, before she had time to think, was pity for Grant.

"Oh . . . " she said. "Poor Grant. That explains such a lot."

"His anxiety to avoid Gaylie Paton, for instance?"

"Yes. That amongst other things. His reticence. His wish to remain aloof from people."

Again there was a long silence.

"Was it . . . was it very long ago?" Elizabeth asked at length.

"He hasn't told you very much, has he? But then, that's like Grant. All the same, hardly fair to you. It was less than a year ago. He'd flown over to England on a matter relating to the preliminaries of floating this big pastoral company he is underwriting. He took a short trip on the continent to investigate the bogy of synthetics and how much they were likely to make inroads on the merino market. Thera Paton was holidaying at the same time. They were driving down one of those hairpin bends in the mountains north of Italy."

"And Thera was killed at once?"

"From what we were told here she never knew what hit her."

"And Grant was not injured?"

"I believe lacerations only."

Elizabeth had finished her tea and put her cup and saucer on the small table beside her. She leaned back in her chair, her head on the back rest, and closed her eyes for a minute. She had to let this information sink in and become a real part of her understanding. The only way it could affect her relationship with Grant, of course, was to ensure that she served him as "paid fiancée" the more faithfully. What shocking bad taste it was of Gaylie Paton and her mother to press their attentions on Grant so early after such a tragedy. No wonder he bought himself a bodyguard.

There had been a long silence.

"You might think I shouldn't have been the first to tell you these things, Elizabeth," Maria said. "As a matter of fact I told you on purpose. It was one of the reasons I asked you to come down for tea this morning. You see, I have lived all my life on Kybarrli. My father was an overseer here with

Grant's father. I was born in what is now the store. In those days it was the overseer's cottage. I know the Jarvis family, all of them, so well. I knew you met Grant on the ship and I could see you had had no experience of the type of men that run outback properties like this and the cattle station Barrli. They are a type—a race almost—of their own. On the day we spent together in Perth I knew intuitively you were sensitive and that perhaps you were a little . . . afraid of Grant. Yes, I know, a silly word to apply to a girl's feelings for the man she loves and is going to marry. But that is what I sensed. I wanted to help you."

"Afraid?" said Elizabeth wonderingly. "Is that what you thought? How strange it must have been to you."

"Not at all. Grant is a very intimidating person. Didn't I tell you the one thing we couldn't imagine him being able to do . . . is make love. Yet oddly enough I love him in a way. In a loyal family kind of way. The Jarvis world is the only world I have known as far as people and personalities are concerned. I want the best for them. I don't quite know why . . . perhaps it is because I feel they are my own people just as Kybarrli is my own home. Because I want the best for Grant I want the best for you."

"And you thought my knowing the truth—the whole story—would help me iron out any small difficulties about understanding . . ."

"Yes. In the long run the truth can never really hurt, because it *is* the truth. Grant would not have told you, because of that terrible reserve of his, for one thing. And for another . . . Thera's death caused a terrible cleavage in the Jarvis family. It was quickly healed . . . I don't know how . . . but it was, thank God. I thought the price was Gaylie Paton to succeed Thera as potential owner's wife of Kybarrli. The families are inter-related, you know. Now, of course, you have circumvented that. But you see . . . there may be difficulties. I *had* to warn you."

"Thank you," Elizabeth said.

What had Maria said about the truth being the only thing that mattered in the long run? Yet here she was, Elizabeth, sitting here and by her own silence deliberately deceiving this kind loyal woman who would evidently give her right hand to help the Jarvis family. Honesty merited a return of honesty, yet her own lips were sealed.

She would have to see and talk to Grant. To play the physical role of mannequin for two or three weeks was one thing.
But to go on deceiving and possibly causing unhappiness to
people like Maria and Flinty . . . and Lalla . . . and yes, even
Mrs. Jarvis, another thing. They might, in the interests of sup-
porting Grant's fiancée, commit themselves to words and
actions that would open again the cleavage which Thera's
death had caused. It would be unnecessary, for in her bones
Elizabeth felt that Gaylie was the inevitable bride to stand by
Grant at the altar. She had everything that was needed. She
had the presence and the beauty and the money. Above everything else she had the knowledge of this strange vast country,
the knowhow of station life and probably the skills that meant
she could light a gum-leaf fire in the night without Old
Flinty's advice; shoot a dingo and strip off her clothes in
front of a fire without thinking anything about it.

Gaylie wouldn't have to adapt herself to a different social
climate and custom. What's more the people on Kybarrli
wouldn't have to adapt themselves to her. They knew her.
Probably had known her for the whole of her life.

It was as clear as daylight—and infinitely more important
—that Gaylie would have the determination and the backing
of her side of the family anyhow.

With reference to the manner of Thera's death she had, as
the saying goes in this part of the world, the wood on Grant.

Meantime she herself, Elizabeth, was only a phony anyway. The pity of it was Gaylie didn't know, at this stage, she
hadn't any real competition.

Elizabeth looked up to see that Maria was watching her
anxiously.

"Have I done the right thing in telling you?" Maria asked.

"Yes, thank you," Elizabeth said. "You have been very
helpful. Now I understand why Mrs. Jarvis was a little cold."

Maria laughed.

"To those who don't know Mrs. Jarvis she is always cold.
I'll tell you something." She leaned forward and touched
Elizabeth's knee. "She likes you."

"Likes me?" said Elizabeth, astonished at the pleasure
these words brought. "But how can you tell . . .?"

"I don't know. I just know. One has to know Mrs. Jarvis
very well to know what she is thinking and feeling. But one
does know."

She probably knows I'm helping Grant out temporarily, Elizabeth thought. She was still convinced that Mrs. Jarvis knew of the temporary status of the engagement. Every mother, no matter how cold a woman she is, is grateful to someone who helps her son. No matter how much Grant was to blame for that terrible accident and for Thera's death, Mrs. Jarvis would never believe her son was in the wrong. No mother ever does. Silently, implacably, she would be on Grant's side.

Meantime, silently, implacably, Elizabeth had to betray Maria Bolton's kindness and honesty with gratitude but dishonesty. She had no other course she could take.

Elizabeth stood up and put her hat back on her head.

"Thank you so very much," she said. "I hope you will always be my friend."

"Of course," Maria said as she went with Elizabeth to the door.

Elizabeth walked slowly back across the great square. She let herself in the garden gate and paused a moment under the shade of the wide-spreading pepper trees whose red and green berries were still shining with last night's moisture. Here, out of the sunshine it was cold. Where the sun's rays touched, everything was dry and warm. Where the sun did not penetrate it was moist and cold. Elizabeth supposed the grey-green of the grass over the plain was due to the moisture of condensation during the night. Otherwise, with no rain for months, it must have all dried out and died long since.

She went up the veranda steps and towards the outside office door. Grant had said he wished to see her. She was obeying the summons.

The heavy office door was open but a wire screen barred the way. Elizabeth hesitated, not knowing whether one knocked or just went in. If it had been Mr. Ashby's office now, there would have been no doubt whatever. But with Grant Jarvis she didn't know at what times she had the privileges of a member of the family and at what times she was in his paid service.

Tentatively she decided to combine both roles simultaneously. She knocked lightly as she opened the screen door.

Grant Jarvis's voice said curtly, "Come in!"

He was sitting behind a large square table with a pile of

papers on either side of him. He was writing. When he lifted his head and saw Elizabeth he stood up rather abruptly.

"I'm sorry," he said. "I did not know it was you." He walked round the table and placed a chair for her at the side of it.

"You said you wanted to see me, Grant. And I felt I must have a talk with you."

"Exactly." He sat down and took out his cigarette case. He did not offer her one. "Do you mind if I smoke?" he said.

"No, please do," Elizabeth answered gravely.

As he bent his dark head to light the cigarette she found herself looking at him with a kind of nervous fascination. She felt as if she had never really looked at him before. Indeed she hadn't. Not in that intent minutely curious way. She could see that under the deep tan of his skin there was a faint spread of freckles. There were more fine wrinkles at the corners of the eyes and the mouth than she had realised. His eyebrows were of thick dark hair and gave his brow that firm well-defined look. He was looking down at the lighted match so she could see the long droop of his lids and the clear straight line of his nose.

This was the man who had driven that car down a hair-pin bend . . . and killed a girl. The girl he was going to marry. Sitting so near him, Elizabeth felt as if the aura of that tragedy was reaching out and enveloping her. She wanted to shrink away . . . not from Grant, but from the grief that must be in him.

He put out his hand to put the spent match in an ash tray on the table. As he did this Elizabeth saw something she had not noticed before. On the inside of his right arm was a long white mark. It reached up and disappeared under the sleeve of his shirt. It was a scar. There was a scar under the line of his chin.

His eyes flicked up to her eyes and in them she read something inscrutable, and distant. They were the eyes of a man who cared terribly, or who didn't care at all.

She, Elizabeth, would probably never know.

"You did very well this morning," Grant said, without preliminary remarks. "To run the gauntlet of the staff wives is an achievement. You managed it with quite an air."

Elizabeth was taken aback. Whatever she had done this

morning had been quite natural and certainly without any conscious straining for effect. She had been engrossed by the interest in all that she had seen and in the quaint procedures of the inspection party; and in the natural interest one woman has for other women's homes.

"Thank you," she said. Then after a pause, "Do you conduct that inspection every day, Grant?"

There was a flicker of surprise in his eyes.

"I'm a very busy man, Elizabeth," he said. "I leave that to other people. I do it before I go away and when I come back. To please the staff."

"To please the staff?" Elizabeth hoped she didn't sound as incredulous as she felt.

"Certainly. It is often their only contact with the homestead in days, even weeks. They like to feel we take an interest. My mother does it generally, when she is here. If absent, then Maria Bolton, Lalla or another staff wife does the job. They take it in rotation."

"Would you mind my asking another question . . . just out of curiosity?"

"Go ahead."

"Don't they mind not having any real privacy?"

"*We* in the homestead have no real privacy. The homestead is inspected every day too. It's the only way to teach the natives how to live as civilised people live. In order not to allow a feeling of discrimination, *every* house is inspected. There is then no reflection on the natives." He paused, shook the ash from his cigarette. "I can assure you it is necessary. The natives when they first come in here are still semi-tribal people. They have to learn how to live in a cottage—properly."

"Oh." Elizabeth felt abashed. She must remember in future not to be too quick with criticism. The white stockmen and their wives were co-operating in a scheme that helped the natives to become accustomed to the white man's way of life. Elizabeth had feared it had been overlordship on the part of Grant Jarvis.

"I'm sorry," she said contritely.

"You're not likely to understand our life here, or how a station is run, in a few weeks," Grant said dryly. Then abruptly changing the subject he went on, "What I wanted to discuss with you was the formality of a vice-regal visit. In a sense it is the same thing as a royal visit in Great Britain. In point of fact the Governor does represent the Queen. There is a certain protocol that must be observed until the Governor signifies he's ready to give it away and become a mere man. When he does that you'll find everything and everyone relaxes. Till then . . ."

He looked at Elizabeth to see if she was following him. She nodded.

"As head of the family, I, of course, meet His Excellency. It will be at the main entrance to Kybarrli homestead. As you are my fiancée and not my wife you will allow me to present my mother first. My mother is still the hostess of Kybarrli."

"Of course," Elizabeth said. "Grant, may I ask another question? Does your mother know that I am only *temporarily* your fiancée?"

"No."

"She may guess it."

"Why should she?"

Elizabeth really smiled, and when she did her eyes had a soft shining look and her nice white teeth gleamed between her red lips. There was a merry look in her expression.

"Our meetings and partings in the morning and evening leave an awful lot to the imagination . . . if we are supposed to be something more than distant acquaintances," she said.

Grant looked at her steadily for a long minute.

"You would like me to embrace you in the morning?" There was a slight cynical emphasis on the word *embrace*. "And in the evening?"

"Oh, no," Elizabeth said hastily.

"It is very easily accomplished," said Grant with such an edge of bitterness Elizabeth hoped she would never say anything amusing again as long as she lived. "We've had one rehearsal. That should be enough."

"I was only joking, Grant," she said. "Please go on about the protocol."

Grant explained at some length just what were the plans for the Governor's visit. The greater part of his day-time would be taken up inspecting the property. The evenings, however, involved the homestead people. On the first evening there would be a dinner for the house party and the household of another station between Kybarrli and Endall. On the second evening there would be a vice-regal reception for the entire district. The homestead, gardens and square would be used. On both occasions Elizabeth would need full evening dress.

When he had finished, Grant stood up. Elizabeth hadn't had her "talk" with him, and now after her little joke about the greetings and partings she felt too intimidated to try. In fact she couldn't remember what it was she wanted to talk about.

"I hope you can find some way to occupy yourself in the next day or two," Grant said.

"I'd like to go down to the school," Elizabeth said on the impetus of the moment. "The teacher said something about a Mrs. Good being away and having the little ones on his hands. Would it be outside protocol for me to go down there and perhaps tell the little ones a story . . . or hear them sing . . . or something?"

Elizabeth found her voice faltering away because Grant was looking at her so curiously.

"Would you really like to do that?" he said at length.

"Yes, I would," said Elizabeth honestly.

"Very well, I'll speak to Mr. Rolfe about it when I go down at twelve o'clock. I myself am riding out to see one of the flocks. You don't ride, do you?"

"No," Elizabeth said regretfully.

"I can send for a riding master from Melbourne. I would suggest one of the stockmen here but they're the world's greatest rough riders . . . their tuition would be very hard on a young lady."

"From Melbourne?" said Elizabeth. "There wouldn't be time, Grant. The *Albany* won't be more than a week or two around the coast of Australia and I must catch it in about two and a half weeks' time."

"There are plenty of other ships," Grant said absently. He was now holding open the wire door for Elizabeth to pass through.

Elizabeth, in the doorway, stopped.

"I have a family, and a job. Remember?"

"Oh, yes. And a young man, too. Well, they can wait. I'll tell you when you can go home."

Elizabeth felt as nervous as if she was standing before Mr. Ashby awaiting orders for the day. Difficult orders that she mightn't be able to carry out effectively.

"I'm sorry, Grant. I must return to England on the *Albany*."

"I will make arrangements with Small and Smallwoods. You could get in touch with your family yourself."

Elizabeth felt a sudden welling of spirit. Just who did he think he was that he could take people as if they were pawns in a game and alter the pattern of their lives for them without consent? Did wealth make all men so power-conscious? Her back straightened.

Grant had let the wire door close behind them and he walked across the veranda and stood looking out over the plain. He put both hands on the balustrade and leaned on it. As he did so Elizabeth noticed again that long fine white scar on his forearm. In her mind's eye she saw that terrible mountain crash; then Gaylie Paton sitting in the hotel lounge looking across the room at Grant under long indolent sweeping lashes. She heard Maria's voice . . . "I love him in a way: in a loyal, family kind of way." Finally she saw herself looking at Mrs. Morgan in the suite on the *Albany* and saying, "I don't know why one should feel compassion for a millionaire."

Yet as she looked at Grant, leaning on that balustrade, staring out over the plain, with that fine white scar showing on his arm, she felt he was, for all his wealth and power, a lonely man. Whether he was isolated by his personal tragedy or by his great wealth Elizabeth did not know. If he required her to stay on she would not raise difficulties. She had a strange and compulsive inclination to serve him. That white scar had probably long since ceased to be painful to Grant. Yet it hurt her.

CHAPTER THIRTEEN

FOR THE next day or two Elizabeth had the curious feeling of being a prisoner. It was quite clear that Grant Jarvis did not intend to let her leave Kybarrli until it suited him. Her freedom of movement in that respect was non-existent.

She found the life around the station homestead immensely interesting. She had written to Mrs. Morgan and told her of Grant's wish that she should remain; and asked Mrs. Morgan for advice. She had written happily to her mother of all the strange and interesting things she was seeing . . . of the great paddocks, the stockmen coming to the homestead each day at daybreak for instructions and at sundown coming in again, dusty and tired. They were a slim, brown-faced, wiry lot. Some of them spent their whole lives in the saddle. Others had taken to jeeps and motor-cycles to get to the out-camps at which they worked. The boundaries of Kybarrli were so remote from the homestead that Elizabeth only caught a glimpse, and then from the distance, of the thousands of sheep that grazed over it.

She wrote to Ralph, and try as she would she could not keep from that letter a note of nostalgia. If Elizabeth had not been haunted by the great distance that separated her from Ralph, and the fear that her absence might bring a change in their shared life, she would have given herself completely to the life on the station.

As it was she felt she was a divided person. Half of her was here, and half of her was there.

Elizabeth was a tender-hearted girl and it was these feelings inspired by her need of Ralph that made her bend more readily to the will of Grant Jarvis. She wished to serve with loyalty where her heart was touched. The head of Kybarrli Station had a need of her services and that made her feel a certain gratitude that someone *needed* her—no matter in what capacity.

It was a wonderful feeling . . . to be needed. Grant Jarvis, in the lonely mountain fastnesses of his own private life, needed her! Elizabeth felt that all her life she would be grateful for that. It gave her confidence.

151

Elizabeth thought that Thera Paton's death, and the part Grant had played in it, had made the atmosphere in the celestial realms where his heart and mind lived, doubly frozen. She would do what she could for him. If back in London Small and Smallwoods thought she was serving them with a singleness of purpose then she was sorry, because they were wrong. Probably Mrs. Morgan was the only person who would know that Elizabeth was something more than a business emissary.

The next day Mrs. Paton, Gaylie's mother, arrived to stay at Kybarrli.

Elizabeth had been out on the run in a jeep with Maria Bolton, seeing one of the huge flocks of sheep that were camped two miles down the creek, when Mrs. Paton arrived. Elizabeth did not see her until they met at the dinner table.

It gave Elizabeth great pleasure to dress for dinner at night. She felt well-groomed and able to face any social occasion with confidence. She was thankful she had taken that shopping spree with Maria Bolton. As Mrs. Morgan had said . . . beauty is armour.

Elizabeth was very conscious of this when she met Mrs. Paton at dinner that night on Kybarrli. She didn't think she was very beautiful herself but she knew her dress and shoes couldn't be bettered.

Everyone as they sat down that night looked well-groomed. Mrs. Jarvis wore a black lace dress, very simple, a little old-fashioned but none the less elegant. Mrs. Paton was the last word in *chic*. Her hair looked as if the hairdresser had just put the finishing touches to it. Her deep green brocade dress was cut high in the front and low at the back and there was a truly French bow draped across the back of the skirt. Grant, who wore a dark charcoal grey lounge suit, looked more striking than usual because the dark colour made his teeth, the whites of his eyes and the snowy whiteness of his shirt seem to gleam. Elizabeth's pure silk dress of deep strawberry-pink roses on a cream background brought out the colours of her hair and eyes and caressed the soft fairness of her skin.

Elizabeth smiled and said, "How do you do, Mrs. Paton?" as she entered the sitting-room before dinner.

"You had better address Mrs. Paton as 'Aunt Mollie',

Elizabeth," Mrs. Jarvis said in her tiny quiet firm voice. "Grant has always done that, although we are not very closely related. It is the simplest way of bridging the connection."

"Of course. If I may?" she looked at Mrs. Paton for permission.

"Yes, you must call me 'Aunt,' " Mrs. Paton said in her slightly clipped tones as they sat down. "It is so much more like a relationship. You are Grant's fiancée."

There was a barely perceptible lift to the end of her last sentence so that it sounded to Elizabeth's sensitive ears like a question—"You are Grant's fiancée?"

Mrs. Paton looked at Elizabeth, smiling in that odd way that showed her teeth as if they were closed. Her eyes were pale blue. They *inquired* when they looked at the girl across the table.

But "beauty was armour" and Elizabeth felt if she was worsted in a conflict of manners and conversation she at least looked the part of Grant's fiancée.

In the dining-room she felt more at ease.

"May I pass you something, Aunt Mollie?" Elizabeth asked. "Have you the pepper and salt?"

"I have everything," Aunt Mollie said politely as she dipped her spoon in the soup. With the spoon half-way to her mouth she looked across at Elizabeth again.

"Do tell me something about yourself, Elizabeth." Again there was that hint of challenge as if suspecting that whatever Elizabeth had to tell would be open for inner reflection on Aunt Mollie's part.

To Elizabeth's astonishment, and before she could answer, Mrs. Jarvis intervened.

"Elizabeth is a young woman engaged to my son," she said quietly and with a finality that brooked no further comment. She turned to Mrs. Paton. "She will be a Mrs. Jarvis in due course. As you know, Mollie, that carries a certain hallmark of distinction."

It could have been a snub except that Mrs. Jarvis said it in a way that invited Aunt Mollie to concur in the principle that the name Jarvis was sufficient for even the Book of Judgment. It also placed Aunt Mollie herself in the hierarchy of those of whom the angels did not ask account, since she was related by innumerable ramifications to the Jarvis family.

Elizabeth stole a glance down the table at Grant. From his manner he might have been deaf to these comments.

"You're a good judge of horsemanship, Aunt Mollie," he said. "I'm having a parade to-morrow of my head stockman's Black Riders. He's got the natives dressed up and mounted on the pick horses for the Governor's visit. It's a sight to be seen." Grant said this with an amused tolerant smile. "They're the pride of Tim's plant. He had them in training at Barrli while he was away but now he's back he's had them brought across here and is putting the finishing touches to the outfit."

There was nothing for Aunt Mollie to do but continue the conversation on the subject of horses, the Black Riders and the Governor's visit.

Mrs. Jarvis at the head of the table was silent. Once, as she put out her hand to take the silver sauce-bowl, when the second course of the meal was served, her eyes met Elizabeth's. Again Elizabeth felt something warming her heart. For the life of her she couldn't think there had been any expression in Mrs. Jarvis's eyes at all. They were like Grant's . . . cold, distant and inimical . . . yet some message had been conveyed. What was it? One almost of conspiracy surely?

But no. Mrs. Jarvis would never stoop to such methods. Aunt Mollie was a connection. The hallmark was on her. Elizabeth Heaton, even in an elegant pure silk dress with a gay pink jacket would not be permitted to see there was a blemish on that hallmark. Yet her heart was warmer, even light. Some day before she went home she might dare to make a joke with Mrs. Jarvis.

Aunt Mollie talked on, lightly, pleasantly and generally but every now and again Elizabeth found her eyes resting on herself. Her eyes smiled but not her mouth; her manner was sweet and amiable. Yet Elizabeth knew that Aunt Mollie was not a friend. Those eyes, though they smiled, sought too much.

Not for the first time Elizabeth felt that Grant was beset by unfriendly omens.

Grant, though reserved and distant, was still the well-mannered host. He turned now to Elizabeth to draw her into conversation.

"How did you find the school to-day?" he asked. "I under-

stand you spent yesterday afternoon and this afternoon entertaining the kindergarten class?"

"I had a lovely time," said Elizabeth quickly. "They entertained me. Bush children are less inhibited and more friendly
than city children, aren't they? As a matter of fact they did
all the talking, and instructing, too. I learned how to tell a
snake track from a goanna track. They tried to show me
how to throw a boomerang but of course I was an abject
failure."

"Very few white people, even those who have lived outback all their lives, can throw a boomerang successfully,"
Mrs. Jarvis said dryly. "It is a gift."

Grant turned again to Elizabeth.

"I heard you sang for them," he said.

"Oh, do you sing, Elizabeth?" Aunt Mollie asked. Her
voice implied this would be a stagy thing to do.

"Anyone can sing for children," Elizabeth said lightly.
"They're so uncritical. And if one sings the wrong note one
can laugh and know that the children are delighted to find a
grown-up human enough to make mistakes." She turned to
Grant. "I sang an old English folk song to them after they
had sung quite a lot for me."

"Were you a school teacher that you take an interest in
the school?" Aunt Mollie asked.

"No," Elizabeth said gently. "I just wanted to be near
the children. I suppose I like them. Mr. Rolfe, the schoolmaster, was really pleased too. He had so much work to do
with the older children he was relieved to have the little
ones out of the way. And, of course, there are the preparations
for the Governor's visit."

"Yes," said Mrs. Jarvis. "The school superintendent is
coming along at the same time. He is showing His Excellency
his outback schools. I expect Mr. Rolfe is on tenterhooks."

Grant was looking at Elizabeth.

"You liked the children?" he asked.

"Oh, I loved them. Who wouldn't? They're so guileless.
So free from all the painful knowledge of being grown-up."
She stopped a minute then added with a laugh, "I mean all
children, of course. Children everywhere. They're dependent,
and innocent and fun-making. They make me feel good.
I mean really *good* the way I was meant to be . . ."

She broke off because quite clearly Mrs. Jarvis and Grant,

from one end of the table to the other, were exchanging a glance.

"I hope you didn't mind my spending my time at the school, Mrs. Jarvis?" Elizabeth said anxiously.

"On the contrary, I think it is a very good idea. We badly need a crèche for the babies in the heat of summer or when the mothers are sick. As it is, the toddlers crawl about in the creek bed and every one of them gets eye trouble from sandfly bites. Blindness is very common among native children, you know. We're always afraid of it."

This was the longest speech Mrs. Jarvis had made since Elizabeth had first met her. Though she gave no outward evidence of feeling, it was quite clear she had feeling for the little ones on the station. And there were many babies and toddlers. Elizabeth had seen that on her first morning.

"We've never had anyone here sufficiently knowledgeable to get some kind of scheme going," Grant said. He cracked a nut and his long fingers flicked away the pieces of shell from the kernel. His voice sounded thoughtful.

"Well, here's Elizabeth on the spot," said Aunt Mollie with an increase of sweetness. "You ought to turn her into a kindergarten teacher at once. I'm sure that would be an ideal position for her."

She laughed and before anyone could make any comment she spoke to Grant directly.

"At what time to-morrow morning are you rehearsing your parade, Grant? And do I go as an equestrian or a pedestrian?"

"At nine o'clock. I think it had better be a foot review, Aunt Mollie, if you don't mind. I haven't had a horse brought in for you yet."

Mrs. Jarvis had risen from the table and Grant went quickly to the door to hold it open for her. He waited while Aunt Mollie went through too. As Elizabeth came towards the door he said:

"Would you wait a few minutes, Elizabeth. I want to talk to you."

"Yes, Grant."

She turned back and went down the length of the dining-room and stood looking out of the window. It was dark, but the yard lights set up a fairyland of shadow and light through the shrubs in the garden. Elizabeth stood watching the motes that were night insects floating up and down the ladders of light that penetrated into the trees.

Grant spoke to the dining-room lubra about bringing two cups of coffee, then he came down the long room towards Elizabeth. She turned to face him.

"I felt Aunt Mollie's suggestion about being a kinder-garten teacher was a broad hint, Grant," she said. She was certain it had put something in Grant's mind too. "Don't offer it to me as a post, please." Rather sadly she added, "I want to go home."

He stood quite still a minute and looked at her. Then with a quick movement he turned the two seats at the end of the table so that they faced one another at angles across its corner.

"Sit down, Elizabeth," he said abruptly. He held her chair while she complied. He sat down in the other chair. He took out his cigarette case. "You don't . . ." He stopped short, and then looked at her. "Or would you like a cigarette?"

"Is it a social grace becoming to your fiancée?" Elizabeth asked. She was unaware there was a slightly rueful smile on her lips.

"Not particularly, but if you would like one . . ."

"I think I would. I might be more successful this time."

He took quite a time and effort lighting her cigarette, hold-ing the match up so that she might tilt her chin upwards and thus avoid getting the smoke in her eyes. Elizabeth felt oddly touched by this evidence of consideration.

"Thank you," she said.

She took care to draw only a very little smoke into her mouth and exhale it slowly. All the same she knew she would never have that confident cigarette-holder air-waving manner that Gaylie Paton had. In spite of what Grant had said, to smoke a cigarette with the grand air was surely very much an added social grace. It marked one as sophisti-cated.

"Why did you say you wanted to go home?" Grant said.

"When you were in England, didn't you want to go home, Grant . . . sometime . . . ?"

"Of course. That is different. My home and my work are here and I have many dependants. Far more than you see around the homestead environs, I might add."

"I have my home and my work, too," Elizabeth said quietly.

Grant made a gesture with his hand.

"You think they are of no consequence?" Elizabeth asked, still very quietly. "They may be of no consequence in the big world, and your affairs are of consequence, of course. But my affairs are important to me. They are my whole life."

Suddenly her eyes challenged his.

Grant leaned back on his chair. His eyes had again the hooded look of the tired man who had yet much work to do.

"I particularly want you to stay here."

"That is a very great compliment. I suppose you are going to adopt Aunt Mollie's suggestion and offer me the job of forming a crèche for the station babies. I would love to do that. But don't you see, Grant? You would be in a very strange position. When this particular role of mine . . . that of being your fiancée . . . is past, it would be awkward for you to have your ex-fiancée working on the place when you bring your next one home."

The expression on Grant's face did not change but his lips went white as he clamped them together. Elizabeth could have cried out at her clumsiness. She had forgotten Thera. She had been thinking only that some day he would marry— Gaylie Paton or someone else—and bring her home to Kybarrli. How would that nebulous person like to feel that the kindergarten teacher at the creek end of the square had once been engaged to Grant?

Now, in her thoughtlessness, she had made it sound as if he was a man with a whole history of engagements before and probably after Elizabeth herself. She lifted her hand as if she would put it out and touch him. But, of course, she couldn't. He was too unapproachable for that. She felt unshed tears of remorse behind her eyes.

Every day someone must innocently say something like this that struck him a blow on his heart and at his conscience. She could not unsay those words. Nothing, no apology could recall them.

"I had not thought of the proposition in those terms," Grant said slowly between half-closed lips. "I had been about to suggest something quite different. But if you feel you must go home . . ."

"Not yet awhile then," Elizabeth said contritely. She could have offered him her right hand in compensation for her cruel thrust. "I will stay as long as you wish." She lifted her eyes up to him. "I would like to be of service to you."

Again there was a long silence. Grant, frowning, looked down at the cigarette as he flicked ash into the ash-tray.

"I have been about to offer something more permanent. Perhaps it is better as it is."

At that moment the lubra brought in the coffee. Both Grant and Elizabeth were silent as she poured the coffee into two small cups and then put the silver cream jug and silver sugar basin within touching distance. They waited until she left the room.

"If you would like me to do something about the crèche while I'm here, Grant, I will. But one shouldn't start something and then walk out and leave it in mid-air. Would you be able to get a successor?"

She had used that dreadful word "successor" again. She bit her lips and wished she could bite her tongue to punish it.

"No. The crèche is something that will come in due course," Grant said. "It really needs direction and enthusiasm and overseeing from the homestead. Everything needs example and overseeing from the homestead. As the years go on I need to spare my mother."

His lips weren't white any more and the look of controlled anger had gone from his face. He was his usual cold and proud self.

"I had thought of quite a different arrangement. However, I'm glad that in the meantime you like going down to the school. It is a help to Rolfe while Mrs. Good is ill. I met him as I was coming up from the stables to-night. He seemed very pleased. If you wouldn't mind carrying on until after the Governor's visit and until after I return from Barrli . . . we'll then be able to make arrangements for your return to England."

He stood up and indicated the interview was at an end. This strict employer-employee procedure would have had its light side for Elizabeth if she still hadn't been feeling her remorse so keenly.

She likewise had risen and they now walked towards the door. She held the unfinished cigarette in her hand. Grant opened the door, his hand rested on the knob.

"Did you say you were engaged to this young man in England?" he asked, standing quite still.

Elizabeth stopped in the doorway.

"Not engaged. Only waiting to be engaged," she said with a half laugh.

"What exactly does that mean? Either you are going to marry him, or you are not, surely?"

"Let's put it this way," said Elizabeth. "I hope I'm going to marry him. When he asks me."

Grant's eyebrows went up.

"Forgive my asking you a question," he said. "Have you known this man very long?"

"Oh, years and years! Always, I think. We grew up together. And . . ." She stopped, looked down at the burnt-out cigarette and wondered what to do with it. "We'll grow old together, I suppose." She nearly added *waiting* but at that moment the cigarette burnt her fingers and she dropped it. Grant bent to pick it up.

"Oh, I'm so sorry," she said.

Grant went back into the dining-room and stubbed the cigarette out in the ash-tray.

When he came back he put his hand on the door again.

"I think you had better marry an outback Australian," he said. "Outback men never wait. They meet a girl one day, become engaged the next and marry the day after."

It was the first time Elizabeth had ever heard Grant say something that she thought was amusing.

"But why?" she asked as they went out into the passage and towards the drawing-room.

"White girls are scarce in the outback. When you do come by one you grab quickly and learn to love afterwards. If you don't get her someone else will . . . that's the principle of courtship north and west of the border country."

"Shock tactics?"

"For some reason it always seems to work," said Grant.

Elizabeth thought he was speaking of his stockmen, of course. In Grant's circle marriage plans were laid down by the families over the christening font. In his own case, for instance. He was to have married Thera but she had died. Now he would marry Gaylie. All he really asked of his love life was that he could have a breathing space between commitments.

Oh, dear, thought Elizabeth as she went into the drawing-room and Grant went on down the opposite passage to his office. I am thinking wrongly again. It's the *system* I reject. But then, when one comes to think of it, is it any more restricted and odd than the meet-ask-and-marry-in-a-day that is the stockman's system?

She crossed the big old-fashioned but beautiful room to the fire and sat down on a bouffant cushion near Mrs. Jarvis who was crocheting. She picked up the wool that had fallen to the floor and slowly unwound a loop of it for Mrs. Jarvis. Aunt Mollie was not in sight though her white cotton crochet work was lying on the nearby sofa, which meant she had gone out of the room for a few minutes.

From her lowly but beautiful comfortable seat Elizabeth looked up at Mrs. Jarvis.

"Your fingers work so quickly," she said.

"Practice," said Mrs. Jarvis. She did not look at the girl until Elizabeth's head had bent again.

Elizabeth continued her train of thought. Is it any more odd, she reflected, than knowing someone all your life and never knowing if and when he is going to ask you to marry him? Isn't the business of getting married odd whichever way you look at it?

She turned her eyes and gazed into the glowing embers of the fire. Love ought not to be odd, she thought. It was something one wanted to give so much. Wanted to *give* . . . more than to *get*.

"What are you thinking of, child?" said Mrs. Jarvis unexpectedly.

Elizabeth smiled.

"I've discovered why we all love cats. It's really that we're grateful to them. They let us love them. In fact, they demand it."

"There are people in the world other than cats that need love," said Mrs. Jarvis. Her eyes lifted from her work and then went back to it. She sat straight-backed, her head inclining rather than bending, her feet placed together as neatly as if they were a pair of shoes in a shoe cupboard. "My son, for instance," she added.

Elizabeth felt a faint shock. Now she must tread carefully. This dreadful deception she had to carry on! Somehow she hadn't realised the ramifications of it all. *Tell one lie*, her mother once said, *and you have to tell fifty to back it up.*

"I am sure he is very well loved," Elizabeth said, looking down again at the wool in her hand and releasing another loop. She was literally hanging her head so that Mrs. Jarvis could not see the flush of guilt that mounted her cheeks. "Maria Bolton was telling me how much she loved Grant. Everyone else on the station must feel the same way."

Elizabeth felt the old lady's eyes boring holes through the top of her own head.

"Do you love him?" Mrs. Jarvis said. The crochet needle did not cease its rhythmic movement nor did the quick movement of the fingers falter by a fraction of a second.

The question went through Elizabeth's heart like a sword. She turned her head to the fire and closed her eyes tight as she did when she was a child and she prayed.

"Yes," she said, hoping for forgiveness for the lie. "Yes. I love him."

Her own words hung like pointing darts in the air; arrows that at any moment would prick and penetrate her own tongue, and yes, her heart too. To lie to a mother was possibly the worst deception of all.

Then suddenly Elizabeth knew that one dart had indeed impaled her heart. Instead of pain there was relief.

She loved him, like Maria Bolton did. She loved him in a loyal, loving, family way. She would be of service to him. She would give him the best that was in herself.

Why?

Why did Maria feel that way? Because Grant lived alone on the top of a mountain, and needed it. Others might love him for his name or his money, his prestige or his power. But people like herself and Maria would love him because he needed it.

There was a tiny shining film of tears along the edge of Elizabeth's closed lids. She opened her eyes, turned her head and looked at Mrs. Jarvis and smiled.

"Yes," she said quietly. "I love him."

Mrs. Jarvis smiled at Elizabeth. It was like the sealing of a pact. They had silently agreed about something. What it was Elizabeth was not quite sure. Possibly . . . probably . . . Elizabeth's duty to love Grant.

CHAPTER FOURTEEN

IN THE MORNING the dress rehearsal of Tim Bolton's Riders went off with a flourish. At the appropriate time Grant, Aunt Mollie and Elizabeth went to the outside homestead gate. Elizabeth and Aunt Mollie stood side by side to the left of the gate as the reception party would stand when His Excellency arrived. This rehearsal was a very serious thing, apparently.

The Riders paraded slowly and gracefully up from behind the stables and formed a line opposite the gate and parallel to the fence. They were quite magnificent and Elizabeth was thrilled with the excitement and interest.

"Don't they look wonderful?" she said to Aunt Mollie.

Grant had moved away to talk to Tim Bolton.

"Everything Grant does, he does well," Aunt Mollie said.

"Tim Bolton must have some credit, too," Elizabeth said. "Grant has been quite a long time in England."

"My dear child, Grant trains his men from the time they come on Barrli or Kybarrli. It would be no particular effort for those stockmen to put on an exhibition. Merely a matter of dressing them up and seeing they had matching mounts."

Aunt Mollie sounded kind but faintly sorry for Elizabeth that she should think this was something rare and out of the way. Aunt Mollie's voice hinted faintly at Elizabeth's inexperience in these matters. She, of course, was born to the way things were done on Kybarrli; to show so much enthusiasm was a little naïve.

But Elizabeth was not going to let Aunt Mollie spoil things for her. It was all new to *her*, and she was going to enjoy it. She would, however, be guarded in her comments.

The Black Riders did indeed look magnificent. They all wore blue shirts and black riding pants. On their heads were hats with very wide brims, wider than those the white stockmen wore and which were often no more than somewhat battered army felt hats.

The Riders sat on matching bay geldings. The harness and saddles were bright with studded silver ornamentation, the leather work shone like new. Each man carried his stock-whip across the front of his saddle.

Grant crossed the space before the gate and beginning at the top of the line walked along and inspected each horse, each man, speaking to each man about his horse and his equipment. Elizabeth thought Grant was as meticulous and imperious as a regimental colonel on inspection parade. And like the legendary colonel, he did not smile.

Then with Tim Bolton by his side he stood back and watched the Riders ride away. A hundred yards across the plain the stockmen began their formation riding, ever gathering speed and widening their circles and their squares. With a shout from the leading man the stockwhips came out and were cracked like so many pistols going off in unison.

Then began what Elizabeth knew was some real horsemanship. Pounding hoofs, cracking stockwhips; fractional judgment as horses came together at a terrific pace and swung away without collision. Dust hung over the paddock like a brown cloud. Elizabeth was entranced. She clapped her hands and said, "Oh, wonderful!" in sheer pleasure. She looked first at Grant, then Aunt Mollie, expecting to read the same excited pleasure, perhaps satisfaction, in their faces.

Aunt Mollie was watching, the lids of her eyes narrowed, the usual fixed smile on her lips. Grant was not smiling but when Elizabeth looked up at him eagerly he turned and looked down at her. However used he might be to outstanding horsemanship he could not now escape the infectious quality of Elizabeth's surprise and pleasure. He smiled.

Twice before she had seen him smile like that . . . the night he was sitting in the officers' wardroom on the *Albany* and days later in Mrs. Morgan's suite. It was the curious shining quality of his smile that struck her again. That, and this time its unexpectedness.

At what time in his thirty-five years of life had he stopped smiling except in rare odd spontaneous moments such as this? When he had inherited Kybarrli? Or after that mountain smash in Italy?

"You think it is good?" he asked her.

Before she could answer Aunt Mollie intervened.

"You know it is good, Grant," she said. And yes, she smiled *her* smile. "Where did you get that bay strain in the geldings? From the stallion Cousin Bob caught loose on the Diamentina?"

Grant's eyes went past Elizabeth to Aunt Mollie. His expression became slightly sardonic.

"The same," he said.

"Dear old Cousin Bob," Aunt Mollie said, never once changing the sweet quality of her voice or smile. "What a horse thief he turned out to be!"

Grant turned back to the Riders' performance.

"When a man comes by an unbranded horse running wild in the outback nobody but that man ever knows whether he 'found' the horse or 'took' it," Grant said. "You probably will have to wait till you go to the particular part of heaven that is the Jarvis and Paton reserve to find out for yourself whether my father was a horse thief or not, Aunt Mollie."

"Oh, come, Grant," said Aunt Mollie, smiling. "He must have told *you*." Her small smile was guileless but her eyes were questing . . . underneath their surface blueness . . . questing.

"Yes, he told me," Grant said evenly. "He rounded up the stallion when he found him running with a mob of brumby mares. Wild."

Aunt Mollie smiled at Elizabeth.

"Oh . . . the doings of those old-timers!" she said.

Grant was standing relaxed as if the inferences from Aunt Mollie's words did not touch him. But they touched Elizabeth. All along the line Aunt Mollie had some little thing against Grant. Some black mark on the ledger. Of course the motor accident was not a little thing. But the history of the horse was, because it happened in another time and generation. Yet Aunt Mollie held it against Grant.

How many of those black marks were in Aunt Mollie's ledger? Would the sum total mean that willy-nilly Grant would marry Gaylie Paton, even though the thought of marrying Thera's sister gave him constant pain?

Moral blackmail, Elizabeth thought. And was delighted she was able to sum it up in such adult terms.

If she, Elizabeth, could go on warding off the day of Gaylie's successful assault on his name and place by keeping up the ruse of this engagement . . . then she would stay just as long as Grant needed her. She would have to keep wary eyes open,

for there must inevitably come a time when Grant's heart
was ready to face the facts of life in the form of a marriage
that was both suitable and convenient. When that time
came she herself must be ready to fade out as quickly as possible. Till then . . .

The Black Riders had finished their exhibition and, their
mounts lathered in sweat, were lined up some distance away.
Grant lifted his hand in a signal to dismiss them. The line
turned and filed away back to the stables.

"If you'll excuse me, Grant . . . Aunt Mollie . . . I'll go
down to the school," Elizabeth said. "Mr. Rolfe needs my
help in quite a big way this time. With Mrs. Good away he
can't get his rehearsals as finished as this one."

"Thank you, I'd be grateful," Grant said.

Elizabeth gave Aunt Mollie a fleeting smile and set off
through the garden towards the west side of the square. As
she turned the corner she saw Aunt Mollie and Grant walking
together towards the homestead veranda. Aunt Mollie's head
was turned up to Grant and she was talking, gesticulating with
her hands. Grant, his hat drawn down on his brows, was
stalking wordless beside her, looking ahead. It didn't look as
if Aunt Mollie was making much impression. One never
knew with Grant, however, just what *was* impressing him.

The next day Gaylie arrived.

Elizabeth had spent the afternoon walking along the creek
bed with the little ones from school, learning more about
bush life than text books could tell. All the afternoon the
sound of small voices and frail childish laughter wafted up on
the still air towards the square and the stockmen's cottages.
The stockmen's wives, often with a tiny tot or baby in tow,
were visiting one another for the daily confab.

"Most times when the visitors come to stay on Kybarrli
they're being entertained at the homestead or are riding out
over the best paddocks on the best horses," one wife said.
"She's different, this one."

"Maybe that's why Mr. Grant picked her out. Do you
think anything will come of it?"

"Come of what? The engagement? Mr. Grant's always
been a man who knew his own mind. Iron-willed and stub-
born, my husband always says."

"He says right, too! Only it seems funny with everything

set for Miss Gaylie to marry him. And there's Mrs. Paton up there at the homestead now."

"Who said everything was set for him to marry Gaylie?"

"I don't know. Everyone. Just took it for granted like. My, she's pretty, is Gaylie Paton. Like something out of a book."

"This one's pretty too. Only nicer. She's got a kind heart."

"How can you tell?"

"Just the way she looks at you. And smiles. It's kinda nice. Gaylie's pretty but this one's got a lovely skin. Makes me think of the Old Country. After all these years in the outback and getting used to sunburned faces it's like seeing a rose growing in a field of poppies . . ."

There was a general laugh.

"Well, you can laugh," rejoined the speaker. "She makes me kinda homesick. I like this one."

"Anyhow, Mr. Grant didn't ask our advice," said the first one, who had asked if they thought anything would come of the engagement. "He must have asked himself which one he liked best."

"All the same . . ." said one of the others. "They're awfully distant when they're together. And you know what? I always had an idea he liked Gaylie Paton better than Thera in the first place. Only everyone in the Paton family sort of threw Thera at him from the word go." She paused, then went on sadly, "Besides, shipboard romances never last."

"I guess that's why Mrs. Paton was pretty quick coming up to the homestead from Melbourne. She's waiting for the moment when Grant and this girl realise that here you can't see the moon rising over the Indian Ocean from a ship's deck."

"When the full moon rises over the paddocks on a clear night it makes the plain look like the sea. I've often thought it. I wish they'd hurry up and get married."

"Who? Gaylie or this one?"

"This one. Elizabeth's her name. I like her. And the children up at the school are all crazy about her."

"My Ben's gone into Endall with the wagon to pick up Gaylie off the day's plane. Grant and this Elizabeth will have to hurry up."

There was a nodding of heads and more than one pair of eyes turned wistfully out of the window and looked down to

the creek bed where flashes of white showed where the children, with Elizabeth, were playing between the trees.

When school was over and the children had gone back to
their cottages Elizabeth walked slowly up the length of the
square towards the homestead garden. She was tired and hot.
The sun was still high and the evening chill had not yet
settled on the land. Looking at the early budding bougain-
villæa that climbed over the roof of the storehouse, and the
brilliant shouting red of the poinsettias in the garden itself,
then out to the grey-green empty vastness of the plain, Elizabeth thought what a strange country of contrasts it was. So
little colour in that endless plain, so much in the big exotic
flowers. So hot in the daytime and so icy cold at night; so
friendly as with the children and Old Flinty and Maria; so
remote and unapproachable as with Grant and Mrs. Jarvis.

All the same there had been some chord between herself
and Mrs. Jarvis that had been touched! What it was Elizabeth did not know. All she did know was that when it had
been touched it had set up frail echoes of warmth and kind-
liness.

Elizabeth refused to think about Aunt Mollie at all.

She went through the garden to the side veranda and in
through a door to her own room. She noticed the station
wagon standing, one door open, before the front entrance.
She wondered if there was a visitor.

Once in her own room she stripped off her dress and picking up her towel and soap-box padded barefooted, in her slip,
into the bathroom.

After she had had a shower she came back into her room,
picked out a pretty slim-line dress of an aquamarine colour
that she had not yet worn, and slipped into it. In her bare
feet she stood looking at herself in the mirror, twisting and
turning so she could see the belt low down on the back. She
liked the hint of her own slim figure outlined by the clever
cut of the dress. While the blouse seemed to envelop her like
an elegant pillowcase, it was very smart.

The thought made Elizabeth laugh. Who ever heard of a
pillowcase looking elegant? Yet, somehow, she knew that her
dress was just that. The loose cut did not make her look big
at all. On the contrary she looked a frail lost thing inside it.
This was very fashionable and therefore very satisfactory.

Something gay was bubbling inside her. Was it the dress or was it the shoes . . . taper-toed and tiny-heeled . . . that made her feel this way? Or the fact she had never worn aquamarine as a colour before and it made her skin very fair and her lips seem redder, and the roses in her cheeks really to bloom? It made her eyes sparkle too. For there was nothing else that Elizabeth could think of which would suddenly so light up her face.

Beautiful clothes and the brave colours so suitable to this country of brilliant sunshine had made a different person of her surely.

She liked looking at herself in the long glass on the wall.

There was something more than colour and cut to her dress. There was some tiny intangible thing on which she could not put her finger that not only made her feel happy but *look* happy.

She hoped that Grant would like her new dress and that when he took the usual drink to her in the sitting-room before dinner he would be content that his "temporary fiancée" looked the part. Somehow, Elizabeth thought, her new dress deserved to win a look of recognition from Grant.

Perhaps he was too accustomed to looking at elegant young women born in the Jarvis "circle"!

She slipped Mrs. Jarvis's ring on her finger and held out her hand to look at it. It too was sparkling. She picked up a silver linked bracelet Ralph had given her on her eighteenth birthday and walked over to the window to clasp it on where she could see to do it by the light.

Three people had come through the side garden gate. They were laughing and talking together. They stopped by a saddled horse tethered to the veranda rail. Aunt Mollie, Maria Bolton and Gaylie Paton! Gaylie wore a small-brimmed casual hat that crinkled round the edges of the brim and because of its very casualness was utterly charming. What the others wore Elizabeth did not see, for she could not take her eyes from Gaylie.

Unconsciously she clasped the bracelet around her wrist.

Gaylie stood, one hand on Grant's horse, and at that moment he too came between the shrubs and trees of the garden to where the three women stood.

He lifted the horse's bridle from the hook on the rail and as he did so he smiled at Gaylie. It was a smile that was half-amused and half-amusing. Gaylie tilted up her face and smiled and talked.

. Elizabeth stood looking out of the window at the group.

Then Grant turned his horse's head to lead him away. Aunt Mollie and Maria left them and came up the veranda steps. Grant moved away, leading his horse, with Gaylie walking beside him.

All the time, till they were lost between the trees and beyond the garden boundary, Gaylie's head was upturned to Grant's. His was turned down to hers. Elizabeth could see only the back of his hat so she did not know if that stern face had relaxed at all. She only knew he had walked away with Gaylie on some mission that concerned them both and which left the rest of the world out.

Far out over the plain the sun sank quietly down to the horizon. It hovered there, a red ball. Then half a ball, then only a tiny crimson arc. The whole western sky was massed with colours so brilliant they hurt the heart as well as the eyes.

Elizabeth, still standing with one hand on her braceleted wrist, watched the sun go down, and wondered was it the colours after all that hurt her where her heart was beating first spasmodically then painfully.

The sun disappeared altogether and the light went out of the world. When Gaylie walked away with Grant the joy that had been in Elizabeth because of her dress and her shoes and the pink roses in her cheeks went out too.

She straightened her shoulders and went back to the mirror.

"Well, at least I look the part," she said soberly. "On that count Gaylie cannot put me out of countenance."

She looked down at the bracelet on her arm and slowly unclasped it and let it drop on the dressing-table.

"Now I am punished," she said, only half understanding what she meant herself.

Then suddenly she turned and went over to the small table beside her bed and took a writing tablet and her fountain pen from the drawer. She drew up a small chair and sat down.

"Dear Ralph . . ." she wrote on the clear white sheet of paper, then sat looking at it.

Why can't I write *"Darling* Ralph"? Why has he never given me the right to write *"Darling* Ralph"?

Fiercely she wrote it twice and stabbed the pen in the paper. Then she tore the sheet from the tablet and screwed it up into a ball in her hand. She put her head down on her hands and wept.

There was a tiny knock at the door but Elizabeth did not hear it. After a minute the door was opened and Aunt Mollie came into the room.

"Why, Elizabeth . . ." she said. "My dear child. What is the matter?"

Elizabeth sat up straight, her back still to the door. She unclenched her hand and let fall the small ball of crumpled writing paper. Then she turned round and began to rise.

"Oh . . . Aunt Mollie. I'm so sorry. Yes, I have been having a little weep but it's only a touch of homesickness. Please promise me you won't say anything. If you'll excuse me I'll just go into the bathroom and bathe my eyes."

She escaped into the bathroom and stood leaning against the door. Then she braced her shoulders and went to the wash bowl.

Inside the room Aunt Mollie picked up the crumpled ball of paper and smoothed it out.

"Dear Ralph," she read. Then underneath it in scrawling writing that looked as if the pen had jabbed into the paper were written the words *"Darling Ralph."*

Aunt Mollie's expression had not changed. It was still as it had ever been, carefully sweet with a small polite smile on lips that parted but teeth that did not. Her eyes were a pale smiling investigating blue. She folded up the piece of paper and slipped it down the neck of her very elegant black lace dinner frock. She crossed over to the bathroom door.

"Take your time, dear," she said. "I promise not to breathe a word. Don't mind shedding a tear or two . . . we all do it some time or other. In fact I'd be surprised if you didn't . . . considering the circumstances."

With that she went back through Elizabeth's room and out into the passage beyond.

At dinner that night Gaylie wore an embossed floral brocade dress in rich shades of gold and pink. It fitted her as if it had been melted on to her. Her fair hair made Elizabeth think, not for the first time, of spun gold; her golden tanned skin was flawless and her eyes and mouth were made up so expertly only another girl would have known they were made up at all.

Elizabeth, who had had a shopping expedition amongst the West End stores of London and Melbourne, knew that Gaylie, besides being lovely in a most enviable way, was also very, very expensive.

Beauty with Gaylie was more a spearhead for invasion than an armour. Never had Elizabeth seen anywhere anyone whose manners were so convincingly charming as were Gaylie's manners that night. In an effortless way, she stole the scene. She kept everyone interested, including Mrs. Jarvis and Elizabeth herself and she did not once appear to be forcing that interest.

She was a beautiful young woman, beautifully dressed, completely natural.

Grant's eyes, inimical and unrevealing, seldom left her face. When Elizabeth thought about this she realised that for that matter everybody's eyes were held by Gaylie.

Deep down Elizabeth's feminine instinct told her it was all an "act." But then what was her own part but an "act"? Again she felt that odd concern for Grant. Was there no one, who circled in his particular orbit, genuine? Not even in the *private* lives of great or rich people was there anyone who could afford to be simply himself. Everyone had a part to play and it was their business in life not to be caught out missing a cue or muffing a line. Otherwise they might be dropped from this precious circle that ensured for them prestige and social consequence.

In the sitting-room first, then afterwards at the dinner table, Gaylie kept the company amused by anecdotes of someone called Julien. Who this Julien was Elizabeth did not know until Aunt Mollie, with an impatient gesture, said:

"Really, Gaylie, I can't understand why you don't give Julien walking orders and be done with it. As far as I am concerned he is just too tiresome."

"Oh, he's useful," said Gaylie, then added sorrowfully, "Poor Julien."

"Yes, I think so too," said Mrs. Jarvis, who rarely spoke

and when she did her words seemed to have some profound meaning which at the moment was not quite clear.

"He's a pet all the same," said Gaylie unexpectedly.

Mrs. Paton quickly looked across the table at her daughter and there was an infinitesimal movement of her head which was a caution not to continue on the subject of Julien. Julien, whoever he was, was evidently taboo in Jarvis circles.

Gaylie laughed and looked down the table towards Grant. "When are we going to Barrli, Grant?" she said, changing the subject. "I never come to Kybarrli without being taken on that little jaunt, you know. I wouldn't miss it for the world."

"It is a dust bowl at this time of the year," said Grant. "And you won't get the comforts of Kybarrli. But I'm going across for a few days after the Governor's visit."

"Goody, goody. I shall put on an old-fashioned dust-coat, two layers of eye-veiling, and do some high riding amongst your cattle thieves out there."

"Why cattle thieves?" asked Grant, unperturbed. He crumbled his bread with one hand and watched Gaylie's face with a mild amused interest.

"Darling, you must know that last time I went to Barrli every stockman on the place wanted to throw his shirt down on the mud road for me to step across that lake. Only, of course, it will be dust now and not mud, won't it?" She looked at him archly. "I didn't mean they were thieving cattle . . . only hearts. Mine in particular." She looked across the table at Elizabeth. "You haven't been to Grant's cattle station, Elizabeth, so you don't know what it means to be the only girl in a bunch of women-haters. I never had so much fun in my life as winning them all over . . . one at a time."

"Is that what you did, Gaylie?" Mrs. Jarvis asked politely.

"They offered me their hearts . . . one at a time. Grant! You're not listening to me. I won them all, didn't I? They would have done anything for me by the time I left, wouldn't they?"

Grant appeared to think about this for a moment.

"Yes," he said at length. "I think that is just what did happen. You have quite a way with you, Gaylie."

Gaylie clapped her hands in a little affected gesture of delight.

"Oh, you do sound serious. I believe you were jealous."

It was then that Elizabeth knew that Gaylie's act was not only for Grant but very much for herself. Elizabeth had been a success on Kybarrli with the children but Gaylie wanted Elizabeth to know, and Grant to remember, that she too could be a success with the staff. That was the first quality Grant's wife would have to have . . . an ability to win the approval and respect of the staff. Gaylie had made a game of this table conversation, but she had also made her point.

Mrs. Jarvis, who did not think it was very good manners for one person to monopolise the table conversation, turned her head towards Elizabeth.

"I would not suggest your going to Barrli at this stage, Elizabeth. The station is a very desolate place in the dry season and you don't ride, do you? That is something that should be attended to before you go to Barrli."

"I will do whatever you and Grant think is best advised," Elizabeth said. "But it sounds a rather exciting place."

"Oh, Elizabeth!" said Gaylie. "Are *you* interested in all those womenless men too?"

"Maria Bolton is there most of the time," said Mrs. Jarvis quietly.

"Yes, but she *mothers* them. You weren't thinking of mothering anyone, were you, Elizabeth? Unless it's the children down at the school." She put her head on one side and pretended to examine Elizabeth kindly. "Yes," she said at length as if she had come to a final assessment of Elizabeth. "I believe you're the care-taking type. Darling, don't go to Barrli. You wouldn't like it."

Oddly this all sounded as if the people at Barrli wouldn't like it.

Gaylie was very clever. Elizabeth almost wished Grant would give up trying to preserve his privacy and would marry Gaylie forthwith. It would save everyone such a lot of effort and it would all be the same in the end. Yet the thought made her feel infinitely sad and she had to bend all her mental efforts for the rest of the evening to appear pleasant and cheerful.

She made conversation with Mrs. Jarvis, and with Aunt Mollie and Gaylie too. Though, when she smiled, she included Grant in that smile, she made no effort to break through his wall of reticence. Gaylie, she thought, could make that effort with competence and grace and not have a conscience about it. Grant at the table was polished and polite, but just a little formidable. Even to Gaylie he was not entirely approachable.

CHAPTER FIFTEEN

FOUR DAYS LATER when the Governor came into the district Elizabeth saw the aspect of the hard-headed man of action that she had glimpsed in Grant on that last day on the ship.

She was so caught up in the whirl of activities that for the next three days she had little time to think of Gaylie except to feel conscious of her presence.

First, the stockmen and staff of Kybarrli were given the day off to ride or drive into Endall for the arrival of His Excellency's plane. Maria Bolton had told her that it would be a holiday. Everyone in Endall would keep up the jollification until all hours of the night.

The children were not to leave the station for the outing, as they were to have their special celebrations when His Excellency arrived at Kybarrli.

Mr. Rolfe, the schoolteacher, was in a very fever of preparation. He had to stage a children's welcome for the Governor and had to have all his school work up to date to satisfy the School Superintendent. Mrs. Good was not fully recovered from a very nasty bout of gastric influenza and Elizabeth felt she could not desert Mr. Rolfe on the day of days.

"Grant . . ." she said, meeting him at the homestead end of the square the morning before the Governor was to land at Endall. "Do you have a very prominent part to play when the Governor lands in the town? I mean, is it one of those occasions when you have to have me with you?"

"No," he replied shortly. "I'll be one of the landowners introduced to him at the airfield. Why do you ask?"

Elizabeth was a little embarrassed.

"It seems," she said, "that when you take a dose of small children it's like poison. You've taken it . . . and then you've got it." She smiled at him hopefully. "Perhaps I shouldn't

have gone near the school in the first place but since I have
—they seem to need me." She said the last few words in a
hesitating manner for fear Grant would think she had big
ideas about herself.

"You mean Rolfe wants you to take care of the small
children while he irons out the rest of his troubles? What are
they, exactly?"

"The Union Jack at the moment," said Elizabeth. "It seems
that when the Governor is in residence it is the Union Jack
and not the Australian flag that is flown. The school
Union Jack disappeared and just an hour ago it was discovered
that the lubra who does the school cleaning thought she would
like it for her bedspread. I've rescued it but it has to be
washed . . . and I'm afraid mended here and there. And
someone has to mind the small children while all the mothers
go in to Endall. Nobody wants to stay home and miss the
fun."

Grant was looking down at her with a faintly quizzical expression in his eyes.

"What about you? Do you want to miss the fun?"

"I've been travelling and seeing different countries. Some
of the stockmen's wives have never been away from the
district all their lives. If I could mind the children . . ."

"Do you *mind* mending flags and minding children, and
worrying whether the stockmen's wives have a good time or
not?" There was a mild curiosity in his eyes.

"I'd like to do it. But I do know my first responsibility is
to you. It is whatever you wish me to do . . ."

"My wishes are that this show is well run," Grant said
abruptly. "The school is an Education Department affair but
it's on my property and I want that end of the reception well
run. If they need you at the school you'd better make arrangements to assist them."

"And you?" Elizabeth asked with hesitation. "You won't
be needing me?"

Grant's mouth seemed to clamp down in its straight line
and his face darkened.

"In my experience there is no one person in this world
who is indispensable," he said abruptly. "If I need you I'll tell
you. In the meantime let Mr. Rolfe know you are available
if that is what you wish."

Elizabeth was about to turn away when she caught again

the expression in his eyes. He had thought she was not looking at him and it was quite several seconds before he let that habitual shade fall over his face. The look in his eyes was tired—and disappointed. Was it because she wasn't as polished for her role as Gaylie Paton? It was the only time Elizabeth had seen Grant's eyes showing that kind of human emotion.

"Grant . . ." Elizabeth said. "If you think I should go into Endall with you . . ."

His eyes showed no feeling now. They were indifferent.

"I've three women . . . my mother, my aunt and Gaylie . . . as well as the entire staff and distaff of Kybarrli to accompany me into Endall. As I said before, no one person is indispensable."

There was a shortness in his tone. Elizabeth's pride was stiffening. She thought she knew what he meant by saying no one person was indispensable in this world. He had loved Thera and he was aware that life on his station went on just the same even though Thera was gone. He was aware that Gaylie was as gay and Aunt Mollie as carefully avaricious for the Jarvis name and Jarvis fortune as if Thera had never been born. Even Thera had been dispensable.

He was bitter . . . with a cold hard bitterness.

Elizabeth let the stiffness flow out of her. She smiled briefly where a moment before she would have looked at him in the same frozen way that he looked at her.

"You want the school's part in the reception to be well done," she said quietly. "I promise you it shall be. If I can take the little ones off Mr. Rolfe's hands, he will work wonders. He's that kind of person."

His eyes softened a shade.

"Thank you," he said. He turned away and went off down the square towards the garages.

Elizabeth turned back to the homestead. Inside the garden Gaylie was standing before the aviary talking to the cockatoos. As Elizabeth came through the gate Gaylie half turned and smiled. It was a cool appraising smile.

"You and Grant seem to do your courting in public," she said with a laugh. "If you can call that recent conversation of yours—courting. I've never seen such a circumspect pair. Off to bed every night without even five minutes alone in the garden. Or is it too cold for you, Elizabeth? Oh, I forgot. You are used to cold, aren't you?"

"It's a different kind of cold in England," Elizabeth said. "And we don't have the glorious hot sunshine in the middle of a winter's day, of course."

"Call this hot? Goodness, you are in for some education *if you stay here long enough.*"

"Do you mean I might be intimidated by the summer heat?" Elizabeth asked, carefully avoiding the meaning in the tail end of Gaylie's remark.

"It can be a hundred and eight in the shade." Gaylie put her head on one side and smiled her amused smile. "But somehow I don't see you staying long enough to test your endurance. Why don't you admit your affair with Grant was a shipboard romance . . . and as quickly over, Elizabeth? You needn't feel embarrassed about it. We all understand, and are really awfully sympathetic . . ."

Elizabeth was at a loss for words. She was incapable of plain undiluted lying. She was trying to think of something to say that would parry Gaylie's words and leave the situation as it was before she had come through the garden gate.

"You know, you blush so easily," Gaylie said merrily. "It's quite a pretty trick and I imagine must have been your most attractive quality when Grant first met you. It's many a year since Grant had anything to do with the blushing kind. Oh, don't look as if I've said something hurtful. I'm really trying to open your eyes. And Elizabeth . . ." She made a pretty little gesture with her hand. "I am your friend, you know."

Elizabeth went to walk away but Gaylie with a quick skipping step joined her.

"I'm sorry," Gaylie said contritely. "I didn't mean to be hurtful. Just my silly way. All the same, Grant is a very knowledgeable and sophisticated man, so don't think of marrying him while you still believe that birds and bees are pretty things that are never cruel to one another. Come, you must have learned nature study in school, too?"

"I don't understand what nature study has got to do with talking to Grant outside the storehouse," Elizabeth said carefully.

"It all leads to human nature," Gaylie said. They had reached the veranda steps and Gaylie stopped with one foot on the first step. "Grant's a man. Understand? You must have known what he was doing in Italy when Thera was killed in that motor accident. They'd been travelling together. A man with Grant's experience generally asks for something more than a cool greeting in the morning and a perfunctory farewell at night time. And Grant *is* an experienced man, you know."

Elizabeth went cold with anger.

"However you may feel about Grant . . . and what manner of man he is," she said quietly, "you should not say that about your own sister. Especially when she can never defend herself."

Gaylie gave a short laugh.

"Thera never attempted to defend herself. She let the whole world know what she did. She flaunted it. If she wanted to travel across Europe with her fiancé she didn't care who knew. Look, Elizabeth, I don't want to hurt you. I like you. It's because I like you I don't want to see you disillusioned. I bet you're not game to tell the truth. You don't really know what Grant is like, do you? You're about as near to him as the South Pole, aren't you? You don't *know* what he can be like as a lover, do you?"

"I think Grant is the most striking man I've ever met," Elizabeth said steadily for want of knowing what else to say.

"Oh, ho!" said Gaylie. "There isn't a young woman who's met him who hasn't said that. But it's the attraction the distant hills have for the traveller, isn't it?"

Elizabeth looked puzzled.

"What has the traveller to do with it?"

"Well, that's just what you were, you know. You were travelling out here to Australia when you met Grant. What sort of a person you were, I can't imagine, that you forgot your former sweetheart for someone you couldn't possibly have got to know closely. Grant rarely lets anyone know him closely. What did you do it for, Elizabeth? What did you engage yourself to Grant for? Even though he's attractive you already had someone you were tied to."

"Gaylie," Elizabeth said quietly, "would you mind telling me how you know about any former sweetheart of mine?"

Gaylie ran lightly up the steps.

"I want to see Grant marry someone of his own kind. Someone who is just as sophisticated as he is . . . and as worldly. And I like you. You're a pet of a girl really. But you wouldn't be happy here. As for your sweetheart . . ."

She laughed. "Even the Elizabeths of the world sometimes talk in their sleep, you know. Would his name be *Ralph*?"

Elizabeth mounted the steps slowly. She didn't know how Gaylie knew about Ralph. Could Dr. Jarvis have told her when they landed from the *Albany*? But surely not. What she had told Dr. Jarvis was in confidence and surely that professional ear was as sacrosanct as the confessional box. Besides, it had been Dr. Jarvis's fun-making that had first led to this situation. He hadn't been in favour of Gaylie Paton as Grant's future wife. He'd been against her. Probably a medical man's dislike of too much inter-marrying amongst families.

She herself couldn't possibly afford to have an open breach with Gaylie. It would make the situation in the homestead impossible. And vaguely she felt she would be letting Grant down if she was the cause of dissension.

"You are very kind, Gaylie," she said. "Thank you for all your warnings. I'm sure you have offered them in my interest."

Elizabeth's hand was on the veranda post and Gaylie put out her own hand and patted it.

"Elizabeth," she said softly, "just let me know if you get too homesick. I'll fix Grant . . . and Aunt Bessie, too. I'll make it easy for you." She now clasped her hand in the crook of Elizabeth's arm and walked along the veranda with her. "You know, you and I've got an awful lot in common really. We like things *neat*. No raggle-taggle ends. Everybody understands about homesickness. And this country really is terribly empty and big and strange for someone who's lived all her life within five miles of the heart of a great city. How some of those English stockmen's wives make out I just don't know. They pay an awful price in loneliness. Well, darling, if you want to go any time . . . there's your perfect excuse. Homesickness! It's so understandable. And of course . . ." She looked up at Elizabeth with a laugh. "And so true, isn't it?"

They had reached the door leading into the east passage and so to Elizabeth's own room. Elizabeth turned away so Gaylie wouldn't see the tears glistening in her eyes.

"Thank you, Gaylie. Your advice is excellent," Elizabeth said.

She released her arm and turned into the passage. She walked quickly towards her room.

The words "homesick" and "Ralph" had been the key words in Gaylie's discourse. Aunt Mollie had come in and found her, Elizabeth crying and she had excused herself by saying she was homesick. She had been about to write a letter to Ralph.

Well, at least, they had very clearly shown their hands. Gaylie had literally invited Elizabeth to go, and had kindly provided her with the suitable excuses. The only thing that Gaylie hadn't known was that Elizabeth was going in any case. What would have happened, she wondered, if she had truly loved Grant, truly been engaged to marry him? Oddly enough, for a peaceable girl, Elizabeth felt she would have made a clean sweep of Gaylie . . . somehow.

As it was, she had no real status in the house and so had had to suffer Gaylie's friendly ministrations in silence. Even so, Gaylie's revelations about Grant's love affair with Thera did have a painful impact. This queer aching love Elizabeth felt for that remote man Grant Jarvis must be the love of *loyalty*, and an honest compassion for one who she knew stood alone in a sea of people all of whom held out their hands, palms upwards.

When she had gone home, and he had married Gaylie—or whoever it was who won in the competition for his name, money and family—he would go on remaining for ever alone. He would never know if anyone loved him for his own sake, even if they did.

Yes. One had to have compassion for a very rich man.

The following day Kybarrli was deserted. The only people left in the huge environs of the homestead were some old natives in a cottage down by the creek, a ninety year old stockman who was living out his last days dozing in the sunshine, Elizabeth, the schoolmaster and the school children.

The day was sunny and still and the children, in the absence of their elders, were able to run helter-skelter all over the square and play dodging games around the storehouse, the garages and the smithy.

The Union Jack had been rescued, washed and mended. Elizabeth assisted Mr. Rolfe in attaching it to its right cords and rehearsing the group of children who were to break it the moment the Governor stepped out of the car that would bring him to the homestead.

Already Elizabeth and everyone else in the district had their gilt-edged invitation on which was printed the vice-regal command to attend His Excellency's reception on Kybarrli. The menus for the Kybarrli dinner party to procede the Governor's function had been discussed. Beautiful old silver and linen had been brought out and orders for its use given. Several more lubras had been brought up to the homestead and put through their paces as house assistants.

In the evening the house party came back late in a fleet of cars. They were tired and dust-covered. Elizabeth herself had seen that a light buffet meal was waiting for them.

Only Gaylie was bright. She recounted everything they had seen and done as if "poor Elizabeth" had been Cinderella waiting at home to hear at second-hand the doings of her elders and betters. Elizabeth, in the pantry shepherding the one lubra who had returned with the homestead party, felt relieved when she saw Grant stalk out of the dining-room and go down the long passage to his office. She heard the click of his door closing. She didn't want to hear herself obliquely portrayed in the role of Cinderella before Grant.

She turned round to find Mrs. Jarvis standing in the door-way. Even tired as she must be, Mrs. Jarvis was still well-groomed, impeccably dressed and very upright. Her small feet in their quaint old-fashioned shoes of beautiful fine leather were as ever placed side by side as if Mrs. Jarvis had always been taught, from earliest childhood, to stand with her feet together.

There was no change in the expression in her face yet her words were unexpectedly kind.

"Elizabeth," she said gently. "We missed you."

Elizabeth flushed.

"That is nice of you to say so, Mrs. Jarvis. But there was so much to do down at the school . . ."

"I know, my dear. But I want you to know we missed you." She paused. "Grant missed you." Then before Elizabeth could catch her breath Mrs. Jarvis turned and went back to the dining-room.

Now what did she mean by that? wondered Elizabeth. Grant, with the lift of his little finger, could command the attention and service of anyone for a thousand miles around. He even had a great firm like Small and Smallwoods wooing him. How could he miss any one individual? He himself had said any one individual was dispensable.

In the morning the first person to arrive at Kybarrli for the celebrations was Old Flinty. He was brought out from Endall in a specially constructed station wagon that was sprung to carry a very sick person as safely as an ambulance.

Old Flinty was lifted out by several of the station hands and carried to a place in the garden, near the path leading to the main door. Yesterday Elizabeth had wondered what that small awning had been erected for. Now she knew. Grant had long since arranged that if Old Flinty was capable of the journey from the district hospital in Endall, he was coming home for the festivities. Grant was human, after all. Elizabeth found it difficult to sort out the contradictions of his personality.

Everyone was dressed ready for the great moment. Far down the home paddock the stockmen were riding about, cracking their whips and occasionally dismounting to give a piece of leather work on their saddles an extra polish. The Black Riders were waiting beside their mounts at the marshalling point behind the stables. Down at the school there were smiling polished faces . . . Such clean pants and shirts on the boys! Such gay coloured dresses on the girls!

Now, one felt, if only His Excellency would come!

Elizabeth returned from the school to the garden where others of the house party were waiting ready. Tea was being served to the visitors from a neighbouring station who had been invited to join the Kybarrli house party.

Mrs. Jarvis was as cool, dignified and unperturbed as if she was about to sit down to a routine morning tea-party.

Elizabeth sat on a garden stool by Old Flinty's bed. She watched Mrs. Jarvis standing under a tree near the gate and talking in quiet composed tones to Aunt Mollie. Aunt Mollie looked exceedingly fashionable in a light suit with a straight cut jacket and skirt and an exotic hat, small and completely covered with tiny roses. She might have just stepped out of the Menzies Hotel, Melbourne.

Gaylie, too, had achieved a kind of dazzling Melbourne smartness with an elegant biscuit coloured suit, and hat, handbag and shoes in a matching blue. Mrs. Jarvis was simply dressed in black with a small black hat on her well-groomed head.

Looking at the three of them there was still no doubt in Elizabeth's mind which was the great lady. Mrs. Jarvis, tiny, erect, correct, was the essence of the châtelaine of a great estate.

Elizabeth was glad she herself had dressed in something simple. It was a blue-grey dress with a white hat that had a drooping bow at one side, and white handbag and shoes. She had seen the look of approval in Mrs. Jarvis's eyes, and that was sufficient compliment.

She sat talking to Old Flinty while they waited.

Grant was outside the homestead gate waiting with Tim Bolton and the overseer. He was dressed as an outback station owner and not as if he was going to the Melbourne Cup. Yet every inch of him was distinguished.

"As long as I can catch a glimpse of His Ex.," Old Flinty said, "I'll be satisfied. I served with him in Flanders. Cripes, that was a heck of a long time ago. Forty-three years."

"Is the Governor the same age as you, Flinty?"

"Don't take account of how old people look outback. You can take ten years off my face. It's the sun in summer and the frosts in winter what puts these wrinkles on my old dial."

Elizabeth laughed.

"I wasn't thinking of what you looked like, Flinty. It's just that they call you 'Old Flinty.' Now why is that?"

The old stockman turned his head on his pillow and winked.

"It's the old-timers who carry all the weight when you're over the borders or north of Twenty-six," he said. "The young 'uns always ask the old-timers for advice. A shrewd man who wants to run his cattle team or sheep flock gets as old as he can as quick as he can. That's the way to keep the young fellas in their place."

Flinty turned his head the other way, and looked down the path towards Grant.

"You take Grant," he said. "When his father sent him up to me to learn the north-west tracks you never saw such a cocksure young shaver as he was. I soon knocked that out of him by sending him up the track on his own. He took his own advice and not mine, so got good and lost. No water and the temperature at a hundred and ten. After that he always come and ask Old Flinty."

Flinty winked again.

"Learning the hard way. That was his father's line. Mine too. That's why he sent Grant up to me to get broken in."

"What was he doing exactly? I mean, what was his job?"

"All the dirty jobs first. Off-sider to the camp cook. If you knew the outback droving tracks, young lady, you'd know that's the lowest of the jobs in the plant. Then I worked him up to off-sider to the leaders. His on-side mate was the toughest and hardest stockman in the north. He cracked the whip over young Grant's head many a time."

"You mean Grant worked as a camp cook and a subordinate kind of stockman? I always thought he had refused to learn his work as a jackaroo."

Old Flinty laughed.

"Jackarooing's the gentleman's way of doing it. Dinner in the homestead every night. I guess after two years with my plant in the Territory, Grant didn't want any softy's job. He knew how tough life can be working in the ranks."

"Oh!" Elizabeth looked down and picked at an imaginary thread on her gloves.

"Did you think he was born up here as Boss Cocky and went on being Boss Cocky all his life?" asked Flinty. "You didn't know his father! Old Grant Jarvis was a ruthless, hard old man. Hardness was a vice with him, like whisky is with some kinds. The only thing I don't forgive him was he never gave that boy . . . or anyone else for that matter . . . any affection. He had a stone for a heart. A raking stone dug right out from under the South Pole."

Flinty lifted his head from the pillow and looked to where Mrs. Jarvis was standing under the trees.

"A great little lady that," he said. "She learned to do without affection. But I sometimes think she kinda hankers for Grant to have what she missed. Not that she'd ever show it. Stoical like." He looked back at Elizabeth. "She never said a word . . . but she never liked that engagement to Thera Paton. But she's law-abiding and her husband said that's how it had to go. So she stuck by him. His word was law. But she never liked it. I could see it in her eye."

"I don't quite understand . . ." Elizabeth said with hesitation. "Why did Grant do as he was told—if that was all it was? He's too strong-minded surely ever to have been the knuckling down kind, Flinty."

"Pride," said Flinty. "The pride of Lucifer. They've all got it. Mrs. Mollie, over there. Gaylie. A host of 'em scattered round the whole country—rich and poor, wherever you find a Jarvis with that or any other name, you find him stiff with pride. The Paton family too . . . and a dozen others . . ." Old Flinty shook his head. "Terrible pity," he said. "That way they don't come by too much happiness, even if they do belong to the reigning family of Jarvis. Anyhow, Miss Thera's out of the picture now and I guess things'll turn out all right for Grant, after all."

Elizabeth looked at Old Flinty intently.

"Why do you say that?" she asked.

"He's got you. You're the first loving heart that's broke into this family in two generations."

Elizabeth felt a faint colour stealing up her cheeks. She liked Old Flinty's compliment. Her heart warmed to it. But once again she had to be the deceiver. She could not explain to this faithful old man that she stood in somebody else's shoes. She never could make up her mind whether she stood in Thera's shoes or Gaylie's. Whose ever they were they fitted her ill. As Old Flinty had said, she had been meant to love . . . and none of the Jarvises were like that. They were all takers. Even Grant, when you came to think of it. He had taken her services as a sort of *quid pro quo* for what he would do for Small and Smallwoods. The only really kind thing she had seen him do was this service of bringing Old Flinty out to the homestead for the celebrations.

Still, it was something. His heart wouldn't be like his father's, *all* stone.

She wished she knew the answer to the riddle of Thera. Why had Mrs. Jarvis not been happy about the engagement? What, after all, did it have to do with her, Elizabeth Heaton? She found it tiresome to keep muddling herself up with the idea she really was Grant's fiancée. She even felt, on occasions, pangs of jealousy as if she had a *right* to have them.

There was a cloud of dust away down the track and a stirring amongst the stockmen everywhere. At the gate, Grant, Tim Bolton, and the overseer straightened themselves. Mrs. Jarvis and the ladies waiting in the garden began to move towards the gate. Elizabeth stood up to join them. Mrs. Jarvis put her neatly-gloved hand on Elizabeth's arm.

"You take precedence because you are Grant's fiancée."

Her quiet blue eyes rested on Elizabeth's face. They seemed to hold no expression yet once again Elizabeth felt as if there had been some communion. It gave her confidence and re-assurance.

I believe she does know, thought Elizabeth. And she wants me to stay this way . . . engaged to Grant. Oh, I wish I knew *why*. And for how long.

Mrs. Jarvis kept her hand lightly on Elizabeth's arm as they went to the gate.

Grant turned and then moved a little to the left so that his mother might stand next to him. Tim and the overseer went farther down the line, past Aunt Mollie and Gaylie, to the right.

Grant appraised them all, his face like his mother's, ex-pressionless. This, Elizabeth knew, was the crowning moment of the whole play she had had to enact from the time the *Albany* berthed at Fremantle until she left again for Eng-land. She had to look and behave as a great lady, born to step into Mrs. Jarvis's place. She glanced at Mrs. Jarvis's straight back and imperceptibly her own straightened. She must remember to keep her chin tilted up as she curtsied. She had practised it relentlessly to the dressing-table, the full length mirror on her wall and even to the door every time she passed in and out of her room. She was quite sure she would go on practising deep curtsies to Kybarrli furniture for weeks to come. It had become a habit.

The three cars in the Governor's entourage rounded the curve by the gum trees at the end of the homestead fence.

Mrs. Jarvis put her right hand on Elizabeth's arm.

"You will take my place, please, Elizabeth," she said quietly. She stepped back and waited for Elizabeth to take the two steps to stand next to Grant.

Elizabeth could not possibly query the decision or expostu-late. His Excellency's car was already slowing down to a stop. She must not disturb the serene appearance of that waiting welcoming line. She simply moved up quietly by Grant's side and Mrs. Jarvis now stood on her right, as she herself stood on Grant's right.

Grant gave her a searching, flickering glance. Elizabeth's chin went up.

Funny . . . but she never felt better in her life. She was on stage now and a new pride poured through her blood-stream. Her head was high, her smile was happy and serene. As Grant received His Excellency and then presented Elizabeth she sank down into a curtsy which was as graceful as it was easy. And there was the largest twinkle in His Excellency's eyes that she had ever seen.

When it was Gaylie's turn to curtsy Elizabeth knew that her own choice of dress had been the better, after all. A curtsy in a full skirt is a thing of grace. In a tight straight skirt it is something quite different. One trembled for the seams. If the tight skirt was not a success Gaylie's conversation was very much so. His Excellency remembered her from some reception at Government House and now they stood, with Grant, and chatted about this occasion. When His Excellency turned to inspect the Riders it was Gaylie, still chatting like a like-able bird, who accompanied him.

What might have been a ceremony too stilted was now made easy and natural by the manner in which Gaylie displayed the splendour of the mounted stockmen. Even Grant was smiling and presently the stockmen too were all showing their big shining white teeth in their polished black faces. The Governor was enjoying himself immensely.

Elizabeth had to admire Gaylie. She carried the whole situation with an air of happy comradeship and His Excellency was enjoying himself and so were Tim and the Black Riders. Grant, too, obviously won by the enchanting figure that Gaylie was cutting, had a relaxed air and joined in the general atmosphere of enjoyment.

Then when the Riders wheeled away to do their exhibition riding Gaylie came back to join the others by the gate. With a faint lift of one shoulder and a tiny flick of one eyebrow she made it clear it had all been as easy as sliding cakes off a plate. The little glance she gave Elizabeth under her lashes implied that she had helped Elizabeth out . . . you see how easy it is when you know how . . . kind of thing.

Grant, walking to the paddock fence on which he and Tim Bolton and the Governor now leaned their arms, looked quite a different person. Once when he looked round he had that rare shining quality in his smile.

Yes, Elizabeth thought, Gaylie has the "know-how." Grant is indebted to her. I suppose I should have gone forward like that. But I'm sure I couldn't have done it the way Gaylie did it.

While the stockmen entertained His Excellency Mrs. Jarvis took her party back through the gate to join the others in the garden.

Gaylie was immensely pleased with herself and looked it. The other guests clustered around her and wanted to know, "What did you say to him, Gaylie? What's he like? What did he say?" and of course, frequently, "Oh, Gaylie, you were wonderful." To which Gaylie replied, laughing:

"Rubbish! I've talked to His Excellency hordes of times before . . . I know him so well."

"What would you like me to do now, Mrs. Jarvis?" Elizabeth asked quietly.

"Will you make sure the tea is ready on the veranda? Perhaps you will take charge of the tea for His Excellency when he comes in . . ."

"Do you think that Gaylie could handle it better?"

"No, my dear. I have other duties for Gaylie."

With that Mrs. Jarvis turned away to consult with the Governor's aide-de-camp who had just come through the gateway.

CHAPTER SIXTEEN

FOR TWENTY-FOUR HOURS life on Kybarrli Station was a whirl of activity. The dinner party at which Grant was the host went off without a hitch and was pronounced a great success. The Superintendent of Schools was delighted with Mr. Rolfe's efforts and with the Governor's surprise and pleasure in the reception the school children had given him.

The cord elevating the Union Jack snapped as it was being pulled and spontaneously one of the native boys went up the flag pole, monkey fashion, and held the flap in position for the whole time. It had caused a laugh all round and a special salute from the Governor. The boy, intent on doing the job perfectly, had kept an expression of graven seriousness.

There seemed so much to do that Elizabeth did not have

time to wonder how she was playing her part. She just went ahead and did it. For twenty-four hours the ladies on Kybarrli really lived a glamorous life. They seemed to be bathing and changing into different clothes every hour or two. Yet all the time they had to look cool and self-possessed.

Elizabeth had only one bad moment . . . and it was a very bad one. It was when the Governor asked her had she fixed the date of her wedding.

"I'll be going back to England shortly, Your Excellency," she said. "I'm afraid there can be nothing definite until then. You see, when I came out to Australia I didn't even know I was going to meet Grant . . ."

"One of those shipboard romances," Gaylie, waving a long cigarette-holder, put in with a laugh. "And you know what they are, Your Excellency!"

"I can't imagine a more delightful way to establish an acquaintance," he replied pleasantly. "I wish you every good fortune. And I think Mr. Jarvis is fortunate too. I've already told him so."

"That is very kind of you," Elizabeth said. "Thank you so much for your interest, Your Excellency."

When he turned away Gaylie caught her eyes and lifted one eyebrow.

"Poor Elizabeth," she whispered. "That put you in a corner, didn't it? Never mind. It can't go on for ever, can it?"

The odd thing was she didn't say this unkindly. It was as if she genuinely felt sorry for Elizabeth. Immediately afterwards Gaylie crossed over to Grant and fell into an eager conversation with him. Elizabeth turned to the other guests.

Late the following afternoon the people from all the surrounding districts began to pour into Kybarrli Station. The square had had awning shelters of striped canvas set up around the three sides opposite the homestead garden. Buffets laden with foods and fruits of all kinds, cool drinks, lagers and light wines were served from a series of small tables. At the creek end of the square a vast marquee was erected for the children where coloured ice cream and ginger beer were served to them in a continuous stream.

In the evening the whole square was floodlit from lights in the gum trees on either side. In the centre a huge bonfire kept everyone warm. The floor of the small specimen woolshed had been cleared and there was dancing to the accompaniment of a concertina and two fiddles.

In the garden several barbecues burned brightly as the fat from lamb chops dripped into the coals. The whole was lighted by strings of coloured lights swinging between the veranda and the trees.

The Jarvis family was able to relax for the first time for this was the Governor's own party and his staff, and caterers, who had been flown up from the capital with a plane load of food, now took charge.

Throughout most of the previous day and evening, and until four o'clock this day Elizabeth had stood by Grant's side at the required times. She had shaken hands with people, bowed to others, talked with many, smiled on the children, replied to questions about her health, her home country, her trip on the ship, and her reactions to life on a station. All the time she was almost touching Grant's shoulder, she stood so near him, yet all the time they did not exchange a glance or even a few words. Both were giving themselves up to the guests.

On the evening of the second day, as the concertina and fiddles made sounds that floated up through the night air to the homestead garden and the fires crackled and the lights twinkled, Elizabeth stood in the garden. She had time now to wonder whether Grant was satisfied with her performance. She could not match Gaylie for gaiety and aplomb, she knew. But she had been genuinely interested in everybody and had tried to show it.

She had just come up from the children's marquee and paused in the deep shadows of an oleander tree, as much to rest as for any other reason.

Thirty yards away Grant passed along the path under the veranda and Gaylie leaned over the railings to speak to him. Elizabeth could see the light shining on the back of Gaylie's golden head and on Grant's upturned face. They stood there talking for some minutes.

Elizabeth found it hard to understand why she minded so much. It was like the day she had been standing at the window putting on her bracelet and had seen Gaylie talking to Grant. There was something so intimate and possessive about it. At the same time, in her own heart, there had been a feeling of possession too. Gaylie was engaging the attention of someone who belonged to Elizabeth. In a way it was a terrible thought because Elizabeth never once doubted her attachment and "belongingness" to Ralph. It was the insidious implications of being "engaged" to a man.

Somehow she must, she *must* put a period to it at the earliest possible date. This way she was not only doing something disastrous to her own well-being and happiness, she was interfering with that of others. Mrs. Jarvis, Tim and Maria Bolton, Old Flinty! Somehow one damaged them when one betrayed their trust. To discover deceits in life is to suffer!

Elizabeth turned away from the sight of Gaylie and Grant talking because it made her heart ache. She walked back down the garden and leaned over the fence looking down to the lighted square and all the merriment that was going on there.

She heard footsteps coming down the path and though, intuitively, she knew they were Grant's, she could not bring herself to move away. He must see someone standing there silhouetted against the lights of the square. One glance and he would know who it was.

The steps came on, left the path, and crossed the short strip of grass to where Elizabeth stood.

"I was looking for you," he said quietly. He stood beside her, looking not at her but out over the square. He leaned his arms on the fence and looked straight ahead. "Are you very tired?" he asked.

"Yes, but pleasantly so. It has all been wonderful." It was Elizabeth who turned to look at him. "Has everything gone as you wanted it, Grant? Are you satisfied?"

"Yes," he said quietly.

Elizabeth ran one finger around the top edge of the fence post.

"I hope I did my part . . ." She paused, then added, "with satisfaction."

The words sounded heavy and inappropriate but she didn't know how to frame them. After all, she was his employee . . . not even a guest.

Grant didn't answer. The silence was long and strained. Grant straightened himself then turned round and leaned against the fence so that he was now facing into the garden.

"I wish," he said very slowly, "that you could continue with it. I wish you would leave things as they are, Elizabeth. And not go back to England . . . at all."

Elizabeth wasn't sure whether she had heard right. Grant's profile was turned to hers and he did not look at her.

"What do you mean, Grant? Go on being an 'engaged' person for ever? Grow old being 'engaged'? Have grey hair and wrinkles and even a walking-stick and still be 'engaged'?"

She was amazed at the pain in her own voice. Suddenly whole wells of bitterness she had never known she possessed seemed to burst open the cracks of her heart.

Like Ralph? Run up the Underground steps to meet him every night for ever and ever? Every night for ever and ever dread that he might not be there? Every night be thankful that he was there and be content with the small crumb of his companionship from the Underground along the long village road past the new housing estate to Rose Cottage?

That was the kind of girl she, Elizabeth, was. Someone who always did the loving, the serving, the doing, the *waiting* . . . for ever and ever and ever.

"No," he said. "I did not mean that. I meant I wished you would stay with me for ever. I have a feeling, a very strong feeling, we need you here."

"Others need me too," Elizabeth said out of her bitterness. "My mother, my job and . . ."

"Yes? And . . .?"

Elizabeth tilted up her head.

"And Ralph."

"Ah, yes. Ralph. The young man we talked about before. The same one that Aunt Mollie spoke to me about."

"He seems to have been well talked about," Elizabeth said, hardly realising there was a cry in her voice as she spoke.

"And I, in my selfish demands for your services, have kept you from him?" he asked, his voice expressionless.

"Well, hardly. The *Albany* has not yet left Australian shores, has it? He didn't expect me back in less than eight weeks. I had agreed to stay on, if you needed me."

"Would you tell me why you agreed to do that, Elizabeth? Had it anything to do with Small and Smallwoods? If so, your sacrifice was unnecessary. I made arrangements about that business the three days we were in Melbourne. Small and Smallwoods would have got the cabled news long since."

"No . . . it wasn't to do with Small and Smallwoods," Elizabeth said in a low voice.

"Then what was it?"

Elizabeth wondered if she really knew the answer herself, and if she did, could she ever tell Grant.

"Why did you agree to stay on?" Grant asked again.

"I thought you needed me. I suppose it is my nature to say 'Yes' if someone needs me. Perhaps I like to be needed."

"You will not stay on now, Elizabeth?" His words were distant, matter-of-fact, yet there was a hint of urgent inquiry in them.

"No," she said. "No. I must go home. Grant, I want to go home . . . soon. *Now* if only it is possible."

"To this Ralph?"

"Yes. To this Ralph."

Again there was a long silence. Elizabeth grasped the railing of the fence with both hands. Grant leaned against it and stared into the garden.

Something like a sob released itself from Elizabeth's throat. She turned her head and looked at his shadowed face.

"Why do you want me to stay? What is it you want of me? What have I to give that others can't give you at a single word of command?"

"A kind heart, Elizabeth," he said slowly. He seemed to be choosing each word. "A heart that feels for other people. Old Flinty; whether the stockmen's wives can have an outing; the schoolteacher's troubles; the children; my mother . . ." He paused half turned towards Elizabeth. "To all, you had something to give. And you asked for nothing. Even me. You were giving, not taking."

"No!" Elizabeth cried. "No, no, no! You are wrong, Grant. I've wanted something, too! For years I've wanted something for myself, too."

Suddenly she put her face in her hands.

"Ralph?"

"Yes. Ralph!"

Grant was silent for a long time. He dug his hands in his pockets.

"If that is what you want, Elizabeth, we must see if we can do something about it. You have done something for me. Now it is my turn . . ."

Elizabeth was amazed at this calm assumption that Grant could do anything about Ralph.

They were no longer on the terms of their first acquaintance. For the first time they were on equal grounds. For the first time Elizabeth could speak to him as she wished and not as she thought correct to the occasion and the circumstance.

"You could not do anything about Ralph, Grant," she said quietly. "He is a man with a mind and ambitions very much of his own."

"I could perhaps help him with those ambitions."

Elizabeth felt a forlorn calmness. And, yes, some kind of despair, too.

"Do you think that by helping Ralph realise his ambitions you would be buying him for me, Grant?" she asked.

"Not buying him. Certainly not. Merely smoothing the path of true love." His voice held an odd cynical note in it now.

"Isn't that *buying* a person? Could you imagine a man having so little pride?"

"You have not consulted Ralph on the issue," Grant answered shortly.

Elizabeth drew in a sharp breath. She waited until she could speak without a tremor in her voice.

"On Ralph's behalf I decline your offer of help, Grant. But thank you for wishing to help *me*. For that I am truly grateful. Now, do you mind if I go inside? I don't think I'll be needed any more to-night."

Why, oh why did she feel it was a terrible personal blow to herself that Grant should think all people . . . all of them . . . could be bought? Wasn't there anyone in all the world who had something to give for nothing?

"Before you go I'd like you to know that Mrs. Morgan is arriving by plane the day after to-morrow. I myself am leaving for Barrli to-morrow but I'll only be away three days. I'm flying both ways. Mrs. Morgan will still be here when I get back." He stopped short, then asked quietly, "You will be pleased to see Mrs. Morgan, won't you?"

"Yes. Yes, indeed I will," Elizabeth answered. "Will this be a business visit?"

"Partly." Now there was an amused note in his voice. "And

partly to see if you have been properly taken care of, I imagine. I'm afraid Mrs. Morgan doesn't trust me."

"Why should you think that?"

"I don't know. Perhaps you know the answer to it, Elizabeth."

For the first time he turned his head a little and looked directly at Elizabeth. In the glow of the lights from the garden his face looked pale and his eyes were dark shadows.

"Perhaps she sensed my wish to keep you here. Probably she is coming to make sure I'm not keeping you chained up in the house." Suddenly he softened. "Go to bed, Elizabeth, if you are tired. I'm sorry I'm such an ogre. I probably won't see you to-morrow. Gaylie with her mother and Maria Bolton are coming with me to Barrli so you and my mother should have the homestead to yourselves . . . and some respite . . . before Mrs. Morgan arrives. Be sure you rest well."

"Thank you, Grant."

"Do you mind if I don't come up to the house with you? I've a few more jobs to do before the night is over."

"Please don't come with me, Grant. I'll just slip away unobserved—I hope. Good night."

She walked away past the oleanders, in between the lighted trees, past people laughing and talking around the barbecues. At the foot of the veranda steps she met Gaylie.

"Where's Grant?" Gaylie asked. "Mother wants to see him about this trip to Barrli. We're leaving in the morning."

"Down by the oleanders near the fence," Elizabeth said.

"Oh, thanks," Gaylie said airily. And she went down the path along which Elizabeth had just come.

It was like a handing-over ceremony.

Elizabeth was woken in the morning by Mrs. Wheeler standing by her bed, holding a breakfast tray.

"Here you are, luv. Really caught you napping this morning, didn't we?"

Elizabeth sat up quickly and shook her head.

"What time is it? Oh, dear, I have fallen by the wayside, haven't I? Breakfast in bed is just not done in the Jarvis household."

"Mrs. Jarvis's orders, luv. And believe it or not she's had a breakfast tray herself this morning. It's only once or twice in a lifetime we have a vice-regal visit to Kybarrli."

"Did His Excellency leave last night?"

"Yes. Eleven o'clock sharp. He's well on his way into the Northern Territory now, God bless him."

She put a jacket across Elizabeth's shoulders and the tray across her knees. Then she picked it up again and put it on the bedside table.

"Mr. Grant hasn't left yet. He just might call in to say 'Good-bye.' Who knows? I think we'll just do that hair. And yes, a warm flannel wiped over your face will make breakfast taste the better."

Mrs. Wheeler went into the bathroom and returned with a flannel and towel.

"Here you are, dearie. There. That's better, isn't it?"

Elizabeth felt like a small child having her face washed. But it was a lovely feeling. She actually felt rather small-childish and the ample-bosomed Mrs. Wheeler was full of warm motherly attention.

"Thank you so much," Elizabeth murmured through the folds of the towel. "How good you are."

"You deserve it, and a lot more. How you stood on those feet of yours all those two days—and talked to everyone and helped everyone—beats me. And you never once looked flustered or tired. But luv, looking round this room I can see just how tired you were."

She was combing Elizabeth's hair now. Elizabeth glanced round the room and smiled ruefully.

"I wouldn't like Mrs. Jarvis to see my clothes are just where I stepped out of them. I'm sure hers all got hung up. Mrs. Wheeler . . ." She looked up at the older woman. "I could never be as able . . . as absolutely right in all situations . . . as Mrs. Jarvis. She's so quiet, and so tiny, and so wonderful."

"Dear girl, there's a lifetime of training and experience behind that. Wait till you've been married forty years, and for forty years run a great Melbourne home and several stations . . . talked for years to Prime Ministers and Ambassadors and State Governors from all over Australia."

Elizabeth shook her head. Once again she had to be silent. But it wouldn't be for long now. Soon, in a few days perhaps, she would be released from living this lie.

Underneath the sense of relief there was, however, she felt, the odd pity of it all. She had but tasted this life; she had had a minor success, she knew. It might have been fun if . . . Yes, *if*! She wondered what it would have been like to stand beside Grant in embassies, at Government House, at the entrance to the vast reception rooms in Jarvis House, Melbourne.

She shook the thought away as Mrs. Wheeler put the tray once again on her knees.

"There you are, luv. Now I'll just pick up these clothes. My, what a way to treat a lovely dress!"

She tut-tutted as she put Elizabeth's things away.

"You are heaping coals of fire on my head," Elizabeth said as she put her spoon into the grapefruit. "I feel so ashamed, but do you know I was so tired I only just remember getting into bed? I don't even remember putting my head on the pillow."

"Of course not. I'm only teasing you, dear. You ought to have seen Miss Gaylie's room! Three days' clothes everywhere. All the drawers open. But then she's had to pack a kit to go off with Mr. Grant."

"They haven't gone yet?" Elizabeth's blue eyes looked over the top of her silver spoon at Mrs. Wheeler.

The older woman stood still and bent her head as if listening.

"No. I can still hear Mr. Grant stamping about. Goodness me, that man is in a high temper this morning. Something's rubbed him up the wrong way because in nine years on Kybarrli I've never seen Mr. Grant in a temper. Not that he hasn't got a temper, mind you. He just doesn't lose it. Bottles it all up inside him. He goes dead quiet and cold as a frog in an ice-bound pool. Terrible to see him when he's like that. You kind of feel that any minute he might break out. Only he never does."

"Except this morning?" Elizabeth asked. She wished her voice wouldn't waver a little on those questions. Yet somehow she had to know.

"Well, not that kind of temper, dearie. What I mean is he's just irritable. But then he's tired, like everyone else. Poor man, he has to behave like a human being some of the time."

"Of course," Elizabeth agreed. "And it is rather hard to be going off on an air flight within a few hours of a big event like the Governor's visit."

"That's nothing to him. Maybe he'll come in and see you before he goes." She stood back and looked at Elizabeth sitting up in bed. "You do look sweet and pretty, luv. The sight of you would do him good."

"I think I'd rather get up first. I suppose I haven't time?"

The bedroom door was wide open and at that moment heavy footsteps could be heard coming rapidly down the passage. Then Grant stood in the doorway.

For the life of her Elizabeth could not help the tell-tale blush that crept up her cheeks. She was thankful Mrs. Wheeler had washed her face and done her hair. She was also thankful for the little pink woollen jacket around her shoulders and the fact that the breakfast tray lay across her knees . . . some kind of symbolic shield.

"Oh, there you are, Mr. Grant," said Mrs. Wheeler. "Now just let me through the doorway, will you? I've a hundred and one things to do."

Grant stood aside and waited until Mrs. Wheeler had left the room. Then he crossed to Elizabeth's bed. He sat down on the end of it.

"I'll only be away three days," he said. "I wanted to make sure you are all right before I leave." He took out a cigarette. "Will it put you off your breakfast if I smoke so early? And is it allowed in a lady's boudoir?"

For no reason whatsoever a devilish question sprang uninvited into Elizabeth's head. But she did not utter it. *If you travelled across Europe with Thera didn't you know what her boudoir looked like*? had been that unasked question.

Elizabeth was aghast at herself. What poison was it Gaylie had instilled into her? And how had it been working secretly that so suddenly it should make its presence felt?

"Please smoke, Grant," she said, keeping her voice steady. "And as you see, I am very much all right. Mrs. Wheeler has been spoiling me, I'm afraid."

"I suggest you stay there as long as you care to," Grant said when he had lit his cigarette. "There's nothing to get up for now. His Excellency gave the children a school holiday."

"Once I've had my breakfast I think I'll feel like getting up," Elizabeth said lamely. Then more eagerly, "At what time is Mrs. Morgan likely to arrive to-morrow?"

"That is what I wanted to see you about. The day plane gets in at midday and I've arranged for Peter Smith to drive into Endall for Mrs. Morgan. With luck she should be here by nightfall." There was a sudden unexpected impish smile in his eyes. "She will not come by any of the out-stations. And I've made sure she won't have to put in her first night on Kybarrli in an old boundary rider's hut . . . in a petticoat and old army overcoat."

Elizabeth smiled in return.

"I've been so busy since I got to the homestead I've almost forgotten that."

"You had better not tell Mrs. Morgan. In her present mood, judging from her letter, she would marry you off to me forthwith. I imagine she would not approve of Elizabeth Heaton sleeping in her petticoat back to back with Grant Jarvis in any circumstances . . . let alone in an out-camp of a station."

Elizabeth's eyes made a joke of this little matter too.

"In that case I'll be careful not to let her know a thing about it."

Grant's face was serious again. The old shutters were down.

"She feels responsible for you," he said. "I expect she has come armed with good advice." He looked straight into Elizabeth's eyes. "I would listen to her closely, Elizabeth. Mrs. Morgan knows the world, and she has a very sound business mind. Whatever advice she gives you will be good advice. I suggest you take it."

With this he stood up. From the foot of the bed he offered Elizabeth a fleeting smile of farewell. It had just enough of that shining quality in it, instantly come and gone, to put a small ache in Elizabeth's heart.

"I'll be off now," he said. "The rest of the party is waiting for me in the station wagon. Look after Mother, will you?"

"Of course. And thank you for calling in."

"Finish your breakfast, it will be cold."

He walked over to the door, lifted a hand, then he went through the door. Elizabeth could hear his footsteps echoing away as he went down the passage across the hall and out to the veranda.

CHAPTER SEVENTEEN

THE FOLLOWING DAY Mrs. Morgan arrived in time for dinner, and in her wake came a young man. Julien Wakely.

Elizabeth was so excited to see Mrs. Morgan it was quite some minutes before she could turn to the other visitor, fussing about his baggage in the wide hall of the house.

Kisses and handshakes over, Elizabeth turned to where Mrs. Jarvis was standing by a very tall, very slim, very excitable young man in a blue reefer jacket, narrow stove-pipe Terylene trousers and black suède shoes that were tied with red shoe laces.

"Julien," Mrs. Jarvis was saying in her quiet firm voice, "leave your cases there. I won't have guests carrying their cases to their rooms."

"Darling Mrs. Jarvis," Julien cried, striking an attitude. "Generally speaking, your word is absolutely law. But wonderful lady, please let me carry just this little one myself. It's got my painting of Gaylie in it. No hand but mine must dare to touch it."

"Oh, very well," Mrs. Jarvis said with amused tolerance. "Now come and meet Elizabeth . . . the girl who is going to marry Grant."

Julien bent his long narrow body over Elizabeth's hand.

"You've no idea how glad I am to meet you." His voice was a really beautiful one, full of resonance. "In fact . . ." He was still holding Elizabeth's hand. "To know you *exist*. I can't get that man Grant married off quick enough. Such a nuisance. A positive menace to other men who want to get married. One no sooner take a shine to a beautiful girl than there looms up on the horizon *Grant Jarvis*. And the girl falls for him. You do see what I mean, don't you, dear Elizabeth?"

Elizabeth was smiling, creasing up her eyes so that they nearly disappeared and tilting her chin in her pleasure at meeting anyone as unusual as Julien, and as amusingly frank. His words hurried on in a stream of excitement and emphasis so that no one else had a chance to say anything. He released Elizabeth's hand and clutched the precious brief-case to his bosom.

"It's utterly charming of you to marry Grant. And, of course, utterly charming of him to marry you. How soon will it be? And, of course, I'm coming to the wedding." He did not wait for an answer but turned to Mrs. Jarvis. "Dear Great Lady of Kybarrli, are we going to have a station wedding with hundreds of people up from Melbourne and Sydney? And, of course, there are a few good families in Adelaide. Just a few. Gorgeous place, Adelaide. All churches and hills. Elizabeth, darling . . . You don't mind my calling you darling, do you?"

Elizabeth, bubbling with laughter, shook her head.

"No, darling Julien," she said.

Even Mrs. Jarvis smiled.

"Come along, Mrs. Morgan," Mrs. Jarvis said. "Katie will take you to your room. And Julien, please find your own way. You're far too confusing for any of the lubras to help you."

"I know exactly where to go," said Julien. "The little room reserved for bachelors at the end of the office corridor. Right? I knew it. As far away from the girls as possible." He made a face of mock distress at Elizabeth. "You see what I mean? Every station house party I go to they have me tucked away out of danger."

He loped off in the direction of the east passage.

"Come with me, Elizabeth," Mrs. Morgan said. "I want to hear all about your visit."

Mrs. Jarvis nodded.

"Yes, do that Elizabeth. We are having a late dinner to-night. And please . . . a light dress only, Mrs. Morgan. We don't dress up on the night of a visitor's arrival. They get in so late."

In the next twenty-four hours Elizabeth felt she had never talked so much in her life. In fact she didn't know she could talk so much. It was wonderful to be with Mrs. Morgan again. They both had forgotten there had ever been an employer-employee relationship. It didn't cross Elizabeth's mind that Mrs. Morgan was a shareholder and director of Small and Smallwoods, and that she, Elizabeth, was a not very important typist in the main office. Elizabeth was back in the company of a trusted friend . . . one to whom she could pour out everything and know it was listened to with interest and even delight.

Mrs. Morgan, watching Elizabeth's face as the girl described Jarvis House, the shopping spree in Melbourne, the plane trip to Endall, the night in Old Flinty's hut, the life round the station, and the Governor's visit, had a light in her own eyes and a smile on her own generous mouth.

Instead of taking a siesta after lunch on the next day they walked together down through the square to the creek. The sun was brilliant and warm and the sky was a pale shimmering blue. Under the trees along the creek bed the shadows lay cool, and where the sun had not penetrated, the undergrowth and the soil were damp from the night's frost. The air was heavy with the scent of flowering ti tree and here and there a lizard sunned itself on a log and water flies flashed in and out the narrow still waterbed of the creek.

They found a clean log and sat down, their feet stretched out before them in the sun, the shade of the gum trees protecting their faces.

"And now," said Mrs. Morgan, "tell me about Grant."

She noticed the quick shadow in Elizabeth's eyes.

"Oh, he has been very kind," Elizabeth said. Then looking at Mrs. Morgan. "Not at all difficult . . . or embarrassing. I mean, when I was with Grant . . . and playing the part . . . I never found it embarrassing. In fact he made me feel quite natural. It was only when I *wasn't* with him . . ."

"Yes. What then?"

Elizabeth looked at her friend with serious eyes.

"I didn't like deceiving Mrs. Jarvis."

"You weren't, my dear. I think Mrs. Jarvis knew or guessed all about it."

"Then she must despise me for accepting her hospitality under false pretences."

"Not at all. To begin with it is Grant's hospitality. He owns Kybarrli unconditionally. And in the second place you quite won her heart. She told me so. I think she would like you to marry Grant, Elizabeth."

It took Elizabeth quite a minute to get over the shock of these words.

"But why?" she stammered.

"I don't know, unless it is something about you that makes her think Grant would be happy with you . . . and the station people would get on with you. Like all mothers she wants the best for her son."

Elizabeth was bewildered.

"But I have no experience . . . I mean, it is a strange

country to me. Their ways and customs are strange. I could make mistakes. Someone like Gaylie Paton is born and educated to a role like that in this country."

"Perhaps Mrs. Jarvis doesn't think that Gaylie Paton would make Grant happy, and that you would."

Elizabeth was silent. Across the creek and up the slow treeless grassy rise a horseman was riding. He disappeared over the ridge. In the queer still air she could feel the reverberations of his horse's hoofs, even though he must be now three-quarters of a mile away.

Then she looked into Mrs. Morgan's eyes.

"It is quite impossible," she said soberly. "You see, I am almost pledged to someone else."

"Almost?"

"Yes . . . almost," Elizabeth said. She turned the diamond engagement ring on her finger.

"Do you know that Grant wants to marry you, Elizabeth?"

"I didn't quite know. He wanted me to stay here—permanently. He didn't mention marriage . . . but I thought he might mean that. I wasn't sure."

"It would be a wonderful thing, Elizabeth. You realise that, don't you? Apart from the fact he is a very wealthy man and could give you everything in life that you want, he is a very fine man too."

So this was Mrs. Morgan's advice that Grant had recommended her to take. What a strange way they did things in this hierarchy of landed families! They had intermediaries who arranged the details of who should marry whom, and why. Grant wouldn't think there was anything odd or strange about it. He'd been through this process before with Thera Paton. He'd been very busy avoiding the process in connection with Thera's sister Gaylie.

She wondered why Grant wanted to marry her. Love, she knew, simply did not come into it. She couldn't see herself with Grant's eyes, or even those of Mrs. Jarvis, so she thought she would probably live all her life and die, wondering. It would be a riddle never to be resolved for Elizabeth.

She lifted her eyes to Mrs. Morgan again.

"You would like it, wouldn't you?" she said.

"On one condition only. That you love Grant enough to know without any shadow of doubt that you will be happy with him. You have to love a hard man a great deal to live happily for ever afterwards with him. Mrs. Jarvis did that. And though Grant is a hard man he is nothing like as hard as his father was."

"I am pledged to someone else," Elizabeth said.

"You said *almost*. Elizabeth, what do you mean by that?"

Elizabeth turned impulsively to the other woman.

"When I left England," she said, "the prospects of this trip were almost spoiled for me by the fact that I feared Ralph might forget me . . . might not be waiting for me when I returned. If that had happened . . . and I had never met Grant Jarvis, or been to Kybarrli . . . it would have broken my heart. It would have been a terrible thing to have happened to me. Can I now do that to Ralph? Can I do the thing that, if done to me, would have almost killed me?"

"Do you love him, Elizabeth?"

"Ralph?" Elizabeth made a little despairing gesture with her hands. "How do I know? So much has happened to me. I don't know if I know what love is. All I know is that the day revolved around Ralph at home and I think that when I go back all this will be behind me and that I will feel like that again."

"And if you do, you will marry Ralph?"

Elizabeth took in a deep breath.

"If he asks me," she said in a low voice.

"*If?* Oh, Elizabeth, don't you see? You are not really sure now that you love him. Yet you are throwing away reality for something that is no more than a mirage on a plain."

"I must do it," Elizabeth said quietly. "I would never look myself in the eyes again if I did anything dishonest to Ralph. You see, I do love him . . . in a way. I know now that there are different kinds of love, even if I don't know very much about them. And any kind of love is enough if it is good. I mean really *good*. So that you want the best for the other person."

"You talk like an idealist, my dear child," Mrs. Morgan said with a sigh. Then she went on:

"Have you got one of these odd kinds of love to spare for Grant Jarvis?"

Elizabeth winced.

"I want to go back home as soon as possible . . . and never

think of Grant again," she said in a low voice. "It is necessary that I do that, Mrs. Morgan. Necessary for any peace of mind I might salvage out of having met Grant Jarvis." Then suddenly, almost fiercely, Elizabeth said, "I not only want to love someone myself, Mrs. Morgan, I want badly . . . for someone to love me."

Then the tears were in her eyes so that she stood up and bent her head while she hastily patted down her skirts.

"Come," she said. "Let's walk farther down the creek. I'll show you where the children have their swimming-pool."

"You don't want me to bring this subject up again, Elizabeth?"

"Please not, dear Mrs. Morgan. I'm so sorry to be a disappointment to you. But please . . . *please*."

"Very well, my dear. And since you have made up your mind I agree with you that you should leave Kybarrli as soon as possible. I think Julien Wakely will obstruct Mrs. Paton's plans for Gaylie for a week or two and by that time Grant will have to make up his own mind about what to do in the matrimonial stakes."

"Julien is in love with Gaylie?" Elizabeth asked as they walked on down the sheep pad that ran beside the creek.

"Quite besotted with her, to use his own words."

"It will be someone else's turn to be a buffer state between lovers," Elizabeth said, not without a feeling of pity for Julien.

On the other hand Julien oddly enough did not really provoke pity. He was so odd, so immensely likeable and seemingly so very much on top of the world that one imagined even the loss of the celebrated beauty Gaylie Paton wouldn't dampen his spirits for long.

"What is your news of home?" Mrs. Morgan asked after they had walked quite a long way and talked of many other things.

"I think all my mail is being delivered to the *Albany*," Elizabeth said. "I haven't heard from home. I knew if anything disastrous happened that Small and Smallwoods would find me, probably through you, Mrs. Morgan."

"Yes, of course. I noticed in the shipping news that the *Albany* was in Melbourne on its way back round the southern coast, the day I arrived there."

"Yes, I read it in the papers you brought with you. How many more ports does it visit before it leaves Australian waters?"

"Only Adelaide and Fremantle."

"When it leaves Fremantle I will feel a painter is cut. I suppose there will be another ship soon?"

"My dear child, if you flew across Australia I think there is still time to catch the *Albany*. In view of what you have told me I believe you should go as soon as possible. I am flying back to Western Australia at the end of the week and I could go with you. We must look up both plane and the *Albany*'s time table."

"Do you think it would be possible?" Elizabeth asked.

Mrs. Morgan noticed there was no lifting of Elizabeth's voice as if in joyous anticipation. The girl wanted to go home because she thought it was the right thing to do and not because she wanted it so very much. Mrs. Morgan cheered herself up by reflecting that whatever happened to Elizabeth she would come out of this journey more poised, and with greater experience. Both gave her an added charm. And her good clothes had proved her a girl of real beauty.

If there was no Ralph waiting for Elizabeth, sooner or later there would be someone else.

But what a pity to have to say "No" to a Grant Jarvis of the world!

When Grant, with Aunt Mollie and Gaylie, returned from Barrli the next day the homestead seemed to be in the throes of entertaining a house party again.

When the station wagon had driven up and Gaylie had jumped out of the car Julien Wakely had swooped down the garden path and swept her into his arms.

"My beautiful child," he cried. He held her back and examined her closely. "Have you damaged that flawless skin? Have you red dust in your hair? Darling, let me see. Any bruises from roughing it out there in that vile place, the cattle station? Stand still, little pest! I want to examine you with careful scrutiny."

"Darling Julien . . . you *ass*," said Gaylie. "Come on, kiss me and be done with it."

He wrapped his arms around her again and Gaylie put her arms about his neck and rubbed her nose in his shoulder.

"Sweetie pie," she said. "I might have guessed you'd be hunting around and about."

"Hunt?" demanded Julien, releasing Gaylie and looking at his most lofty. "My darling child, I don't know how to hold a gun. When I kill things, it is with charm." He took Gaylie's arm. "Come along, thing. I have things to say to you." He turned as if just remembering some thing.

"Dear Mrs. Paton, how do you do?" He held out his hand in an elegant fashion. "Well, I hope?"

He looked balefully at Grant who was lifting three suitcases from the wagon.

"Drop dead, old fellow, will you?" said Julien.

Grant grinned tolerantly.

"I'll think about it someday," he said.

"Mighty nice of you. Do it before you marry any of my girl friends, will you? Oh, Elizabeth, darling . . . so sorry. I forgot. Of course you're going to marry the fellow. All right, Grant. You may live."

Elizabeth was laughing and when her eyes met Grant's the laughter was still in them and there was an answering amusement in his own. Julien was literally dragging Gaylie up the path towards the veranda steps.

"Quite impossible!" said Mrs. Paton crossly.

Grant smiled, but he said nothing. When he came to the gate, a suitcase in either hand, he stood looking at Mrs. Morgan and Elizabeth. He put down one case and raised his hat.

"Well, Mrs. Morgan," he said. There was that old touch of sardonic amusement in his eyes. "Welcome to Kybarrli."

"Welcome home to Kybarrli, Grant," she said, quite at ease.

While the two ladies chatted Grant turned to Elizabeth.

"Well?" he said, flicking one eyebrow up. "Have you taken Mrs. Morgan's advice?"

Elizabeth was surprised. This was such a very public place to talk about who was going to marry whom. Besides, the sight of Grant as the station wagon drove up had made her heart leap and then seem to sink to a slow death somewhere at the level of her feet. Only Julien's antics had been able to take her mind off the sudden pain of it all.

She looked at Grant now as if she had never really seen

him before. How very fine-looking he was . . . much, much more so in that khaki drill outfit with the open-collared shirt showing the fine thrust of his brown neck, the wide stockman's hat that still carried some of Barrli's dust on its brim, and the very dust-laden stockman's boots.

Everything about him seemed to thrust a dart in her heart. His tall figure, the wide span of his shoulders, his sun-weathered face with the edges of his white teeth showing between his lips, and his grey-blue eyes that did not have the shades down. They were looking at her closely, inquiringly.

"No, Grant," Elizabeth said soberly. "You see, I can't do that. I must go home."

They looked at one another for a long time. Then Grant bent and picked up the other case. When he stood up his eyes were cold and as impersonal as they had ever been.

"In that case," he said, "we must do something about it at once."

"Thank you," Elizabeth said.

The party turned and went towards the homestead where Mrs. Jarvis was waiting on the veranda to greet the returning travellers. Gaylie and Julien had disappeared inside but their voices could be heard laughing and arguing together in the hall.

Three days later, Elizabeth with Mrs. Morgan and Grant left Endall by plane for Melbourne.

When Grant was moved to action he moved very quickly. By the evening of the day of his return from Barrli he had been in radio communication with the *Albany*'s shipping company and the trans-Australian airline. By flying out from Melbourne on Friday they could catch the *Albany* at Fremantle, the first and last port of call for ships coming to and from Australia via Suez or South Africa.

When he had told Elizabeth and Mrs. Morgan of his arrangements he said he would accompany them to the west coast. Elizabeth protested but on that point Grant was coldly implacable.

"I took you off that ship at Fremantle," he said. "I'll see you safely back on board. It is my responsibility."

Telling Mrs. Jarvis, and parting from her, had been the hardest part for Elizabeth.

The little lady was sitting in a small arm-chair in the sitting-room, upright as if she was about to receive an ambassadorial presentation. Her crochet was on a table beside her but her hands were lying still in her lap when Elizabeth came in. The large bouffant cushion was near her chair. Elizabeth sat down on it.

She turned the diamond ring once on her finger and then slowly took it off. The tears were very near as she lifted her head and held it out to Mrs. Jarvis.

"You gave it to me," Elizabeth said simply. "I must give it back to you."

Mrs. Jarvis took it and put it on the table beside her. For a moment there was silence.

"I am very sorry," Elizabeth said. "I wish I could tell you how ashamed I feel, Mrs. Jarvis."

The older lady looked at the girl steadily.

"Why do you feel ashamed, Elizabeth? You did something my son asked you to do. And paid you to do."

Elizabeth flinched. Then she held her head up and met Mrs. Jarvis's eyes.

"I am not ashamed of that. It was a contract of work and both Grant and I were party to it. No, it is not that . . ."

"Then what is it?"

"That I deceived you."

"You did not deceive me, Elizabeth. I knew from the moment I first met you that you were not the deceiving kind. Don't allow that to trouble you. I'm glad you were of service to my son, if that is what he wanted."

"May I thank you for your kindness, and your hospitality, Mrs. Jarvis? I would like you to know I am truly grateful."

Mrs. Jarvis nodded her head thoughtfully.

"We shall not part enemies, my dear girl," she said at length.

Then with great dignity she stood up. Elizabeth stood too. Mrs. Jarvis looked at Elizabeth for a long time.

"I should like to tell you something, Elizabeth," she said at length. "I, too, am sorry. Very sorry. I would have liked you to marry Grant."

She turned away and walked towards the door. At the door she stopped and turned again.

"You were very welcome," she said. "I hope you have enjoyed your visit."

Then she went out of the room. The diamond ring still sparkled on the table beside Mrs. Jarvis's chair.

Elizabeth went through the door into the hall. Once she had turned into the passage leading to her room, she ran. In her room she sat down on her bed and wept her heart out.

CHAPTER EIGHTEEN

THEY HAD one day in Melbourne though on this occasion they did not go to Jarvis House. They booked in for the day at the Menzies Hotel and in the early hours of next morning left that hotel for Essendon airport and the plane that would take them across Australia.

This time they flew by day and Elizabeth could see the great vast treeless span of hundreds and hundreds of miles of plain and desert that was the heart of Australia. On this strange map below her Elizabeth could see the thin straggly line of odd water courses, the blue shining blots of salt lakes and then at Kalgoorlie the miniature steel stacks and sand dumps that were the gold mines.

They flew into Perth airport an hour after sundown. She was back where she had started from, and Grant Jarvis was still by her side.

The next day Mrs. Morgan and Grant accompanied her to the ship at Fremantle.

On board Elizabeth found she had her old cabin. On the table by the bed was a small stack of letters. They had been waiting for her.

Mrs. Morgan and Grant had both come on board with her. "Oh, look," Mrs. Morgan said. "Nobody in our suites, Grant. Don't those closed doors look too bad? I almost feel like staying on board and going back now."

"There's a short passenger list at this time of the year," Grant said. "It's the off season. The ship is going into the English autumn . . . and that's not a good time for tourists."

"Darling, I hope you won't feel too lonely," Mrs. Morgan said to Elizabeth.

Elizabeth had picked up her letters and quickly flicked through them. They were four from her mother, one from her aunt and one from Bessie Wainwright of Small's office. The other two were from Ralph. She put them all in her handbag and turned to exchange last-minute farewells with Grant and Mrs. Morgan.

At that moment a mesenger girl appeared with an enormous bouquet of flowers.

"Miss Heaton? Cabin 69 A Deck?"

"Yes," Elizabeth said, and held out her arms for the flowers. "Thank you so much."

She slipped the card out of the tiny envelope tied by a ribbon to the bouquet.

With love from Celia Seaton Morgan and Grant Grant Jarvis.

Elizabeth flushed. She blinked hard.

"Thank you," she said again. "Thank you both very very much."

"That's all right, dear," Mrs. Morgan said. She took the flowers from Elizabeth and put them on the table. "Now you have a brush up while Grant and I see if we can find that red-headed rascally cousin of his. You remember Dr. Jarvis? Then we'll go off the ship, but you come up on to the top deck and wave us farewell, won't you?"

"Of course," Elizabeth nodded.

Mrs. Morgan kissed the girl tenderly.

"We'll meet again," she said. "I'll be back in London next year. But you're to write. You understand? Write nice long, long letters. I want to know every single thing you're doing."

"I will," Elizabeth promised. "Mrs. Morgan, I wish I knew how to thank you . . ."

The whole time, ever since they had come into the cabin, she had been avoiding looking at Grant. He stood, his back against the door jamb, his hat dangling in one hand, the other hand in the pocket of his tweed coat. He was looking out of the porthole, his eyes as incommunicable as ever.

"Don't try," said Mrs. Morgan. "Grant and I thank you. Now good-bye again, dear. And come up on deck when the ship begins to move, won't you?"

Mrs. Morgan kissed Elizabeth again and went outside the door. Grant drew himself up and then held out his hand.

"Good-bye, Elizabeth," he said.

She had to meet his eyes now. In them she saw an odd stubbornness.

She put her hand in his. She had a mad moment when she thought of lifting up her face so that he might kiss her. But she kept herself in rein. Grant made no attempt at anything so sentimental. Indeed, Elizabeth realised that by the aloof way he held himself, such an act on his part was unthinkable.

He turned away into the short passage. Elizabeth followed him past the closed door that had been Mrs. Morgan's suite, past the closed door that had been his suite. As they reached the entrance into the main alleyway he turned towards her and this time his eyes relented. He was smiling. Then he said:

"So long, Elizabeth. I'll be seeing you."

He turned and walked away down the half mile of long passage. She watched his tweed-covered back until he turned into the lift lobby. He was gone.

"I must not cry," Elizabeth said to herself, but she knew that in the not far distant future that was just what she would do.

She went back into her cabin. Standing beside the table she lifted up the flowers and buried her face in them.

Beside them was a small square box. She picked it up and opened it. When the lid flew back on the tiny jewel case the diamond ring she had worn as Grant's engagement ring flashed up at her. There was a card.

To Elizabeth Heaton from Elizabeth Grant Jarvis. I would like you to have this ring, with my love.

Elizabeth slipped the ring on the third finger of her right hand.

She mustn't shed tears! Not yet. Not *yet*. She had to put on a smiling face. She took off her hat and went to the wash basin and washed her face and let the wet flannel rest on her eyes like a soothing pad. Then carefully she stood in front of the mirror and made up her face. She did her hair and then stood back from the mirror and surveyed herself. She had insisted on giving back Mrs. Morgan's fur coat and she wore now a light olive-green coat over a biscuit-coloured dress.

She picked up her white handbag. All the time she was in a daze.

She remembered her mail.

She sat down on the side of her bed and opened her bag. She couldn't bring herself to read Ralph's letters yet. Somehow she couldn't bring herself to open them. There was something perfidious, feeling the way she felt now about seeing Grant's receding back going down that gangway, and then opening Ralph's letters and reading them. It was like betraying Ralph.

Instead she took up her mother's letters. It would be twenty minutes before Mrs. Morgan and Grant got off the ship. It was crowded with visitors and they would want to speak to Dr. Jarvis first. She looked up at the clock. Yes, there was time to read her mother's letters. She opened them all and placed them in the order of their dating.

As she read of the everyday doings of Rose Cottage, the scent of the flowers Mrs. Morgan and Grant had given her stole up into the air and wove a kind of sadness round her heart. Once she stopped reading to break off a rosebud and put it under the marcasite pin on her lapel . . . a present from Mrs. Morgan when Elizabeth had insisted on giving back the fur coat.

Several times in the first three letters her mother mentioned seeing Ralph, and that he was well and seemed very interested in his new job. At the end of the fourth letter there was a strange cryptic sentence.

"By this time you will have heard from Ralph about his new venture. We all think it is a wonderful opportunity for him but both Aunty and I are worrying about how you will take the break."

Elizabeth read it again. Then suddenly she tore open Ralph's two letters. She read the one of the earlier date. She raced through its rather stilted sentences and itemised account of what he had been doing. Her eyes flew up to the clock. Ten minutes to go. How long did it take to get through those gangways and up in the lift to the top deck?

She dropped the letters, except Ralph's second letter, and hurried out into the passage.

There was a press of people at the lift and Elizabeth had to wait for its return. When she entered it at last there were only two other pasengers in it.

"Top deck, please," she said to the man who was pressing the buttons.

The door closed. Elizabeth looked down at the letter in her hand. It was already opened. She began reading.

The word "Canada" leapt out at her and she shook her head and blinked her eyes and began reading again.

The lift stopped at the lower deck and the two passengers got out. It went up, then stopped. Then it whizzed down again into the bowels of the ship. Somewhere at the back of her mind Elizabeth realised she should have got out when it stopped earlier.

Three people got in.

"The top deck, please," Elizabeth said again mechanically as one of the passengers started pressing buttons.

She couldn't read the letter properly. She might forget to get out again. The feel of the ship's engines under her was altering. There was a rhythmic purring now.

"Dear God . . ." she prayed. "Don't let me have missed them."

She waited till she got out of the lift and then read the letter again. *He was going to Canada. He hoped she would soon fill the gap it would leave in her life. He had found it not too bad after she had gone away. After a week or two it was wonderful the way other interests began to creep back again into one's life.*

Creep back again.

As if those five years had been taken up with frivolous things that had kept at bay the important things of life.

Elizabeth went white.

Five years!

"Oh, no!" she cried aloud. "Oh, no! And I've sent Grant away!"

"Are you all right, miss?" It was a solicitous steward.

"Yes. Yes, thank you. Which way do I go? To the deck, I mean. I've forgotten. I can't find my way. *I can't find my way any more.*" There were tears in her voice.

The steward pointed through the open companionway. She stumbled over the brass step, then almost fell across the width of deck to the ship's side. She leaned over the rails, searching desperately for those two faces.

There they were.

She clung, white-faced, to the rails.

Their faces were upturned and they were smiling. Every now and again streamers held by the other passengers obstructed her view. It was like a gala ball, only it was in the middle of the afternoon. Streamers, confetti, laughter, music, the band on the wharf playing "Aloha" then the band on the ship playing "Waltzing Matilda."

Elizabeth couldn't wave. She needed both her hands to hold her steady to the rail. She needed all her will-power not to cry out across that ever-widening gap between the ship's side and the wharf; not to lie down and die because a widening sheet of water was separating her from Grant. The ship was moving. The tug was pushing the great liner out into the harbour. Smaller grew the upturned faces on the wharf. They were a white blur now.

With the letter clenched in her hand she grasped the rails.

"Are you all right, miss?" It was the steward again.

"Yes. Yes, thank you."

She did not look at him. She only looked at the width of harbour water that now lay between her and Australia.

Slowly, laboriously the tug began to turn the ship. Slowly the wharf angled away. In a minute it would be hidden by the bow of the ship.

The faces were going . . . going . . . gone!

With a sigh Elizabeth slid down on to the deck floor in a dead faint.

When she opened her eyes Dr. Grant Jarvis was standing over her. She was lying on a sofa in the purser's office.

"You're a fine one!" said Dr. Jarvis. "Able to sit up now? Good. We'll get the nurse to take you below. Here, drink this first."

"I . . ."

"Shut up, my sweet child. I'll tell you when you can talk. Oh, there you are, nurse! I think Miss Heaton will walk with a little help. Take her into the sick bay, will you? I can keep an eye on her there."

"The passenger dropped this letter, sir," the steward said.

"Thank you," Dr. Jarvis said. He put Ralph's opened letter in his pocket. "Now, are you ready, Elizabeth? Good. Then up you get."

The next morning they were well out into the Indian Ocean.

There was a heavy swell but in bed in the sick bay Elizabeth felt nothing but a wish that she had never woken up from that faint.

Dr. Jarvis came in half-way through the morning and sat down beside her.

He took out Ralph's letter and gave it to her.

"I read that," he said. "I couldn't think what it was or what it was doing in my pocket. So I read it. You dropped it when you fainted out on the deck. Now, tell me, young lady. Is that what made you faint?"

"You are supposed to look after my body, not my heart, Dr. Jarvis."

"I'd say baloney to that except that your heart is very much part of your body. If it doesn't function properly, *you* don't function properly. And by that I mean the mythical heart as well as the physical heart. Now tell me something else. Why didn't that engagement to Grant come off? Didn't you fall in love with him?"

It took three days of persistent questioning at odd intervals before Dr. Jarvis broke down Elizabeth's resistance. Then, in a long sad flow, the whole story came out.

"You see, Dr. Jarvis, I felt the strain all the time. I was like two persons. All the time I was in a dilemma. I had to choose. First of all I had to choose whom I really loved. Then I had to choose what was the right thing to do. Not the thing I wanted to do . . . but the *right* thing."

Dr. Jarvis leaned back in his chair and folded his arms. Elizabeth was still in the sick bay but was sitting up in an arm-chair by the porthole, a light rug across her knees and a pretty pink bed jacket giving her cheeks a little more colour than they had by rights.

"Well, now I'll tell you something," Dr. Jarvis said after a pause. "Mrs. Morgan thinks you were mistaken in leaving Grant. She told me. You see, she wanted to make sure I'd keep that old weather eye of mine on you on the way home. But I think you did the right thing. Do you know why?"

Elizabeth shook her head.

"Because your conscience would never have given you any peace for the rest of your life. Right?"

"Yes. You are right."

"Good. Well, now that there is no more dilemma you will

get well again and soon. The strain will be off. That's what has caused the collapse. That letter of Ralph's was like springing a trap. The waiting was over. Well, it's all over now. To-morrow, we'll get you up on deck in the sun. We're getting up in the hot latitudes and there's plenty of fun to be had in the deck life. You've got to join in. I'm going to make you join in. By the time we reach Ceylon you're going to have learned to face life gallantly. Do you know why?"

Elizabeth shook her head.

"Because you're a very gallant person. That's why."

He patted her hand. He was sitting in a chair beside Elizabeth and he now leaned forward and took a chocolate from a box he had brought Elizabeth the previous day. He put a chocolate in his mouth, then held out the box to Elizabeth.

"Eat one," he commanded.

"I . . ."

"Eat one. Doctor's orders," he said, smiling.

Elizabeth took a chocolate and put it in her mouth.

"That will do you good and keep you quiet while I tell you something. I won't ever bring the subject up again . . . but I want to tell you something which, when you think it over, might help to make you happier. Ready?"

Elizabeth nodded.

"First. Forget Ralph. He was a self-centred young man who had better luck than he deserved when he won your affection."

"I'm not worrying about him any more," said Elizabeth.

"You can't talk properly with a chocolate in your mouth, my dear girl. I'll talk and you listen."

Elizabeth exchanged a fleeting smile with the kindly red-headed doctor. How very bossy were these Jarvis people! Somehow it was rather a relief to be bossed. Elizabeth felt she had no will of her own yet.

"Don't forget about Grant Jarvis, however," said the doctor, looking over the chocolates and picking himself one that had a soft centre. "Even if you never see him again he is someone worth remembering. He's a man of character."

"Yes. I know that."

"I am going to give you an example of it. You knew he was engaged to Thera Paton?"

Elizabeth nodded.

"I heard the story, and about the car crash," she said.

"I suppose you heard the version in which Grant was driving the car when Thera was killed?"

Elizabeth's startled eyes met the doctor's. She nodded.

"Grant let that story stand to protect Thera's name."

Dr. Jarvis selected another chocolate while he let that remark sink in. He did not look at Elizabeth but at the chocolate in his hand.

"This is why I'm fat," he said. "I always eat my patients' chocolates." He held out the box. "Take one before they're all gone," he commanded.

Mechanically Elizabeth put out her hand and took a chocolate.

"That was a trumped-up, arranged engagement, anyway," said Dr. Jarvis with his mouth full of chocolate. "Grant was doing it for peace sake . . . and because Thera needed someone to keep her steady. Thera was doing it just for the heck of it, I think. Anyhow she broke off the engagement and Grant and Tim Bolton flew across to Italy to see if she was all right. Grant felt some kind of responsibility for her. She'd fallen in love overnight with some Italian racing magnate. She gave out at the hotel that she was engaged to this man. It was he who was driving the car. Grant hadn't got there."

"But then . . . how did everyone come to think it was Grant?" asked Elizabeth. She wished her heart wouldn't pound the way it did, and that her hands would stop trembling.

"The Italian press had it written up. The English press wrote it up that she was with her fiancé. The Australian press, unaware the engagement with Grant had been broken, wrote it up that she was with Grant. That is all. Simple as that!"

"I still don't understand why Grant didn't tell his own family . . . and Thera's mother."

"Because Grant is a gentleman, and Thera's Italian fiancé turned out to be a married man."

There was a complete silence in the sick bay. Then a little sigh escaped Elizabeth. She turned her eyes to Dr. Jarvis.

"Thank you for telling me," she said. "I won't forget Grant. It was wonderful knowing him. I'll always be glad."

"Now, I'll tell you something else. You know that the News Sheet that is distributed every day on the ship gets its news by radio from Australia until we reach Ceylon? Well, this morning's radio news included a few items from the social pages of the Sydney and Melbourne press. Gaylie Paton has announced her engagement to someone called Julien Wakely, an art collector and the owner of a private gallery in Melbourne. He appears to be quite somebody in the Art world."

"I've met him," said Elizabeth. "He was at Kybarrli." Again her eyes met those of Dr. Jarvis. "Do you know . . . I'm glad. I couldn't help feeling they were ideal for one another. Gaylie wasn't really the right person for . . ."

"Grant?"

"Yes," said Elizabeth. "For Grant."

"Exactly. That's why I told you. I don't think you need bother about Grant being dragooned into a Paton net again. Trouble about Grant was that he's got a chivalrous streak in him . . . well hidden, of course. Those Patons really bothered him. You see, their estates in some of his pastoral companies are tied up with Jarvis estates. There was always a Paton round and about somewhere in his affairs. There was a family tradition on both sides of marrying into the right circle. It would have been a bit of a slap in the face for Grant Jarvis, the king-pin of them all, to turn his back . . ."

"Yes, I understand," said Elizabeth. "Thank you for telling me everything. It does help to make my recollections of Grant, and of Kybarrli, happy."

The doctor stood up and Elizabeth smiled up at him.

"I feel happier already," she said.

"Good girl. Always salvage the best out of any experience. It doesn't leave any painful scars then. Do you mind if I take the last chocolate? My figure doesn't matter, but yours does."

Elizabeth laughed.

"That's a sound I like to hear," said Dr. Jarvis. "Don't forget . . . to-morrow, back to your own cabin and then out in the sun on the deck. Doctor's orders!"

He gave her a cheery wave with his hand and a minute later had gone through the door.

In the morning Elizabeth sat in a deck chair under the shade of the awning and watched the flying fish sparkling through the air over the incredible blue of the Indian Ocean.

Dr. Jarvis had set her an assignment. By Ceylon . . . that was only three days away . . . she had to learn to face life. Already she had accepted the first fact. She no longer thought of Ralph but only of Grant. It was better to have loved and lost, than never to have loved at all, she thought. If love never came her way again she would remember that she had had this rich and rare experience of loving, and being wanted, by a man of such distinction and gallantry that even his relatives had a slightly hero-worshipping attitude towards him.

She knew now that whatever she had felt for Ralph before had been as mistaken as Ralph's own allegiance to her. They had been caught in the web of custom and habit just as Grant Jarvis had been caught in the Jarvis-Paton web of custom and habit. She had had to be freed of that web before she could see the world, and other people in it, clearly. And Ralph, too. Freedom had given Ralph his opportunity in life.

Slowly, through those three days, Elizabeth won herself back to taking part in the shipboard life of the *Albany*. She knew she had salvaged happy memories out of this strange voyage but she thought too that she would always have to walk through life with an aching void in her heart. She had to learn to live with that void. Thousands of other people had had to do that. She must do it, too.

Sometimes in the night she wondered how long the lesson would take to learn.

The day before the ship entered Colombo, the port of Ceylon, she noticed the door of the suite that had been Grant's was open. When she glanced inside, the steward was dusting it and preparing it to be occupied.

He came to the door as she passed.

"Is someone coming into that suite at Colombo?" she asked.

"Yes. It's been reserved by cable, madam. A married couple."

"Oh!" said Elizabeth.

She wished it would be a real Indian prince . . . and his wife. No one was worthy of that suite other than Grant Jarvis . . . or an Indian prince. How Mrs. Morgan and Hetty would love the news if she were able to write and say: "Their clothes are encrusted with precious stones and they eat only from gold plates."

Hetty and her joke about Grant being like an Indian prince!

In the morning the ship was already at anchor when

Elizabeth woke. Sometime in the night she had felt the engines stop. Funny how the cessation of sound and movement had woken her as much as if it had been noise instead of silence. It was like that for two minutes on Armistice Day in London. When the roar of London stopped it was eerie. In the port of Colombo Elizabeth woke to the eeriness of a ship's engines stopping.

She rose early and had a quick bath and then dressed herself in the blue suit she had worn the day she had gone with Grant Jarvis to see the Wells of Aden. She thought she might take a Cook's tour to Mount Lavinia or Candy. She had to live with life and by doing things she might one day forget, if only for a few minutes, that void in her heart.

To begin with, she had to make the best of her appearance. That took time, filled moments. And beauty was armour . . . this time with which to face life instead of people like Mrs. Paton.

She took care doing her face and hair and then she put the blue hat and handbag and gloves on her bed ready.

Perhaps if she wore all the things she had worn that day in Aden she could pretend just a little. Pretend that Grant Jarvis, silent, inimical but full of that rare courtesy of his, was beside her.

When she went down the little passageway she saw there were two cases already inside the doorway of that suite. The Indian prince was already aboard then!

When she turned the corner into the main alleyway she saw him.

He was coming down its full length. He was carrying that broad-brimmed hat and wearing that tweed coat. His shirt was brown and his tie khaki . . . like he wore them on the station; and he wasn't an Indian prince.

He was Grant Grant Jarvis of Kybarrli.

Or wasn't he? Had something happened to her head? Was she just a little mad? She put out her hand and steadied herself against the hand rail.

On he came, and he was real. She stood quite still and waited, her face a little white, her eyes straining not to be strained.

He came on and his face wore an amused, almost ironical smile but when he came right up to Elizabeth it seemed as if he had no words. There was nothing to say. Nothing in all the world that could be put into words. He looked down into Elizabeth's eyes, then with a sudden movement took her hand off the hand rail and took her into his arms. Her face was buried against his shoulder and her heart pounded against his heart.

She knew that he was real because the tweed of his coat hurt her nose, and she could feel the great power of his arms as he crushed her to him.

"Red Jarvis sent me a cable . . ." he said at length. "I flew to Ceylon ahead of you . . ."

His voice went on. Something about being married to-morrow through the Australian High Commissioner's office in Ceylon. Then catching the ship again from Bombay. The tweed of his coat was getting wet from her tears . . . not because she was getting married but because he had *come*. He had come.

The incredible had happened. Someone in the world had crossed continents and flown oceans to get *her* . . . Elizabeth Heaton, typist.

"Grant," she said into his coat. "Did you get that job for Ralph in Canada?"

He stroked her hair.

"Yes," he said. "I scattered cables across two hemispheres. I wanted you. You belonged to me. I wasn't going to let you go . . . far, at any rate."

She lifted her head.

"How *could* . . ."

Their eyes met. He bent his head and his lips met her lips. For a long moment Elizabeth had the taste of heaven on her mouth.

"We'll argue that out ten years hence," he said at length. "Come into my suite, Elizabeth."

"It's . . . it's for a married couple."

"That's what we'll be to-morrow."

He smiled his rare shining smile and held her hand lightly as he pushed open the door of the Indian prince's suite.

THE END

Historical novels by
Marjorie Bowen

author of more than 60 memorable works of fiction and nonfiction, including the "Joseph Shearing" mysteries.

THE QUEEN'S CAPRICE

The four men in Mary Stuart's life carried her to pinnacles of glory, to the very throne of Scotland—and finally to a terrible death. "A highly colored and dramatic novel . . . well and vividly written."—William Rose Benet, *Saturday Review of Literature*

THE POISONERS

Paris is terrorized by a series of gruesome murders—and the trail leads straight to the glittering Versailles of Louis XIV and its decadently sinister aristocracy.

DARK ROSALEEN

The romantic, tragic story of one of Ireland's greatest patriots, Lord Edward Fitzgerald, and the lovely wife who offered him a choice that would have meant abandoning his ideals. "It throws into vivid relief one of the many stirring periods of Irish history and should be read by all interested therein."—Mary Ellen Chase, *Commonweal*

To order, send $1.30 for each book to Dept. CS, Beagle Books, 36 West 20 Street, New York, NY 10011.